# THE FOREST GODS' REIGN

# THE FOREST GODS' REIGN

ALEXANDRIA HOOK

New York

# THE FOREST GODS' REIGN



Published in New York, New York, by Morgan James Publishing. Morgan James and The Entrepreneurial Publisher are trademarks of Morgan James, LLC.
www.MorganJamesPublishing.com

The Morgan James Speakers Group can bring authors to your live event. For more information or to book an event visit The Morgan James Speakers Group at
www.TheMorganJamesSpeakersGroup.com.

A **free** eBook edition is available
with the purchase of this print book.

CLEARLY PRINT YOUR NAME ABOVE IN UPPER CASE

**Instructions to claim your free eBook edition:**

1. Download the BitLit app for Android or iOS
2. Write your name in **UPPER CASE** on the line
3. Use the BitLit app to submit a photo
4. Download your eBook to any device

ISBN 978-1-63047-446-1 paperback
ISBN 978-1-63047-448-5 eBook
ISBN 978-1-63047-447-8 hardcover
Library of Congress Control Number:
2014917330

**Cover Design by:**
Chris Treccani
www.3dogdesign.net

**Interior Design by:**
Bonnie Bushman
bonnie@caboodlegraphics.com

In an effort to support local communities, raise awareness and funds, Morgan James Publishing donates a percentage of all book sales for the life of each book to Habitat for Humanity Peninsula and Greater Williamsbu--

Get involved today, visit
www.MorganJamesBuilds.com

Dedicated to

J.H., S.N., K.V., E.B., H.A., I.C.,
and Peter O.

# PROLOGUE

More than two thousand years ago, the Greek gods of Olympus were born or molded by the hands of the Titans. You know the myths. Or at least you think you do. When the Olympians had gained control of the world, however, they didn't rule just from the heavens above, but also from the earth, in the form of humans.

Although they were always far too entangled in their own personal affairs, the gods earned much respect from the Greeks. In human form, the gods were all-powerful but, just like everyone else, completely mortal. At the same time that the first generation of Olympians died, their spirits, which had embodied their superhuman powers, took over the bodies of human babies. This is how the ancient world functioned, and how the modern world still functions.

Unfortunately, with the rise and fall of the Roman Empire, the Greeks were rendered lost and helpless among the clamor. For salvation, many turned to new, monotheistic religions instead of to the gods who had failed them. During this process, they gradually lost the ability—the Sight, as the Greeks called it—to believe in the impossible, to see the terrifying monsters for what they really were.

But a handful of believers still remained. Among them were relatives of the famed Greek heroes, lesser-known demigods, and a few people who had been so blessed as to catch a glimpse of the gods or monsters themselves. To avoid persecution, those believers set out to find a space where they could live and honor the Olympians in peace. Eventually they founded a long-lasting society called the Knowing. It even branched out to different countries, making it a bit easier to find each new generation of gods, which would root itself in a unique location each time of reincarnation.

However, the Knowing did not account for the fact that the world population was growing exponentially, and horizons were expanding with it. The Knowing could no longer keep track of each new generation of gods, for there were simply not enough people with the Sight left to accomplish a task so daunting. Ages passed without much action. As the generations of gods came and went, so did the generations of devoted humans. Occasionally members of the Knowing would stumble across a new generation of disinterested gods, but decades, even centuries, at a time passed in which the gods were nowhere to be found. As a result, a few of the Knowing members began to doubt the truth of the Greek myths. Some moved away from the Knowing camps and lost the Sight altogether. Even the biggest, strongest camps became corrupt.

Drastic measures were required to get the Knowing and their beliefs back on track. At the very least, honor needed to be restored to the gods of Olympus, if only to bring hope to others. This is the story of those drastic measures. This is the story of the Forest Gods. But in order to fix the Knowing, this new generation of Greek gods needed to fix themselves first . . .

# Part One

# "THE GODS"

## Chapter 1

# INTO THE FOREST (AND BACK OUT AGAIN)

*Beep. Beep. Beep.* My eyes flew open as I rolled over on my bed to punch the black alarm clock that sat on my nightstand, glaring at me with its red numbers: 5:00 a.m., it reminded me. Yawning, I dragged myself out of bed and pulled on a casual pair of jeans and a simple blue tank top—not in the least bit flashy, but definitely comfortable to move around in. I lazily tied up my long, wavy, dark-brown hair in my usual side ponytail before stopping by my open window to look outside at the quiet forest on the other side of the empty street, across from my house. I couldn't help but smile as I grabbed my little black pocketknife and walked downstairs and out the front door to meet my friends, thinking about that crazy day three years ago, the day that had completely changed my life . . .

The four of us—that's Zach, Connor, Luke, and I (Ashley)—were only six years old when we became the first people ever to go into the mysterious woods and come out alive. I always thought our young age was one of the reasons why we survived, the other being luck, but maybe there was another reason too; we just didn't know it.

We lived in the Woods, named after the sprawling forest that stood rooted beside the wonderfully rugged establishment. Although the forest itself was huge, the town was very, very small—only one main road lined with six tired-looking shops facing the forest and twenty-something ancient houses lined up in rigid rows to the south. There were no real stoplights, and all the children were forced to take a twenty-minute bus ride to the school in the bigger town nearby, called Pine Grove. Naturally, the Woods was one of those cute but clichéd towns where everyone knew everyone else, no one had fences of any kind to keep each other away, and gossip traveled like wildfire.

The bad part about living in such a small town, however, was that someone was always poking his nose into somebody else's personal business. Keeping secrets was awfully difficult when all the families had known each other for generations.

Yearning for freedom and new experiences after high school, most teenagers went to out-of-state colleges or traveled the world with friends. Somewhere out there, in those huge, unfriendly concrete jungles called cities, they would find jobs, settle down, and possibly even start their own families. However, one day in the future, each would receive a call that he knew deep down inside himself to be inevitable, a call that would inform him that his parents were aging faster than ever. Most of these formerly hopeful teenagers would then return to the Woods, perhaps bringing their own new families along to settle permanently in their exact same childhood homes, or perhaps they would rekindle a relationship with a still-single high school sweetheart who had come home for a similar reason. They would take over their parents' beloved shops simply because they hadn't realized how much they missed the playful gossip and the lazy atmosphere of the Woods, but even more so because they felt obligated to keep the old businesses alive, thus passing down both the businesses and the houses from generation to generation, creating a timeless fog surrounding the tiny town. It was far too comfortable and easy to cross into the hazy isolationism of the Woods.

The fact that the growth of our beloved town had been stunted in this fashion was only partly due to the forest being a real death trap. Before Zach,

Luke, Connor, and I went in, more than forty people had walked in confidently (the last one had gone in more than thirty years ago) but had never come out. Decades ago, someone finally decided to put out a large DANGER, DO NOT ENTER sign in front of the forest. However, the sign didn't help as much as the former mayor had foolishly expected, and so the devastating disappearances did not cease; just as families in past centuries had more children in the hopes that some would survive long enough to reach adulthood, the families in the Woods began to do the same, often involving the whole town with the decision—it takes a village, as the saying goes. Still, children of all ages were constantly reminded by their elders never to go into the forest, and most children listened. Until the four of us beat the odds, that is.

That sunny day had started out like any other Friday. Zach, Connor, Luke, and I had walked to the school bus together like we always did. There was no fear of kidnappers preying on young children in the Woods, since word of a stranger in town would spread in a matter of minutes. Plus, the four of us lived in the only houses on our side of the street, and we had been best friends since we had first met. We would race to back each other up in a heartbeat if trouble should ever arise. It didn't matter that I was a girl; the guys had learned early on that although I was of the opposite gender and most likely had cooties, I was not to be messed with. My bite was just as bad as my bark, if not worse.

After school that day, the four of us raced home from the bus stop, eager for the weekend to be ours. We lived for the freedom to do whatever we wanted, whether it was going shooting with my BB gun or having a war with our wooden swords. In a beautiful, sunny place like the Woods, we hardly ever spent any time inside. We saw less of our parents that way; it was better for them and for us.

When we reached our street, we stopped to catch our breaths in front of Zach and Luke's quiet house. The two were twins, though they didn't look much alike. They were about the same height and argued a lot, but the similarities stopped there. Zach was a natural-born leader, and with blue eyes and dirty-blond hair, he was a total girl magnet (just how he liked it), though once in a blue moon he liked to take a break and go sulk in a corner somewhere when his popularity became too much to handle.

For Luke, on the other hand, the party never stopped, and he would mess with his brother all day if you let him. However, his short temper was a beast not even his brother would dare provoke on a daily basis. Luke's hair was slightly longer than Zach's and jet-black, and he had teal eyes that matched the color of the sea. Unlike his brother, who preferred staying on land, Luke had no fear of the water. Even though he had been to the beach only once, and had swum only once or twice in a swimming pool since then, the water was obviously his true home. He still dreamed of visiting it again, and he talked about it all the time.

When we had all caught our breaths a minute later, Zach grinned at us, showing off his pearly-white teeth, and said, "We should go into the woods today, I think." Luke, Connor, and I rolled our eyes immediately. After all, Zach liked to suggest this idea to us at least once a week, but we had never listened until that fateful day.

I shook my head. "You know it's against the rules." As the smartest one in the group (and the smartest person in the entire *world*, though I didn't know that yet), considering my gift for absorbing every piece of knowledge I had ever come across, I was responsible for giving the boys reality checks every once in a while.

Zach only laughed and stuck his tongue out at me. "I bet you're just scared," he teased.

I shook my head again and stepped back, gesturing toward the dark-green forest behind Connor. "If you want to die, go ahead. But I wouldn't recommend it." That time, for whatever reason, they didn't listen to my words of wisdom.

"I think I will," Zach said, raising his dark eyebrows at my challenge. Then he turned on his heel and ran straight toward the forest, with Luke following close behind. I simply watched in shock as their red and white shirts disappeared into the trees.

My jaw dropped open, as I found myself too surprised to speak, but Connor, who was usually my comic relief, snapped me out of my trance when he yelled, "We can't let them go in there alone!" The next thing I knew, I was running with the blond son of the town's mayor past the first few moss-covered trees.

We were about two hundred yards into the dark forest when Connor and I bumped right into Zach and Luke, who stood like statues gaping at something to our left. Slowly, Zach raised his tan, shaking arm, and I followed the invisible line to where he was pointing and found myself looking straight at a large, black creature sniffing at a dusty human skeleton lying in the grass about a hundred feet away. The monster had the torso of a man but the legs and head of a bull, complete with huge horns that curved upward. This creature was a Minotaur, although at that moment I wasn't too concerned with what it was called, only that it was going to kill us.

The four of us stood frozen, scared (though we were too proud to admit it) that we would make even the slightest noise, thus causing the Minotaur to come after us. I thought we were surely dead meat when a shirtless boy who looked about our age popped out from behind a tree.

Well, I thought he was a boy at first, but then I noticed that he had short goat legs covered in reddish-brown fur. "Psst," he whispered. But all of a sudden, when he realized he had our attention and we were distracted, he grinned and yelled out "Boo!"

With that, the Minotaur looked up in our direction, and its red eyes instantly locked on its next targets: us. I had just enough time to turn around and glare at the half-boy, half-goat, who was cackling uncontrollably as the Minotaur ran straight at us. Deep down inside, I knew little kids like us could never outrun a giant bull creature, so without really thinking about what I was doing, I picked up a small stone from the ground and threw it as hard as I could.

To this day, I honestly don't know how I mustered the strength to do it, but the high-velocity stone hit the Minotaur squarely between the eyes, actually *denting* its skull, and the confused monster paused just long enough for Zach, Connor, Luke, and me to get away safely. The young half-boy had already disappeared deeper into the misty woods, probably thinking we were as good as dead.

Breathless, we tore out of the woods and across the empty street toward Zach and Luke's newly repainted dark-green house with white trim. Through the kitchen window, I could see their mother wearing a horrified expression as she watched us trample over her freshly mowed lawn and burst into her humble home.

Their mother, a blue-eyed woman with dark curly hair, stepped into the living room, hands on her hips. Her name was Martha, but she was like a second mother to Connor and me, so most of the time we called her Mom as well. It was just easier that way. Usually she was calm and kind, but not at that moment. "What in the world were you children doing in those woods? Do you realize you could've been killed? Were you even thinking about what that would mean to your families?"

Still too shocked to speak, the four of us exchanged frightened glances, silently agreeing never to tell anyone about what we had seen. We were six years old, but we weren't stupid; we knew no one would believe us. Monsters weren't supposed to exist, even if we still believed.

Luke and Zach's mother paused to shake her head and smooth out her wrinkled red skirt, then continued, a bit calmer this time, "No, obviously not. Luke, Zach, you're both grounded. Up to your rooms, now." Obediently, Luke and Zach left the room and walked up the stairs, looking back at Connor and me, their eyes filled with a mixture of sorrow and fright. "Connor and Ashley, I will be talking to your mothers as well. That was a very dangerous thing you did today," I heard Martha say, but I wasn't really paying attention to her anymore.

By the end of the day, our respective punishments had been formally handed down. Yes, the four of us were grounded for two weeks, and although our parents tried to keep things quiet, news travels fast in small towns, so by the next morning the entire county knew that four first graders had beaten the odds. We had even made the front page of the newspaper and were interviewed multiple times, but none of us kids had much to say and the county was so small that this really wasn't much of a feat. My unstable father, secretly proud of me, still kept a few of the newspaper articles, but he had hidden them behind a bookcase in my room long ago, for my mother was still terrified at the mere mentioning of the wretched forest. Her sister had been lost in its depths when she was only my age.

That week, more than twenty people of all ages (including two former classmates of ours) from all over the state went into the forest, thinking that they too could beat the odds. None of them came back out. None at all. After that devastating week, the woods were once again free of humans; no one in the entire state of Washington could deal with more deaths.

Of course, the fact that we were the sole survivors only made the four of us cockier and more curious than ever. Our rebellious teenage years came early, Martha liked to say. Within that week, we started sneaking out of our houses late at night to meet by a large tree behind my house, where we would discuss the day's events, like who had died and when exactly they had gone into the forest. We would talk about why we were the only ones to come out of the forbidden forest alive and, yes, when we would go back in. It was probably a stupid idea, but we had to find out if it was just because of luck that we had survived or not. To be honest, I always thought the four of us were too brave for our own good.

---

When our punishments had finally been lifted and it was summer, the four of us decided to go back into the woods. But this time we were prepared, more or less. Armed with wooden toy swords and a compass, we strode across the street while our parents were working, or maybe shopping, but it didn't really matter to us as long as they weren't watching.

"Ready?" Zach asked nervously, halting just outside the forest. Even our fearless leader seemed to doubt himself for once. Connor's signature goofy smile was absent for probably only the second time in his entire life, and Luke was just biting his lip and dragging his foot through a small spot of mud. Nevertheless, the three of us ignored the fear tugging at the back of our minds and reluctantly nodded in unison.

Zach let out a shaky sigh and stepped past the first tree. We stopped and looked for monsters both to the right and left of ourselves, as if we were crossing a busy street. I heard Connor take a deep breath in relief, and then we stepped past the second tree. Again, we stopped to look for monsters, and again we saw nothing but pine trees, lush grass, and silver mist. Slowly but surely, we made our way through the thick brush, paving our own trail. We were undisturbed except for the occasional call of a bird . . . and the random bloodcurdling screams, which made all four of us stop in our tracks every single time we heard one. We could only hope that the shouts didn't belong to anyone we knew.

Suddenly I heard an awful crunch to my left, and Connor screamed. A high-pitched, girly scream. I couldn't help but laugh. Zach and Luke quickly joined in as I said, pointing to Connor, "You scream like a girl!"

Connor was frowning, and his hazel eyes looked very upset as he defended himself. "I just stepped on a skeleton! I bet you would be screaming too." Zach, Luke, and I then glanced down at Connor's red Converse shoes where a bunch of old, cracked bones lay next to a skull, covered in leaves and grass and cobwebs. The decomposed body had obviously been there a very long time.

Noticing the same thing I had, Luke snorted and shook his head. Zach apparently took this as a sign that everything was okay, and he was about to step forward when someone, or rather, *something* popped out in front of us. We all jumped. It was the same half-boy, half-goat who had almost gotten us killed before.

"You guys came back here?" He sounded amazed and wore a shocked expression on his face, his bushy eyebrows raised in perfect parabolas. He narrowed his brown eyes and continued, "Gods, you four are tough. I like that. I can't even believe you escaped the Minotaur. And my screaming didn't scare you at all?"

Zach shook his head in amazement and confusion. "No! What's a Minotaur? Wait—what are you anyway?"

The half-goat gasped and covered his mouth with his dirty hands, appearing moderately offended. "My name is Pan. I'm a satyr, of course. Haven't you ever heard of them? We live all around here."

Luke snickered. "Pan? What kind of name is that?" I quickly punched him in the arm to keep him from saying something that might get us killed, but Luke just laughed harder, his bright eyes shining.

Connor sighed and said, "Ignore him," but I could tell he was trying hard not to laugh as well.

Meanwhile, Pan the satyr frowned and ruffled the mop of curly brown hair on the top of his head. "Sounds like you freaks need to study your Greek history."

Not too far off in the distance, we heard the crackling sound of branches, and the four of us turned to see a giant, dark-brown wild boar race past, followed by a gleaming white horse with wings. Simultaneously, a flock of giant birds with metallic wings took to the skies, making bewildered screeches that sounded like nails being dragged across a chalkboard. This time we didn't even stop to think about what in the world these powerful beasts were; Zach, Luke, Connor, and I were already becoming accustomed to the mystical forest. But the creatures had obviously been spooked by something, and we didn't want to stick around to see what had scared them.

Pan looked down at the wooden swords in our hands, obviously thinking a similar thought, then whispered, "I like you four, so I'm going to help you get out of here while you still have the chance. And if you plan on coming back in here again, bring some *real* weapons or else you *will* be killed." He gave us a very serious look. "I mean it." Then the strange satyr waved his arms at us and we turned around and quickly but silently jogged out of the forest along the same winding path we had created on the way in.

We returned to our respective houses unnoticed, and I immediately walked to the computer that sat on a desk in my living room to do exactly what one would expect a brainiac like me to do. I searched for Greek history on Google, with no luck finding anything pertaining to what the four of us had seen in the mysterious forest, until I clicked on a link for Greek mythology.

It was then that I realized that everything adults believed was a lie—religion, monsters, and a whole lot of science. I wrote earlier that one of the reasons we survived was because we were young, young enough to still believe that monsters were real. Even though we didn't know it, we were prepared for the unexpected in a way that older people weren't.

However, it wasn't until much later that the four of us realized our true role in the future of the forest . . . and in saving the world. Though there are plenty of other stories I could have told, this book (as well as the one following it) is a record of those particular events, the most important ones. I figured someone would want to know the truth eventually.

## Chapter 2:

# OUR FIRST KILL

For three years now, the four of us nine-year-olds had been going in and out of the woods without being harmed, other than a couple of scratches from tree branches and undergrowth and whatnot. We had convinced all of our parents to buy us pocketknives when they finally realized they couldn't keep us out of the forest, but we had mostly been staying out of the way of the monsters hidden in there. Our running and tree-climbing skills were excellent as a result of this. It's safe to say that we had become much more accustomed to the ways of living in the forest, and we had even begun to split up and wander alone, communicating with expensive waterproof walkie-talkies which we had automatically deemed the best birthday presents ever.

Over the years, we learned to tell direction and approximate time by looking at the shadows and the moss on the north sides of the trees, and we had almost the entire forest mapped out in our heads, which was a hell of a lot of land, mind you. We even knew the hangout areas for the different breeds of monsters, as well as for our friends, the nymphs and satyrs, specifically Pan.

However, Pan wasn't just a satyr but also the god of the wild, as I had found out from researching Greek myths online and from recalling mysterious dreams. Strangely, for three whole years, our good friend had never told us himself. Naturally I wondered why Pan was keeping his immortality a secret, so one day, when the subject came up, I decided to ask him.

I was walking alone along one of the paths we had blazed, heading north toward the center of the forest and keeping a close eye out for any movements in the bushes or in the trees. (You never knew when a monster might pop out to kill you, after all.) Suddenly, the black walkie-talkie attached to a belt loop on my blue jeans crackled to life. I grinned when I heard Zach's breathless voice say, "Connor's making a run for it! Heading south toward the meadow. Over."

We were in the middle of playing our invented game, which we liked to call reverse hide-and-seek. One of us hid anywhere inside the woods, while the other three of us split up to find the hidden one, communicating only by walkie-talkie. However, the person in hiding also had a walkie-talkie to listen in on the conversation, and he could make a run for it and hide again if one of the seekers was getting too close. One round of our game could take hours to finish, depending on how good someone hid—and how often the seekers had to change their course to avoid being attacked by some mythical creature. I was the best one of us at hiding, because I was nimble and quick and could climb trees easier than the boys, and Zach, Luke, and Connor would often give up after a couple of hours.

Quickly, I ran forward, knowing that the meadow was not too far ahead of where I was, meaning that Connor was running straight toward me from the opposite end of the forest. I knew I could catch him before he tried to hide again, and so I ran on the uneven path as fast as I could, trying not to trip. Breathing hard, I saw the sun's rays just barely shining through the treetops before I ran out into the open, and then Connor was running at me head-on, his white shirt and jeans covered in dust and small green leaves. He caught my eye and threw back his head in anguish, knowing he had been caught, and the soft glow of sunlight glinted off his sandy-blond hair as he slowed to a stop.

Zach ran up behind Connor and stopped next to him, breathing a sigh of relief. I grinned and checked my watch as I joked, "Only took us half an hour. Was Connor hiding on the east side of the hill *again*?" Zach nodded and laughed, while Connor just frowned at me. But it wasn't my fault he needed to be more creative with his hiding places.

We sat down on an old fallen pine tree situated at the west edge of the sunny meadow, waiting for Luke to meet us. The last time I had heard from him was when he was in the west part of the woods, searching for Connor near the river, so it took him a while to reach us. Eventually he walked out of the trees behind us, breathing heavily and using a long tree branch he had whittled into a spear as a walking stick.

"I didn't realize how far away this meadow is from the river," Luke complained, smoothing out his black hair. Zach shrugged dismissively, ending the conversation there.

Luke was about to sit down next to me on the log when we heard an extremely loud, panicky wail that only Pan could have made coming from behind us, inside the tree line. We leaped to our feet, facing the trees, Connor, Zach, and I with our sharpened pocketknives open, and Luke with his spear poised above his head, ready to attack if need be. We probably should have run away, like we usually did, but we also wanted to save our friend, assuming he really was in danger. As I mentioned before, we were too brave and too curious for our own good.

But the danger wasn't in front of us—it was above. The four of us looked up just in time to see a large birdlike creature spiraling down from the cloudless blue sky. It was a harpy, a monster with the head and torso of a woman, but also with the dark wings, tail, and talons of a huge bird. A snarl on her face, the harpy flew down toward us, her rough, sharp talons outstretched. Connor, Zach, and I turned to sprint away, but Connor tripped and fell, screaming helplessly. With a grunt, Luke instinctively chucked his spear into the air at the harpy, just as she swooped down to grab the fallen Connor, and it stuck in one of her leathery wings with a loud *thunk*. She screeched and fell back into the wind, her long black hair blowing wildly around her pale face. But somehow she managed to stay in the air and continued her dive toward us, aiming for Luke's head now.

I gulped, abruptly realizing that this harpy was not going to give up the fight so easily. She was perhaps the monster who came the closest to killing us in the three whole years of our being in the forest. But there was also no way to outrun her, since the quick and powerful harpy was obviously not bothered very much by the wound Luke had inflicted upon her. Plus, she would certainly be able to trap at least one of us kids in those spiky talons of hers and carry him away while the rest ran for cover. This meant that we had no choice but to fight back for the first time, to kill the monster before she could kill one of us.

Connor gasped beside me as I threw my small black pocketknife up at the monster in determination, and it made a deep cut on one of the harpy's feet, just above a claw before falling to the grass about eight feet in front of me. Following my lead, Zach threw his red pocketknife at the harpy, and then Connor did the same. Zach's pocketknife struck the harpy in the head, right on her cheek, and Connor's slashed her neck.

Using Zach and Connor's attack as a distraction, I dove for my knife just in case the harpy would continue her own attack and desperately hoped the boys' pocketknives wouldn't cut me as they fell back down to earth. I grabbed the blade with my left hand as I stood up, but just then, the harpy hit the ground in front of Zach and Connor with a big thump.

I stood staring at her with the guys as the harpy gave short, uneven gasps for air and slowly bled out in front of us. Monster blood—golden, with an unusual tinge of green—flowed steadily from the four wounds we had inflicted upon her and created tiny streams along the creases in her leathery wings, but still she did not give up the fight. Using her shredded wings and curled talons as leverage, the harpy pushed herself toward us, a cold glare in her dark, beady eyes. Panting, the three boys and I started to back away from the monster, retreating to the trees, and I wondered what kind of grudge she had against us. Whatever it was, it was obviously very strong.

Finally, the beautiful beast shuddered one last time and was still. It was eerily silent for a moment, but then the harpy suddenly crumbled to dust, disappearing into the soil without a trace. The four of us had just killed our first monster, and I had a strong feeling that it would not be our last.

"Well, she'll be in the Underworld by now, I expect," said Pan quietly, walking out into the sunlight from behind a tree. My human friends and I jumped, too focused on the dying harpy to notice him trot over.

"Oh, so *now* you come out of the tree cover?" Zach asked Pan, annoyed.

Pan opened his mouth to defend himself, crossed his arms, and objected, "I didn't have a weapon!"

Suddenly angry that Pan had kept his secret from us for so long, I frowned and shouted, "You're the freaking god of the wild! Surely you could have done something! Who was it that told us to carry weapons around all the time anyway? Oh, that's right, it was *you*!"

I took a deep breath, glancing around at the boys. Luke, Connor, and Zach looked surprised that I had lashed out at Pan so uncharacteristically, while Pan just looked hurt. I felt the slightest twinge of shame and remorse, but I pushed the feeling away and looked at him expectantly. Looking back on that moment now, I probably should have held on to those feelings a little longer before they went away forever.

Pan simply chewed his chapped lips and stayed quiet, as if deciding whether or not to tell us something. It seemed like it had been ages when he finally sighed and admitted, "I don't have all the powers you may think. I'm not immortal, for one. I'm really more like a . . . *protector* of the woods."

Connor's curiosity and impatience got the better of him, and he blurted out before Pan could elaborate, "Well, what about the rest of the gods? What do they do?"

Luke and Zach also seemed much more attentive to the conversation all of a sudden, and it was not often that someone held their attention for long periods of time. But don't get me wrong—they were great fun to spend time with, even if they preferred being at the center of attention.

Pan studied us carefully, and then his brown eyes darted around the edge of the meadow, as if he were looking to make sure we were alone, which was probably a smart thing to do. "The major gods aren't immortal either. They're just reincarnated every generation, taking over the bodies of humans. This generation has planted itself here, in the town of the Woods." He paused, then looked at each one of us in turn, letting this information sink in.

I glanced at Connor, Luke, and Zach, checking to see if they knew what Pan was really trying to say, but their expressions were blank and slightly confused. I sighed, knowing that the three of them could sometimes be thick-headed and that I was just going to have to put two and two together for them. So I said,

"You're saying that anyone your age who lives here could be a reincarnation, including us?" But it was really more of a statement than a question.

I already knew the answer, of course, and it was confirmed by Pan eagerly nodding his hairy head. Connor and Zach could do nothing but gasp in surprise as Luke nodded at us while exclaiming, "No way! I bet we are. Why else would we have survived in here?"

*Duh,* I thought, rolling my eyes as Zach snorted, and my gaze met Pan's, lingering as a silent conversation passed between us. I could tell he had a guess as to which god each of us was, and I slowly nodded in agreement with him, sure that his inferences were the same as mine.

It was quite simple, you see. Just as humans have different personalities, so did the Greek gods. For example, Luke was Poseidon, the god of the sea, earthquakes, and horses. As I mentioned before, Luke had a temper and had always loved the beach, even though he had been there only once. If we let him, Luke would probably fish for hours on end in the river in the northwestern part of the woods.

Zach was Zeus; it was unarguable. Who else could be so popular as to take control of an entire school in first grade? Just like an experienced politician, he knew the perfect ways to manipulate certain people to get what he wanted. His one ambitious dream was to be the president of the United States someday, and, in my opinion, there was no one better, as long as I was by his side. Zach was optimistic and quite charming most of the time, and some people even went so far as to say that the abnormally good weather in our town often mirrored his mood. No one from outside the forest realized how true that was before then. The elder satyrs and nymphs, I perceived, had had an ulterior obligation three years ago when they permitted Zach, Connor, Luke, and me free reign over their home.

Connor's Greek counterpart was Apollo, god of the sun, healing, prophecy, and music. He rose with the sun, waking up at the crack of dawn every day and crashing right when the sun disappeared behind the horizon. Even though he lived in the house next door, he woke me up almost every morning when he started playing his guitar or his flute. Or his saxophone. Or his violin. Or pretty much any instrument you could name.

And I was Athena, obviously. Somehow I knew things that I shouldn't, and I didn't understand how I could have known them in the first place. Even at a young age, I was destined to forever carry the burden of knowledge. In my dreams, I often had sudden flashes of what I realized then were someone else's memories, and in school I was asked for answers to problems endlessly, much to my annoyance. As added work, it was often my job to bail the guys out of trouble, when possible.

But right now all four of us were in a whole new kind of trouble, the kind that involved monsters, unimaginable powers, and much, much more.

Zach interrupted my thoughts. "We should find the other gods," he mused, stroking his chin. Connor, Luke, Pan, and I nodded in agreement. It was as good an idea as any, and it would be a benefit to us in the long run, although I thought it was kind of sad that we probably wouldn't have the woods to ourselves any longer.

I looked back down at my pocketknife, which was still partly covered in the harpy's sticky blood. Since we had killed the harpy, I had a feeling that our days of simply running from the monsters were over. As gods, we would no longer be restricted by the threat of monsters in our own forest. And I knew that if we were going to start actually hunting and killing the monsters to protect ourselves, as well as the satyrs and nymphs, we would need much better weapons. A word of wisdom: even a god cannot kill every monster with only a pocketknife.

"We should go to the antique shop first. I think we could use some better weapons, and I bet we will find something we can each use there," I suggested, and the others agreed.

So then Zach, Luke, Connor, and I slowly made our way out of the forest, striding east toward Main Street. And no, we didn't see any more monsters. Thankfully.

# Chapter 3:

# THE PROPHECY

The four of us strode across the empty street, not even bothering to check for cars. We then headed toward the antique shop, which was owned by my mother and stood between our town's small clothing store and the restaurant run by Zach and Luke's parents. Its simple façade made the shop look like it was built as a set for an old Western movie, but the inside, which was decorated with faded tapestries, looked more like a storage room in a medieval castle.

I pushed open the door, and as the tiny silver bell rang to signal our step through the wooden doorway, the familiar smell of leather and dust filled my nose. My mother looked up from her desk in the back, and her brown eyes met my gray ones for only a split second before she walked into the back room. Apparently she didn't feel the need to supervise us poking through all the miscellaneous junk.

On the right side of the room was a montage of mismatched furniture, mostly ancient wooden chests and tables with intricate designs. The left side of the room held more miscellaneous items, such as swords and small metal sculptures, bearing witness to the fact that my mom and dad had gone through a long phase of a medieval obsession before I was born. There was also a ship in a bottle, along with a large broken grandfather clock that had supposedly belonged to Benjamin Franklin. Where my mother found all these things was a mystery to everyone, including me and my father.

The four of us began picking through the dense pile of stuff on the left side of the room. After a few minutes, we hadn't found much, but Luke spontaneously decided he liked an old, rusty black trident, and I frowned, supposing it could be cleaned up somehow. A laughing Zach had just picked up a metal sword that was way too long for him and was swinging it about wildly when I heard the tiny bell ring, meaning someone else had just walked through the door.

I turned to see who it was and recognized the owner of the gas station, a muscular man with caramel-colored hair, squeezing through a small opening between two tables, heading to my mother's desk in the back of the room. My mom must have heard the bell too because she walked out of the back storage room and sat down in the leather chair before politely greeting the man. "Hello, Robert, how can I help you today?" Just then, I noticed his daughter standing in the small walkway behind him, looking quite bored and sending sympathetic glances toward the boys as if she pitied them for their blatant immaturity.

Her name was Camille, one of the quieter ones in our small class. I didn't know her as well as Zach, Luke, and Connor, but she was nice and we talked often. She had flushed cheeks and wavy, blonde hair usually held up in a tight bun, with hazel eyes almost exactly like Connor's. In fact, the two of them looked so much alike that people who didn't know them might mistake them for siblings, maybe even twins.

*Twins.* My eyes lit up as I saw her carefully pick up an antique wooden bow and study it curiously. Instantly I knew who she was: Artemis, the maiden goddess of the moon and the hunt, a daughter of Zeus, and the twin sister of Apollo.

Feeling excited to have found another goddess, I glanced over my shoulder at the guys. Luke was busy inspecting his trident, and Connor was rummaging through some old junk, but I caught Zach's eye and jerked my head toward

Camille. He must have understood that I suspected she might be a Greek goddess, because he nodded and followed me over to her almost immediately.

"Hey, Camille," I started, and she looked up to meet my gaze. "Have you ever been in the woods before?"

She raised her thin eyebrows and challenged, "If I had, do you really think I would still be standing here alive?"

Okay, so she had a point.

"Maybe," I answered honestly, thinking about our godliness, and Zach quickly nodded his head in agreement.

Then I looked down at the bow Camille was still holding and noticed how beautiful it was. It had a design of a flower vine running down it, and the wood was still in very good condition. I also noticed the faded leather quiver full of arrows that sat on a chair next to Camille and asked, gesturing to the bow, "Have you ever shot before?"

Camille looked back down at the bow, then back up at Zach and me, and shrugged. "Once or twice."

"Are you any good?" Zach piped up cheerfully.

"Maybe," Camille responded shortly, narrowing her eyes at Zach again.

Zach exchanged uncomfortable glances with me, but I gave him a nod of encouragement and he said, "How would you like to come with us into the woods tomorrow? I promise you won't get killed, as long as you stay with us."

Camille studied us suspiciously, debating her options. Then she checked behind her to make sure her father wasn't listening and said in a low voice, "All right, I'll admit I'm curious. What time?"

"Ten. In the morning, that is . . . and you may want to bring that with you," I said, pointing at the bow and arrows, but then her dad called for her again. She wordlessly raised her eyebrows at us one last time as she followed her father out the door, leaving the bow on the chair. When she winked at Zach and me, I knew she would come back for it later.

Meanwhile, Zach walked back toward the other end of the shop, continuing to look for a suitable weapon. I picked up a small spear that I decided I liked well enough and was going over to meet the boys when I saw a shiny, convex, round metal object with a large golden Medusa head on the front of it. From the two hooks embedded in the backside, I could tell that the former owner had used it as a wall decoration, but I saw it for what it really was: a shield. Athena's shield, an *aegis*, to be specific. *My* shield. So I picked it up, knowing I could find a way to fix it.

I walked outside with the guys after Zach had settled on a jagged piece of metal, which had a strange resemblance to a lightning bolt, and I knew that when it was charged with electricity, it would do some serious damage to whatever unfortunate creature was in its path. Connor had decided he would find a weapon later because he hadn't seen anything he really liked yet, but there was no real rush. We did not have to pay, since my mom owned the store, but I wasn't sure she had even noticed us leave with the weapons. That was probably for the best; she became too overprotective of me when she was worried.

We turned left, walking on the sidewalk past Zach and Luke's parents' restaurant, the Fire Pit, when we saw another classmate sitting alone outside at one of the small, round, green tables set for two.

"What in the world are you guys doing with those spears and . . . is that *Athena's shield*?" questioned the husky voice of Shane, a boy who used a wooden cane due to being disabled since birth. Whenever he wasn't using the cane, he walked with a jarring limp that just looked plain painful. Most kids stayed away from Shane because of this, but he was nice if you got to know him. His hair was dark and, for some unknown reason, speckled with gray, making him appear much older than he really was. His parents were the county carpenters, automatically making them good friends of my mother's, and he was also quite gifted in that particular skill set.

Zach, Connor, Luke, and I looked down at what we were holding in shock, surprised to find out that he knew about Greek myths. It was not often a kid of our age was into that sort of thing, but I supposed he might have extra time around the house, since he was unfortunately restricted from doing things a normal kid might otherwise enjoy.

With an indifferent shrug, Zach told him vaguely, "It's for the forest."

Shane raised one of his bushy eyebrows at Zach, but he continued to eye my shield at the same time. "I could fix your shield, if you want."

That was an offer I couldn't (and would be stupid to) refuse, so I handed him the shield as Connor asked, "Hey, do you think you could make me a bow and some arrows?" When Shane nodded thoughtfully, as if already forming a design in his mind, Connor thanked him.

Then we waved goodbye to the boy who I was certain was Hephaestus, the smith god, and the four of us hurried to get home. We were ready for the next day to come so we could go into the woods again, this time with another god or two.

---

The next morning, we had a quick breakfast of pancakes and sausages at Connor's house, and then we raced to meet Shane outside the restaurant. "Here you go," he said, handing me my newly polished shield (minus the hooks, thankfully), to which he had attached thick leather straps. He also gave Connor a brand new wooden bow and a quiver full of arrows. All I could think about was how on earth Shane had managed to build all of that in a single night.

Just then, Camille walked out of the antique shop behind us, holding the bow she had been looking at the day before in one hand, with the worn leather quiver slung lazily over one shoulder. Shane's jaw dropped. "You too?" he asked Camille, and she just shrugged. Apparently she didn't feel bothered enough to offer up an explanation.

Shane shook his head in wonder before asking, "Are you all going in right now?" We all nodded, and Shane looked down at the concrete, thinking quietly to himself for a minute. Then he declared, "I'm coming too."

"What?" we all exclaimed at the same time, staring at Shane in disbelief. I was sure we were all thinking the same thing: could he really make it with his bad leg?

But Shane seemed to have read our minds, because he responded firmly, "I can make it."

I had to admit that he was pretty tough. Still, Shane must have been really curious to know what was in the forest, and I couldn't blame him. At a loss for words, Zach and I looked at each other, shrugging. Neither of us really wanted to tell him no.

Suddenly, I heard the slapping sound of feet hitting pavement coming from behind us. We turned around to see yet *another* classmate, a girl with reddish-brown hair, wearing a purple tank top and a pair of skinny jeans. I sighed when I realized it was Alicia, a slightly snobby girl who had latched onto Zach during our very first day at school. Because she was so fond of Zach, she was often rude to any other girl who tried to get close to him, especially me. I really wasn't sure why, because I had never thought of the relationship between Zach and me as romantic. It was purely a brother-sister type of relationship . . . or father-daughter, if you were referring to our godliness. However, Alicia's jealousy made her the perfect candidate for Hera, Zeus's powerful wife.

"Is there a party I wasn't invited to?" Alicia asked, but she didn't wait for anyone to answer her. "Because if there is, I'm inviting myself." Everyone but Alicia groaned. Although she was popular, she didn't get along well with too many kids. We had to let her come, though, even if we didn't particularly want to; we had an ulterior motive unknown to Camille and Shane.

A few minutes later, all seven of us were making our way along a narrow path in single file. It was slow going, however, since we kept having to wait for Shane to catch up with the rest of us. Even with his trusty cane, he was still stumbling and tripping all over the place. As if to dampen our mood even more, we were heading east toward the meadow when the light suddenly got darker, much darker than it usually was under the cover of the trees.

We looked around wildly as a thick mist rolled in out of nowhere, swirling around us like the walls of a tornado. It sounded as if wind was whistling through the tree leaves, but there was no wind to speak of, not even a breeze buffeting our hair. Behind me, I heard Camille mutter something like, "I knew I shouldn't have come." But I just ignored her and raised my spear because the mist, still thickening, was forming into the unmistakable shape of a human. Luke and Connor too looked prepared for a fight, and out of the corner of my eye, I saw Alicia cling desperately to Zach's arm, as if he could protect her from whatever was descending upon us.

Looking closer, I saw that it was a girl . . . or something that looked like a girl. She was barefoot and wore a deep purple dress and shawl. The only skin showing besides that on her feet was on her tan face, which bore large eyes that were glowing bright green, with no pupils or irises. She had thin, plucked eyebrows, and her lustrous black hair was tied in a side braid, entwined with lavender ribbons. Her hand rose up into the air to ask for silence, but we gods were too bewildered to say anything anyway.

She opened her mouth and more lime green light emanated from within her as she spoke: "I am the Oracle of Delphi, here to deliver a prophecy." Her voice sounded strange to me, but I couldn't figure out why. I didn't have time to dwell on it, though, because she continued to tell us the prophecy as the mist billowed into thick gray clouds behind her.

"In six years' time will come one god's prime,
And he will be tired of being under fire.
He will fight for what he thinks is his right,
But it could tear apart the balance that's fair,
And the duty will fall upon you all
In order to save the world."

Then the girl, who looked about one or two years older than us, fell silent, and the silver mist swirled around her again, swallowing her up until we could no longer see her. As the mist slowly faded away into thin air once again, we saw the girl collapse in a heap onto the soft ground, and the glowing light that had been projecting from her green eyes faded, leaving her with the closed eyes of a regular person.

Suddenly the truth hit me, and I realized why the Oracle's voice had sounded so weird to me: she had been speaking a different language. Yes, she had been speaking in Greek, but somehow we all seemed able to understand her perfectly. That alone proved we were gods.

Still incapable of stringing together complete thoughts, the seven of us stood gaping in complete shock at the spot of grass on which the Oracle of Delphi had just collapsed. We had to save the world. In six years. *Wow,* I thought to myself in disbelief. At least we had time to prepare, to find the other remaining gods.

I was finally brought back from my thoughts when Camille demanded, "Okay, does someone want to tell me what's *really* going on here?" Unsurprisingly, Shane and Alicia looked just as confused, and so Zach launched into a long story about how he, Luke, Connor, and I found out we were gods, which took quite a while. At least there weren't any monsters around.

Meanwhile, Connor had been attending to the Oracle, who still had not woken up from whatever kind of sleeping trance she was stuck in. Connor patted her cheek gently at first, but then he started to slap her more violently. I turned around, eyes wide with horror, and without even thinking, I said in perfect Greek, "Apollo, what do you think you are doing?" Connor only shrugged, and I was pretty sure I saw him smirk.

At this, the Oracle's eyes flew open, and she quickly tried to sit up, but her purple robes were tangled around her legs and thus prevented her from bolting upright. "What happened?" she asked in broken English, and I could tell she did not normally speak in our first language. When no one answered her right away, she said slowly, "You are them . . . the gods, no?"

"Well, some of them," Zach replied blandly, studying her closely. "I've never seen you around here before, but I thought we knew *everyone*. Where do you live?"

The Oracle of Delphi sighed, and her green eyes looked into Zach's blue ones extremely seriously. "Deep in the forest, to the northwest. I only come out when I need to deliver a very, very important prophecy." Nodding at Camille, she explained further, "Lady Artemis's huntresses bring me food. They are the ones who told me about you."

I smiled to myself as Camille's pretty face lit up and she immediately raised her eyebrows with a look that read, *I have huntresses?* She appeared to be a mixture of surprised and impressed.

But then the Oracle abruptly leaped up off the ground, obviously spooked by something unknown to the rest of us. As she hurried off unexpectedly, she yelled back over her shoulder in Greek, "Do not be afraid of the future now! Embrace your godliness here!"

"Well, that was weird," Shane remarked, scrunching up his nose in confusion as we watched the Oracle disappear into the trees and the mist, leaving us alone to ponder the mysterious prophecy and the rest of the gods.

"Understatement of the century, my friend," Camille agreed, shaking her head and patting Shane's shoulder. "Understatement of the century."

Chapter 4:

# THE REST OF THE GODS

We continued trudging through the forest along the narrow paths covered with dead leaves and thick tree roots. We were now heading west toward the rushing river to introduce Alicia, Shane, and Camille to Pan. I was interested to see how they would react to meeting him, since he would be the first mythical creature they would see besides the Oracle, if you even counted her.

Eventually we walked out onto the damp riverbank, and we followed the river north for a ways, until it flowed around a bend and suddenly dropped off at a small waterfall, where the water collected in a small, deep pool before slowly continuing on its course. This was the only place in which the river had almost no current, so it was a popular swimming area for water nymphs, and it was Pan's preferred hangout.

We stumbled down the steep hill, climbed down the slick rock sides of the waterfall, and turned to face the pool. There were currently two teenaged nymphs, wearing bikinis made of leaves and long blades of grass—attire that would have been considered downright scandalous by anyone from the Woods—

swimming lazily through the cool water, with their long, brown hair flowing out behind them. I could tell that they were both water nymphs because of the slight blue tinges to their skin. Tree nymphs, on the other hand, tended to have very light greenish tinges.

Meanwhile, Pan was eating grapes and sitting on a makeshift throne made of large rocks, which were covered with soft, bright green moss he had collected from nearby pine trees. The way Pan was splayed out across all the rocks made it look as if he were tanning his bare chest, but it was actually pretty dark out because the pool was so well covered by trees that formed a sort of shade tent, catching the rays of sunlight before they could reach us.

When the seven of us stopped in front of the pool, however, both of the nymphs and Pan looked up, staring at us in surprise. Although seeing Zach, Luke, Connor, and me there was definitely not uncommon, seeing three new people was.

It was silent for a moment as Pan carefully studied Camille, Alicia, and Shane one at a time. Then, without even looking at them, he ordered the nymphs, "Leave us." Quickly, the two nymphs heaved themselves up and out of the water, and they walked away barefooted, trying to wring the water out of their long hair. Even though Pan was younger than most nymphs and satyrs, they all knew about and respected our godliness.

"Let me guess," Pan started again, and he pushed himself off his rock throne and brushed bits of moss off his hairy goat legs. He pointed in turn to Shane, Camille, and Alicia. "Hephaestus, Artemis, . . . and Hera." When Zach nodded to show that the guesses were right, Pan stuck out his hand to each of them. "Pan, god of the wild, at your service." He even did a little bow. Although he was indeed a god, Pan was only a minor god; he did not sit on the Olympian Council of the twelve most powerful ones.

I watched Camille, Shane, and Alicia closely as they shook Pan's rough hand in mild shock. They were all staring at his goat legs, slightly bewildered, and I smirked, remembering how it felt meeting Pan for the first time. But I interrupted the moment by letting out a small cough to get Zach's attention and nodding toward Pan.

"Oh, right," Zach said. "So, we were on our way over here and suddenly the Oracle of Delphi shows up and—"

Zach was interrupted by Pan, "Ah, she finally told you the prophecy. Yeah, she told it to me after you four first showed up in the forest." He looked at Zach, Connor, Luke, and me in confusion before asking, "You've really never met her before?" We shook our heads, and Pan shrugged, not worried at all. "Oh well, anything else?" We all shook our heads again and Pan checked his wrist, as if he had a watch, then said, chuckling, "Well, I have to go catch up with those nymphs again. Come back when you find more gods." With that, Pan winked at us and trotted off in the direction that the two nymphs had gone.

*A lot of help he was*, I thought to myself. *Not.*

At last, the seven of us turned to walk back east toward Main Street. There was still a lot of time left in the day to search for more gods, but our trek took a while because we had to walk back to the town from almost all the way on the other side of the forest. We hid all of our new weapons in hollow logs near the edge of the forest, so our parents would never see them again, and I sighed as we all walked out into the bright sunlight from under the trees. As usual, the street was empty and quiet, but then two laughing boys our age suddenly turned the corner and started running in our direction.

The boy with curly brown hair, who happened to be winning the little race, was wearing an old pair of soccer shorts and a plain white T-shirt with the Nike swoosh on it. His name was Josh, and he ran everywhere. And I mean *everywhere.* He did own a very nice bike, but for some reason he preferred running, and that's how he chose to deliver the newspapers to people in our town almost every morning. I was already considering him as the prankster messenger god, Hermes.

The second boy, who was following close behind, was Josh's best friend and partner in crime, Cole. I was also good friends with him, so I was secretly hoping he was a god, but honestly, I just wasn't sure. He didn't really have the standout qualities of any of the gods we had left to find, but he had many qualities from all the different gods. He was smart, pretty tough, and a funny guy overall, at least from what I had seen.

My gray eyes met Cole's brown ones and I waved, and he just grinned with Josh as they slowed to a stop in front of us, still cracking up at an inside joke.

"Well, if it isn't the Monster Watch . . . and others?" Josh said questioningly while eyeing Shane, Alicia, and Camille.

I recognized the tone of his voice immediately—curious and slightly confused. After all, the Monster Watch was well known to be an exclusive club, and not one for the faint of heart. You see, the Monster Watch was the county's loving nickname for Zach, Luke, Connor, and me, given to us because we were always going into the woods, which was rumored by children to hide terrible monsters, although no one but us knew how true that was. A clever reporter came up with the name when we were six, though it didn't catch on until about a year later, when our parents finally realized that they couldn't keep the four of us out of that terrible forest.

Luke only smiled at the mention of our nickname and asked politely, "What are you two up to?"

Cole and Josh exchanged mischievous glances and started laughing again. "We just pulled a prank on Matt. Man, he's going to kill us!" Cole managed to gasp between his laughter, but Camille and I just rolled our eyes. We both had little tolerance for mischief, but unlike me, Camille seemed to try to avoid most boys as much as possible for this reason, which, in turn, was a reason I hadn't gotten the chance to spend as much time with Camille as I would have liked.

Just then, we heard a very angry yell coming from down the street, "Arrgh! I'm going to kill you freaks and eat you for dinner!"

As if on cue, Matt, the biggest bully from our school, suddenly rounded the corner and stormed toward us. I saw that his brown buzz cut, red shirt, and jeans were covered in paint of all the different colors of the rainbow. I had to admit he looked pretty ridiculous, so I started snickering along with the rest of the Monster Watch, Shane, and Alicia. Camille, however, was just frowning.

"You know, cannibalism isn't tolerated in America!" Josh shouted back at him, and we all started laughing again. I had to admit that kid had some guts, messing with Matt. But the unfazed Matt only continued to stomp toward us, his face getting even redder by the second, and I could have sworn that I saw steam blowing out of his nose and ears. He really did look like he might kill them, or at least beat them up. This unwavering ruthlessness made Matt the perfect candidate for Ares, the angry war god.

Josh and Cole were just thinking about taking off and hiding from Matt when a police car slowly rolled down the street and stopped to talk to Matt. It was one of only three police cars in the entire county, and it happened to be driven by Alicia's father. "What do we do? You two could get in so much trouble," Alicia hissed at Josh and Cole, knowing how strict her father could be at times.

Frowning, I watched Matt turn to the officer and begin to tell his story, waving his colorful arms around his head as he spoke in a raised voice. I knew that if Josh and Cole were going to make a clean escape, there was only one place Alicia's father wouldn't go.

"Into the woods. Now," I whispered.

Camille, Alicia, Josh, and the rest of the Monster Watch immediately turned and took a step toward the woods, the safe haven for our godliness. Cole, however, stood frozen in place, his brown eyes wide, and Shane simply sighed as he leaned over on his cane. With a dismissive wave, Shane ordered, "Just go without me. I'll slow everyone down, so I'll only go in there when I'm truly needed."

The rest of us nodded in understanding, but Josh still looked over at Cole expectantly. Stuffing his hands in his pockets, shoulders slumped, Cole shook his head apologetically and said, "Sorry, dude, but I'm not ready to die yet." He spun on his heel and took off down the road without another word, Shane hobbling along slowly behind him.

*Yet,* I thought wishfully. *But maybe later.*

I pushed the thought of Cole out of my mind as the seven of us left hid only a few yards inside the forest behind some trees, just long enough to make sure Alicia's dad was gone and to tell Josh about the prophecy that the Oracle of Delphi had given to us. At first, he thought we were absolutely crazy, but then he caught a glimpse of the Minotaur from afar.

When we finally walked back out onto Main Street, the police car was gone, but unfortunately, Matt was standing there on the cracked sidewalk, still waiting for us and still covered in paint. He quickly stomped up to Josh and prodded him in the chest. "One day I *will* get you. I'll make sure of it."

Zach only sighed irritably, pushed the bully away from Josh, and growled, "Get over it, Matt. We have to tell you something." And so, for the third time that day, we had to explain our godliness to a classmate. But unlike the dubious

Josh, Matt's face immediately brightened at the thought of being a Greek god. I knew power was everything to him; he bullied everyone he saw as a threat.

Later, we left Matt on the street outside the antique shop and slowly headed back toward our houses on Maple Street. Obviously in a hurry, Camille peeled off to the left toward her small, white home down the road, while the rest of us stopped at Alicia's house, which was on the corner.

Lucky for us, Alicia's father wasn't home, and her sister, Madison, was kneeling outside in the grass next to some beautiful flowers. She wore a yellow summer dress that matched her happy mood, even though the hem was covered in soil, and her long blonde hair was held up in a ponytail, a freshly picked daisy tucked behind her ear. The five of us had talked it over earlier in the forest with Shane, Alicia, and Camille, and we had all decided that Madison, who loved gardening, would make a perfect Demeter, the goddess of the harvest and fertility.

Zach smiled and greeted her kindly, "Hey, Maddie. What's up?" Madison returned his smile and blushed, while Alicia just glared at her. I was not the goddess of love, but I could tell when someone had a crush going on. Sensing trouble, I simply shook my head and looked down at the freshly mowed grass under my shoes, leaving the rest of the Monster Watch and Alicia to explain everything to her.

As the conversation went on, Madison's bright brown eyes grew wider and wider, until I thought they might burst. She was definitely surprised, to say the least. By the end, all she could say was, "Wow."

Afterward, Zach, Connor, Luke, and I left the sisters alone to quarrel about Zach and headed across the street to our own houses. We had all agreed that it was time for a snack. Chattering excitedly, we went to Connor's house first because we thought his mother would make us ham and cheese sandwiches, but unfortunately for us, no one was home. Although we were quite capable of making the sandwiches ourselves, we nine-year-olds were much too lazy and impatient. Besides, we knew that none of the rest of our parents would be home yet either, so we retreated into the woods to play a couple rounds of reverse hide-and-seek. While we were still hungry, there were delicious berries to munch on inside the forest, if you knew where to look and which ones were safe to eat. I then tried to convince them otherwise, but the guys forced me to hide first, which was a big mistake. They searched for a full three hours before giving up, when I had just been hiding in a tree near Pan's hideout. Zach and Luke had also taken turns hiding, but we had found them fairly quickly and with no real problems.

By the time we came out of the mysterious forest, the sun had long since set in the sky, and it was dark, with the first stars just beginning to shine. Wasting no time in returning to our human families, we bid each other goodbye and I quickly ran up the stairs to my front porch, clutching my stomach after realizing how hungry I was. Something to eat besides berries would have been nice.

Humming softly to myself, I opened the screen door and stepped into the kitchen. It was surprisingly dark at such a late time of night, and so I began frowning in confusion almost instantly. Sure enough, I heard a sniffling sound coming from my left and turned to see my mother, her silky brown hair covering her face as she tried to hide her tears. I only frowned deeper and looked past her into the next room, where I saw my father lurking, still standing tall but slightly hunched over. He was rummaging through the piles of papers strewn about the living room and grumbling loudly to himself, like a bear, about many unrelated things all at once. By the way he was stumbling around the dimly lit room, I could tell he had been drinking, probably beer of some sort. I couldn't say I was surprised, though, as he had been labeled an alcoholic a long time ago.

When my father was drunk, he often yelled and fought with my mother, and every once in a while he would even take off in the middle of the night to an unknown location, sometimes even out of the country. But he would always return a few days later with a fancy antique in hand as a gift for my mother, acting like nothing bad had ever happened between the two of them. No one knew where he got these fancy possessions, most of which were paintings, but no one really wanted to ask, out of fear that his mysterious adventures sometimes involved illegal dealings. And he wasn't native to the town, a fact that seemed to make him even less trustworthy in the eyes of others.

At such a young age, I was already growing to hate my father and was fed up with his immature actions, which would even force me out of my own house occasionally. I remembered spending many nights at Zach and Luke's house, curled up on the floor of their bedroom and wrapped tightly in Zach's extra blanket. If having a sleepover with two boys was a strange thing for a nine-year-old girl to do, Martha didn't seem to think so. Out of worry for my safety and emotional health, she often invited me to stay there if my parents were being especially loud and possibly violent, no matter how old I was, and I was always grateful to her.

Of course, my mother tried and failed to keep these fights a secret from me and from the rest of the town. When I wasn't camping out next door, I spent sleepless nights sitting at the top of the stairs, quiet as a mouse, listening to my parents fight for hours on end. When I was four or five years old, I used to get frightened, but I was now accustomed to their bickering and did not scare so easily anymore. Needless to say, I had seen far worse in the forest.

Therefore, I just bit my lip, thinking that it was probably time I confronted them about their arguments anyway. Unsure of exactly what to say, I awkwardly patted my mother's shoulder and whispered, "It's okay to cry, Mom."

She pushed the hair out of her eyes and gave me a broken smile. She was looking down at me, and it wasn't just because I was shorter than her. "Then why do you never cry anymore, sweetie?" my mother said as she stroked my hair lovingly.

I cringed and gritted my teeth in silence, closing my eyes to avoid meeting her sorrowful eyes. To be honest, I hated when she called me sweetie because, in case you hadn't noticed, I was definitely not sweet. I hadn't been sweet in three years. Truthfully, I was armed and dangerous, but I knew I could never tell my parents about what really happened in the woods. And that secret was eating me alive.

So instead, I took a deep breath and replied seriously, "Because I realize now that I've never come across anything worth crying over."

Then I simply turned on my heel and walked upstairs to my room. I had nothing else to say to her.

---

The next day, Connor and I met Luke and Zach at their parents' restaurant, the Fire Pit, which was named after the elaborate fireplace in the back of the room that was kept burning all day during the frigid winters. Together, we sat down in our own comfortable booth at the back of the restaurant, chatting happily and sipping the fresh, ice-cold lemonade for free. I always swore that the Fire Pit made the best-tasting lemonade in the world, but at that moment, the four of us were not savoring the sweet drink as much as usual. In fact, we were in the middle of arguing over who would hide first in that day's round of reverse hide-and-seek when a classmate of ours strode into the room with a swagger to her step.

It was Becca, doing her best runway walk. At our age, she was already the prettiest girl in the state—probably even in the entire world—and she knew it. People of all ages would stop and stare at her whenever she strutted by, mystified by her elegant beauty, her seemingly innocent sensuousness. She was obviously the gorgeous goddess of love and desire, Aphrodite.

Becca's soft blue eyes lit up when she spotted us from the doorway, and she flipped her silky, strawberry-blonde hair with confidence before heading over to our table. "What are you boys doing here?" she asked flirtatiously.

I was only slightly annoyed that she chose to ignore me, as usual. Meanwhile, Luke flashed his white teeth and answered her, "Not much, Aphrodite."

Becca wrinkled her nose in slight confusion. "What did you just call me?" she asked, and I couldn't say I was surprised to find out that she was not familiar with any Greek myths. I guessed she probably spent all of her afternoons painting her nails or going shopping at the mall a few towns away, not studying Greek history.

*Great,* I thought sarcastically when her eyes began to light up as Zach continued with our story. *We just gave her an even bigger ego.* I sighed and shook my head. Shane suddenly staggered through the doorway and came over to sit down with us, but Becca only looked down disapprovingly at him and his cane. She could be nice at times, but so snobby at other times, it was unbelievable. Unsurprisingly, she quickly excused herself and went to sit outside, though I couldn't say I was too disappointed.

Luke, Connor, Shane, and Zach continued their conversation while I looked around the room. Over at one of the tall bar stools, our classmate Jack was on his third large glass of lemonade. I had honestly never seen someone drink so much at once, so I knew he had to be Dionysus, the god of wine. I just frowned, however, and decided that we would fill him in a bit later, when he was slightly more stable.

"So, who's the last god?" Shane asked, tilting his head, and I turned back to face the boys. Finally, a topic worth my attention.

"Hades," Zach replied, his brow furrowing, fists clenching.

So far, we had found no one who would match the personality of the ruler of the Underworld, but I suddenly remembered a newspaper article about missing people, specifically the mention of a classmate or two, from the week when the Monster Watch had first gone into the forest. I was beginning to think that we would not find Hades here in town. Instead, he would be stuck under the ground, perhaps lounging around in a large palace all by himself, living exactly like he had since he found out from someone else—the Oracle, most likely—that he was a god.

"Don't forget Hestia," Connor added, referring to the goddess of the hearth.

I snapped my fingers and exclaimed, "Haley!" Zach let out a whoop and high-fived me, obviously agreeing. Feeling extremely motivated, we left the restaurant quickly, even though we had no real reason to hurry, and headed to Haley's house, where she spent most of her time outside of school. It also happened to be right next door to Alicia and Madison's, which would definitely be convenient later on in our godly careers.

A few minutes later, the five of us arrived at her house, a little one-story building painted a soft lavender color, almost gray. We stepped up on her porch in unison, and Zach rang the doorbell. The screen door creaked open almost immediately, and Haley tentatively poked her head out, her long, light brown hair flowing in the slight breeze and her nimble fingers gripping the doorframe. Even though it was very warm outside, she wore a purple cashmere sweater, which she only hugged tighter around her. She always managed to stay cool and collected. I couldn't remember ever seeing her lash out at anyone for anything, to be honest.

"Um, hi," Haley said meekly, obviously not expecting to see us. Admittedly, she did not get too many visitors.

"Let's take a walk," Zach suggested as Shane politely stuck out his arm for her to take, and Haley glanced back over her shoulder, deeper into her mysterious house, before silently shrugging and taking Shane's arm. Together, we aimlessly walked down the streets as we told her our story, and she silently listened to us. I thought she was taking the whole thing very well, better than any of the other gods had (or at least more calmly), and I was eager to see what she would think of the monsters when she visited our lovely woods.

A few minutes later, we bid Haley and Shane farewell, and the rest of the Monster Watch and I headed back into our second home, the forest. For now, our work was done. But now what? We had found all the gods (except for Hades, who was left to figure out all this on his own—if Zach could avoid a problem like Hades, he would) remarkably fast, which I thought was quite strange, even though we lived in such a tiny town. As it turned out, there was a good reason for this too. However, we didn't find out why we had been so motivated, why the Fates had been on our side that day until six years later, when we were fulfilling the prophecy . . .

# Part Two

# "THE KNOWING"

*Six Years Later*

# Chapter 5:

# PERSEPHONE

*Clang!* Ares grunted, and his thick sword blade hit the golden Medusa head on my shield as I raised it up to block his swing. Taking advantage of his open position, I swung my spear down and to the left, and the tip caught in Ares's heavy armor as he stumbled backward, just out of my reach. But I knew he would be back for more.

Suddenly I heard a high-pitched whinny come from somewhere above me and looked up to the dark, cloudy sky to see Zeus atop the gleaming white horse, Pegasus, whose wings were outstretched, spiraling down toward the meadow. In one of Zeus's rough hands was a lightning bolt, shining so white-hot that it almost looked blue. His perfectly toned muscles rippled as he threw the bolt toward the ground, aiming at no one in particular.

My vision turned completely white for a couple of seconds due to the blinding lightning, but I didn't panic. This was nothing new. But when color finally returned, I saw Ares running straight at me again, just like I knew he would, his reddening face twisted in anger. I thought quickly and prayed silently to Zeus as I pointed my spear at Ares's chest. Right on cue, a bolt of lightning erupted from the sharp metal tip of my spear, hitting Ares exactly where I had aimed.

As he was blown at least thirty feet backward, I caught sight of Poseidon on the other side of the meadow, his golden trident raised above his head, ready to bring it down any second now. Then the trident's blunt end hit the ground, and as the earth gave a tremendous shake, I somersaulted into the trees for cover, hoping none would fall on me. I simply paused, waiting for the world to stop shaking, and hid behind a tree while I caught my breath and looked around.

A battle was currently ensuing between Poseidon and Zeus, and all I could see were bright flashes of light as I felt multiple small tremors in the ground, one after another, throw me off balance. The fraternal twins always liked to take out their anger at each other here, where they didn't have to worry about destroying a house.

Meanwhile, a few yards away from me, two other goddesses were having an equally epic showdown. When Demeter placed her arm out in front of her, her hand clenched in a fist, a thick vine shot up from the ground and wrapped itself around Hera, squeezing her tighter and tighter, like a snake would a mouse. All of a sudden, a flash of purple light blinded me, and when my vision cleared, I looked up to see Hera standing free again, the charred remains of the vine lying at her feet.

From across the way, close to Zeus and Poseidon, Apollo shot an arrow straight at Aphrodite, who was standing alone out in the open, cleaning off her small dagger with the bottom of her designer workout jacket. She ducked her pretty little head at the last second, and the arrow missed her by mere inches. "Hey! Watch the hair!" Aphrodite yelped as she smoothed down her golden locks. I smirked when I saw Apollo do the same. This was supposed to be a real battle, after all.

Throughout all of this action, Hermes was running circles around the rest of the gods so fast that I could barely see him; he was just a colored blur. In fact, his battle strategy was usually to run circles around the opposition until he or she just gave up the fight. Although I was in awe, I simply shook my head to refocus and continued surveying my opponents, trying to decide where to join the attack. Then, on the other side of the meadow, I saw a small flash of movement from way up in one of the tall pine trees. I immediately recognized Artemis's blonde head and grinned, certain about what she was planning to do. Sure enough, a slim wooden arrow shot gracefully out of the tree from where she was positioned and hit Hermes right on his heel, and he went tumbling to the ground. He finally stopped rolling in front of Dionysus, who tripped and fell down on top of him, cursing like a sailor.

Once Dionysus had pushed himself off the poor messenger god and moved on to join the fight against Demeter, Hermes began struggling to pull the arrow out of his dirt-covered winged shoe, even though the arrow had a pink suction cup at the tip instead of metal or rock. We were only practicing, after all—well, all of us gods except for Hestia and Hephaestus, who usually opted not to fight. And no one was ever supposed to get seriously injured.

I was heading back out into the open, ready for Ares to come at me yet again, when Zeus threw his hands into the air and shouted in Greek, "All right, that's enough!" He had just fried Poseidon with another lightning bolt, and looking at the angry expression on Poseidon's face, I knew it was not a coincidence that Zeus decided to call it quits now.

I shook my head and groaned as Poseidon teased Zeus, "What? We're quitting *now*? Are you scared of losing, Mr. King of the Gods?"

Zeus just crossed his arms and replied smartly, "Do you really want me to beat you up even more? Because I could, if you want."

Poseidon grumbled something that I didn't catch in response to his brother, and then we all headed east toward Main Street, bickering among ourselves excitedly. It was a sweltering afternoon, and we all craved a cold glass or two of the world's best lemonade.

We were trudging through the thick undergrowth, about halfway to the street, and chatting about nothing in particular when we heard the crackling of branches come from somewhere off to our left. We all drew our weapons in unison, ready to face and kill whatever monster was on our trail, and slowly turned to face the huge boulder a few yards away.

But it wasn't a monster.

The seemingly ordinary gray boulder was set into the small brown and green hillside, and the side facing us was hollowed out, creating a tiny cave, a cave we had walked by a thousand times before. But this time we all watched in awe as a pale arm, skin as white as pearl, reached out from the shadows and pushed a girl who looked about our age into the forest. As she stumbled forward, a thin, low-hanging branch caught in her straight, light brown hair, and she quickly turned around to free the strand of hair. The rest of the gods and I stayed silent, holding our breaths as if our lives depended on it. Thankfully, the girl did not seem to notice us yet, but we were standing at least fifty yards away, barely visible through the thick foliage.

Finally, the handsome pale person who had pushed the girl came out of the shadows, revealing himself to us for the first time. He squinted like it was very bright, though we could barely see the sun through the trees, which meant he obviously wasn't used to light. But instantaneously his expression changed from confusion to one of hurt and anger, his black eyes glaring at the girl as he chewed his lip in anguish. Exasperated, he ran his right hand through his jet-black hair before saying loudly to the girl in Greek, "Well? Aren't you going to leave now? Leave me, like you always do this time of year to go visit your goddamn mother!" His voice cracked with a hint of remorse.

A few yards away, the girl stood facing him, standing tall and trying to look brave, though she was trembling like an autumn leaf about to fall off a branch. "Oh gods, Hades! Don't yell at me! You know I can barely even remember meeting my mother, but you throw me out to live with the Oracle every summer anyway," she argued in a small voice.

I should have known. Hades, the one and only god of the dead, ruler of the Underworld. Which meant the girl was most likely Persephone, a daughter of Demeter whom Hades had kidnapped eons ago out of love for her. However, in most of the myths I had read, Persephone did not love him back, seeing him instead as her own personal prison warden. It looked like that was the case here too.

To be honest, I was not surprised that the rest of us had never seen Persephone in the forest before, since she said she lived with the Oracle, whom we rarely visited and who had probably been the one to tell the two that they were gods six years before. Our relationship with the Oracle was strictly one of business regarding the prophecy. We didn't often have a good reason to stop by her camp, except when we were hunting down the occasional monster for fun in her neck of the woods.

"Nothing I do pleases you! Not ever!" Hades shouted back at Persephone. He shook his head and rested it for a moment on a small crystal skull that topped off the tall, black staff he was gripping tightly. He then took a deep breath and lifted his head, but as he turned to face Persephone once again, his dark, cruel eyes locked on us.

For a few seconds, we stared at each other in stiff silence, wondering if Hades would make the first move or not. But instead, it was Persephone who whirled around to see what Hades was looking at, and she gasped when she saw us, her mouth forming into the shape of a perfect *O*. She looked baffled, overcome with so many emotions at once.

Then Persephone took a hesitant step toward us, her long white dress swaying elegantly around her ankles. "Mother Demeter?" she asked in almost a whisper, staring right into Demeter's soft brown eyes. Somehow she just *knew*, even though she hadn't remembered ever meeting Demeter until just then. I guessed it was instinct, a daughter's love. But I wouldn't know. In the myths, I had originally hatched out of Zeus's skull, already fully matured and clad in battle armor.

Rendered speechless, Demeter only nodded, and Persephone ran and hugged her long-lost mother. The air around them radiated with pure happiness, but then I glanced back over at Hades, who was now glaring at all of us even more intensely, his fists clenched tightly by his sides. Unlike Persephone, he did not make even the tiniest step to come meet us; he just stood silent and still, much like a rock. When Persephone had finally let go of Demeter and turned to stand next to her, facing him again, Hades growled at all of us angrily, "What are you all doing here?" We had obviously interrupted a deeply personal conversation, one not meant for our ears.

Seemingly unfazed, Zeus stepped forward and responded in a commanding Greek voice, "This is *our* forest, not yours. And besides, I could ask the same of you."

Hades frowned, looking very unimpressed. "It is spring now. Persephone is yours . . . for the time being. This is the agreement we made more than two thousand years ago, is it not?" Zeus nodded reluctantly, and we all returned to a state of awkward silence.

Eventually, Persephone broke the ice that had frozen over the fluid waters of our conversation. "You can go back to your palace now," she demanded, her voice tight. She was obviously eager to get rid of Hades, and I could understand why.

Sensing that he was no longer welcome in our realm, Hades silently glared at us one last time before turning and walking back into the cave, where he disappeared back into the Underworld. With that, Persephone let out a big sigh of relief and turned to face the rest of us. One by one, we introduced ourselves, though I'm sure she could have guessed all of our identities herself. She asked what we were doing here, and we told her everything, including the prophecy. But Persephone just nodded, appearing unsurprised, and explained, "I heard the Oracle mention the prophecy a couple of times when I used to stay with her."

After we had filled Persephone in about the current events in the forest, we all started to continue on our course back to Main Street, while Persephone eagerly continued to catch up with her mother and the rest of the gods. Meanwhile, I was silently pondering the prophecy, wondering who would be the god to turn against the rest. Maybe it was too early to guess, but I was thinking that I wouldn't be very surprised if the god in question were Hades.

Finally, we all reached the edge of the forest and hid our weapons and shiny armor among the trees, still chatting and bickering excitedly, in our usual manner. But then Persephone stopped dead in her tracks and pointed out, "I can't go out there. I have lived in here almost all of my life. It would look strange if a random girl showed up in such a tiny town, especially if I walked right out of the forest."

The rest of us nodded in understanding, figuring that she could use some time to set up some new living arrangements with Pan. Demeter also told us to go on without her, since she wanted to spend more time with her daughter and new best friend. So, after a short farewell, the rest of us stepped out of the dark forest and into the bright sunlight that shone over the town.

"Hey, Ash, can you do my math homework for me tonight?" Connor asked me in English.

I let out an exasperated sigh, thinking about school tomorrow and wishing for summer to come quickly. During school terms, it was even harder than usual to have good control over our double lives. You see, as soon as we were out of the forest, we no longer spoke in Greek or called each other by our god names. We knew very well that we could not let anyone learn about our secret identities, or else we would become human lab rats for the rest of our lives. How would we be able to save the world then?

"For the two hundred and forty-ninth time, no!" I replied (and yes, I had been counting), slightly annoyed with him, but Connor just grinned, obviously not expecting a different answer.

Together, the rest of the Monster Watch and I headed over to the Fire Pit, while Josh, the messenger, took the job of telling Shane and Haley what had happened in the woods that morning. The others said goodbye and returned to their homes after Camille announced she was going to take a long nap, which probably meant she would be going hunting in the woods later on that night. She was the only one of us gods, besides the members of the Monster Watch, who went into the forest regularly. For whatever reason, the others chose to venture in only when we had battle practices.

When we walked inside the old restaurant, the rest of the Monster Watch and I took a seat at our usual booth in the back of the dining room before ordering ourselves some lemonade. Luke took one quick sip and then leaned back in his seat, his blue-green eyes shining. That movement alone, subtle but commanding, would have been enough to capture the attention of thousands.

"Persephone's kind of cute, huh?" he observed as he slowly ran his fingers through his black hair, and Connor and Zach grinned mischievously, obviously in agreement.

I just groaned. "Don't even think about it, dude. Maddie will kill you," I lectured Luke, but he simply shrugged at me, still smirking.

Zach was about to add something in Luke's defense, but then he saw Cole, who still didn't know about the truth of the Greek myths, making his way toward us. So Zach quickly changed the topic to the first thing that came to his mind. "I love clouds, don't you? Today, I saw one that looked like a bunny."

Of course, Luke and Connor cracked up involuntarily, but I just shook my head in defeat as Cole gave Zach a dubious look. I knew I probably should have changed the topic myself.

In slight confusion, Cole ruffled his brown hair, which was about two shades lighter than my long, dark hair. As he began to make me feel even more awkward, I thought of my own hair and nervously adjusted my ponytail before pushing the bangs out of my eyes. Luke snickered.

"So," Cole started as I settled down again, looking specifically at me with his soft eyes. I frowned and bit my lip, not quite sure yet of what to think about the provocative way he had stared at me, while he continued, "Have any of you seen Josh lately? I haven't heard from him today."

Without thinking, Connor answered promptly, "He went to talk to Shane and Haley."

Cole frowned and ruffled his hair again, then wondered aloud, "Why would he need to do that?"

Although his statement may have sounded slightly rude, Cole did have a good point. Outside of the forest, Josh didn't really know Shane or Haley very well. I had to admit that although our town was small, people still acted quite cliquish, specifically the Monster Watch, but I liked to tell myself that this was just an inevitable result of how the newspapers had portrayed us nine years earlier. I didn't see much sense in completely changing the status quo so many years later, when it would only cause more issues to arise.

"He found a . . . hairband! In the street, yeah, and he thought it was one of theirs," Connor said as he caught sight of my ponytail from the corner of his eye.

*Note to self: When possible, don't let Connor/Apollo or Zach/Zeus lie or change the subject.*

Luke, Zach, and I simply shook our heads, wondering why in the world he had said "hairband." Obviously just as bewildered as the rest of us, Cole gave Connor a strange look of disbelief, knowing full well that Shane's short, cropped hair was nowhere near long enough to need a ponytail, and so Connor continued sheepishly, "Yeah . . . it's probably not Shane's." Then he put his head down nervously and started quietly sipping his lemonade again, which was probably for the best.

"Well, do you mind if I join you?" Cole asked. We all reluctantly said it was fine, and then he sat down next to me, with a tall glass of lemonade in his hand. Once he had made himself comfortable, we started a new conversation that had absolutely nothing to do with clouds or hairbands. Thankfully.

## Chapter 6:

# THE KNOWING

A few weeks later, everyone in the entire county was getting restless, especially all of the kids who were stuck in school for a few more hours. The next day was the start of summer vacation, after all. So when the last bell finally rang, students immediately poured out of the double doors at the front of the large, brick school building and raced to the buses as quickly as possible. After the ride home, the rest of the Monster Watch and I hung back and waited for the other students to disperse and the school bus to drive away, leaving us alone in the dust. Obviously, this didn't bother us one bit.

As soon as the four of us were completely alone, we exchanged excited grins with each other. "Race to Pan's hideout?" Zeus suggested in Greek, raising one eyebrow. He took off without even bothering to wait for an answer, and Poseidon and Apollo let out loud whoops from behind me as we sprinted across the empty street and into the woods. We didn't stop running until we had reached the hideout by the waterfall.

For the rest of the afternoon, we played a few rounds of reverse hide-and-seek and then happily chatted with Pan, Persephone, and a few nymphs as we munched on some delicious juicy berries. Needless to say, the rest of the Monster Watch and I headed back to our houses late that night with huge smiles on our faces. When we reached Maple Street, I bid them farewell and walked up my porch steps, opening the screen door with a creak. I didn't see either of my parents, so I heated up some leftover pasta from the night before and ran up the stairs to my room. I then sat on my bed and began eating as I pulled out my laptop.

I was video chatting with Zach and Luke, trying to decide when to have our next battle practice, when my dad suddenly walked into the room. He leaned against the door for a moment, and I quickly signed off the chat. Whenever my father came to tell me something, I knew it was important, since he almost never stopped by my room for a visit and I certainly never stopped by his. I didn't appreciate him poking his nose into my business anyhow.

I slowly turned to face him, and he took a deep breath before he said, "Your cousin Katie and her parents are coming to visit tomorrow."

I cursed. But not out loud, of course, not in front of my dad. You see, I despised Katie. She got to travel the world with her parents year-round, and she always acted like she was so much better than me, even though we were the same age. Not many people would describe her life as normal, but it was far more normal than mine. Most of the time we were together, Katie was constantly annoying me by trying to give me a makeover, but contrary to her belief, even Becca admitted that I dressed perfectly fine, except for the fact that I didn't own any fancy skirts or dresses. Anyway, I seriously doubted that Katie had the guts to kill a monster, and I knew for a fact that I was way smarter than she was, so I didn't believe she had the right to give me any lectures at all.

Naturally, I didn't tell my father any of this. Instead, I just gritted my teeth and tried to hide the annoyance in my voice as I asked, "How long are they staying?"

"Just three days," he answered, and I groaned. That meant three days of being banned from the forest. Three days too many, in my opinion.

My dad ran his fingers through his thinning, light brown hair and mumbled, more to himself than to me, "I just don't get why you think your cousin is such a problem. She's a very nice girl."

*Yeah, nice to you, but not to me,* I thought to myself bitterly, but again, I didn't answer him out loud. Instead, I turned to face the glass doors that opened to my tiny balcony. Across the lawn next door, I could see a light on in Zach and Luke's room. I wished I could go over there for a while, if only to get out of my house and finish our conversation, but I couldn't exactly do that with my father looming there in front of me.

I held my breath as the awkward silence lasted a couple more seconds, and then my dad left the room without saying anything more. He was probably going to get drunk, as usual. The only mystery was if he was going to go out to the Fire Pit, or if he was planning on staying home. But I knew the answer when I heard the screen door slam shut a few seconds later. Sighing to myself, I turned off the light and went to bed a few minutes later, ready to get the next three days over with.

---

I heard an arrow whiz by my head as I stabbed Ares's chest plate, but he still yelled in agony. Like him, I was breathing heavier and getting even more tired as each minute passed by. We had already been fighting for two hours, nonstop. PE class definitely did not get us in shape for this kind of exercise, if you could even call battle practice an exercise. It was way more than exercise. That was like comparing an ant to a blue whale—not even close.

To my left, Artemis shot an arrow at Poseidon, but the earth suddenly shook under her feet, and her body crumpled to the ground. Meanwhile, Dionysus was trying to whip and trap Demeter with his grapevine, but she turned it against him, and so Dionysus was flung backward into Hera, who had been fighting with Zeus and Apollo. At that particular moment, Apollo was trying to shoot arrows at Hermes, who was running faster than a rocket. Literally. And Aphrodite . . . well, she was nowhere to be seen. Maybe she was chatting in the woods with Hestia, who had actually decided to come to practice this time. Hephaestus, however, was in his basement workshop making us some new weapons.

"Okay, fine! We're done!" Zeus shouted at us in Greek as we finished our battle practice, and I checked my watch to see that it was eleven o'clock, which meant only half an hour until my cousin and her parents were scheduled to arrive in the Woods. I took a deep breath, wishing I could stay in the forest forever, but I knew I couldn't. I figured I would just have to walk back home as slowly as possible.

So Dionysus, Ares, Hermes, Hera, Demeter, Aphrodite, Hestia, and Artemis headed east toward Main Street, and Zeus, Poseidon, Apollo and I decided to follow them for the time being, just to avoid going home for as long as possible. Hera was giving me dirty looks because my left arm kept brushing up against Zeus's right arm, but I just chose to ignore her because I was talking with Zeus about going to see Pan soon and the trail was so narrow that our accidental touching of arms was inevitable. And, to be honest, I didn't really mind the comforting, tingling warmth of his skin on mine anyway.

Suddenly, a man's bloodcurdling scream cut through the quiet forest like a knife. We knew this was not one of Pan's games of trying to scare us; Pan's voice was more high-pitched, and we knew it well. This was real. Someone—probably another satyr—was being attacked by a monster, although I thought it strange that I wasn't hearing any prayers for help echoing through my mind, like what usually happened when a satyr or nymph was in need of my wisdom or guidance in battle. But then again, whoever was in trouble could have been praying to a different god just as easily.

Without even looking at each other or confirming a plan, we all raced north, in the direction of the scream. We were gods, which meant we protected our people, of course. That had been our most important job for six years now.

However, the trail that the Monster Watch and I had blazed long ago was very narrow, so most of the gods were not even bothering to use it. Like a herd of elephants, we trampled over bushes and fallen branches as we sprinted through the thick forest, just hoping we would get there in time to save whoever needed to be saved.

Hyperventilating, we ran over the top of a small hill and found ourselves staring straight at the huge Minotaur, although his back was facing us. It's black, furry, humanlike hands were completely covered in dark red blood, and in the long grass a few feet in front of it there lay a body, a *human* body, bloodied and unnaturally twisted. The older man's dark eyes were still open, but they were glassed over. He was obviously dead. We were too late . . .

Or maybe not.

I saw movement from behind a tree a few yards past the Minotaur, and when a head nervously poked out, I found myself looking at a boy our age. He appeared just as surprised at seeing us as we were at seeing him. His frightened, bright blue eyes met mine for only an instant before he looked down with concern at the dead body.

And that was when I noticed what he was looking at, what he was contemplating retrieving: a shiny sword, lying next to the dead man. There were only a few drops of red human blood on it, so the sword had obviously not helped the dead person at all, but it was a sword all the same. And it did prove one thing: this boy and the dead man had come prepared, sort of. Somehow, they *knew*. Knew that the Greek myths were true, and knew where they could find us, the gods.

*How the hell did they know?* I asked myself, quickly deciding that I had to save this mysterious boy no matter what, even if I just wanted to find out his secrets.

Obviously having heard us gods run up behind it, the Minotaur turned around to face us, its red eyes widening. It knew it had already been beat and was turning to run away, but I wanted to *vanquish* the threat, not just chase it away. With only a split second to think, I eagerly called out my plan, "This one's mine!"

I hurled my spear at the Minotaur with as much force as I could muster. The spear dug into his chest with a dull thud, and the Minotaur fell forward onto his bull face, turned over, and grasped the spear's shaft in an effort to pull it out. I saw the greenish-gold blood slowly ooze out from the giant body, but the monster was still alive, breathing shakily through flaring nostrils that were the size of my fists. Not taking any chances, Artemis quickly shot an arrow at the beast, and when it pierced the Minotaur's thick skull, we all sighed in relief. The Minotaur died immediately, and it crumbled to dust before the second wound could even start to bleed.

For a moment, the only sounds one could hear were of us trying to catch our breaths after running so hard. Most of the gods were staring uneasily at the bruised corpse lying in front of them, although the only obvious wounds were a broken neck and slits on his arms and torso from when the Minotaur had pried the sword out of the man's grasp. We had seen plenty of monsters die, as well as a couple of nymphs or satyrs, and we had seen our own blood gushing out of us too, but this was the first human death we had witnessed, the first body that didn't crumble to ashes as soon as its life was destroyed. Not surprisingly, Aphrodite threw up and sank to her knees as she continued to forlornly eye the dead body, and many of the gods looked away from the scene in disgust, but then the sight of the discolored remnants of the love goddess's lunch caused Hestia to vomit as well. As the boy with dark hair nervously stepped out behind the tree, however, I noticed that he seemed to have much better control over his stomach than a few of the gods, and so I wondered if he had seen someone die before in this fashion.

The teenager gulped before he took another step forward and knelt down in front of us, bowing his head. His actions only confirmed my suspicions that he knew we were the infamous gods of Olympus. "Who are you?" Zeus demanded in English, still breathless.

"My name is Alec. I am honored to be in the presence of my gods," he responded immediately, still kneeling. He sounded almost like a robot, like he had practiced saying this one line a thousand times.

"Do you speak Greek?" Zeus asked. When the boy nodded, Zeus continued, this time in Greek, "I give you permission to stand." Obediently, Alec stood up and looked Zeus in the eye. "Who is the dead man?"

"That man is, I mean *was*, my father, Edmund," Alec reluctantly answered him in Greek, his voice filled with pain.

Before anyone could utter a word of sympathy, however, Zeus fired off questions at Alec without taking another pause. "Why are you here? Where did you come from? How did you find us?"

I was about to tell Zeus to kindly slow the speed of his interrogation, but then Alec took a deep breath and said, "I came from a big camp in Kentucky, where my people live and train to be heroes—but of course, only you gods can actually label a person a hero. Anyway, we are a secret society of people who have the Sight and know that the Greek myths are true, and we are called the Knowing. Most of us are children and grandchildren of demigods or the real heroes who knew past generations of the gods."

All of our eyes were wide as we intently listened to Alec's story, and I began racking my brain, trying to remember if I had ever read anything about Knowing camps like Alec's. However, Dionysus suddenly interrupted, "Whoa! Did you walk here all the way from Kentucky?" I just rolled my eyes along with Artemis, thinking about how stupid it would have been if Alec had walked from Kentucky to the Woods, which was in the middle of Washington.

Alec shook his head. "No, sir. My father and I rode a bus to the airport in Kentucky, and then we flew to Seattle, but we just hitchhiked and walked off and on for the rest of the way. We didn't know what to expect at the end of our quest."

A few of the other gods' jaws dropped in shock. The Woods was at least one hundred miles from Seattle.

"Continue with your story," Zeus said with a sigh of amazement, waving for all the gods to be silent once more.

"Okay, sir," Alec started again. "I had to find you because I had a vision, sent to me by the Oracle of Delphi. In the dream, I saw directions, leading me here into your forest. Her voice told me that I had to help you fulfill some prophecy, or else all would be lost."

I sighed. Hera narrowed her brown eyes at Alec as she mused, "Interesting. The Oracle never mentioned *you* in the prophecy." She paused and shrugged before saying rudely, "But we don't need you right now, so you can just go home and cry to your mommy." Alec's jaw dropped, too shocked to be offended.

"Hera, what is your problem?" I asked her angrily. "Just because nothing has happened yet doesn't mean something won't start! Give the guy a chance, for crying out loud!" The rest of the gods nodded in unison, agreeing with me.

"Yeah, he's *cute,*" Aphrodite added, and Alec blushed bright red, glancing down at his worn-out shoes.

Hera frowned and glared at me, pushing a stray piece of reddish-brown hair back behind her ear, trying to calm herself down. "Anyway," Hestia started, clapping her hands together to try to get us all back on topic, "we can't really let him go home now, if he's only going to come back later. And if we let him wander around the forest on his own, he'll surely die. That would be a total waste of resources, as I'm sure Athena was about to point out."

"But Athena should also know that if this so-called war is really going to erupt among the gods, this boy here doesn't stand a chance against our powers. Ultimately, he'll be killed in either case, even if he is a little more likely to live longer in one," Hera responded hotly, glancing over at me to back her up for once.

Frowning, I looked back at Alec, his wild blue eyes seeming to flicker with flames of uncertainty that mirrored the ones in my own eyes. I had a very bad feeling about him, but for some reason I found myself turning to face Zeus and announcing in a strangely calm voice, "He stays." Hera groaned.

"You sound awfully certain about this," Zeus remarked.

"Really?" I asked. "Then you must have misunderstood my tone. I've honestly never been so unsure of anything in my entire life. This kid could be dangerous, after all. Actually, I *know* he's dangerous. But I certainly don't want his premature death on my conscience, and you probably don't either."

Zeus immediately raised his eyebrows but narrowed his stormy eyes at me in concern, knowing I was almost never hesitant in making a decision. "Is there something else you would like to share with the rest of us?" he questioned, guessing there was more to the story, and murmurs about me were immediately passed along among the other gods.

Once again, I risked a glance toward the dark-haired boy, whose bright eyes were still innocently wide and unblinking, which is how I realized that he didn't know much about the whole prophecy at all. And I was *not* planning on enlightening him.

I tore my eyes away from Alec's, after they had lingered on him just a moment too long, and with an indifferent shrug, I lied, "No, there is nothing left to be shared."

After I heard Alec let out a sigh of relief and noticed him nervously tug at the collar of his shirt, silence ensued for a minute or two longer, until Demeter piped up, "Okay, that's fine, but what are we going to do with him?"

More whispers were exchanged, but the answer seemed easy enough to me. "We'll leave him with Pan and Persephone. Pan's hideout is probably the safest place in the forest," I reasoned, and the rest of the gods' faces brightened again.

Artemis was the only one who didn't seem to agree. She complained, "That just means I'll have to hunt even more than I already do. As much as I love hunting, Athena, I have to leave some food for the natural predators."

Apollo only snorted and told his twin to quit being so whiny. When we had all finally agreed on leaving Alec with Pan, who had been keeping an eye on Persephone since she had been released from Hades, and had piled some rocks on top of Edmund's body, we headed over to his pool to introduce them. As usual, Pan was lounging on his rock throne and eating purple grapes, while Persephone was swimming in the small but deep pool with some water nymphs. Unsurprisingly, all of their jaws dropped when they saw Alec.

After Zeus filled them in, Persephone politely greeted Alec. The poor human was having trouble restraining himself from staring at the pale-skinned goddess, who was still wet from swimming and who was wearing nothing but a bikini handmade out of leaves.

I, however, was keeping a close eye on Alec. He was still frowning over his father's death, but he seemed guiltier to me than sad because of the way he was nervously running his fingers through his dark hair. I made a mental note of it.

"So, Alec, do they have monsters where you live? Or was this the first time you saw one?" Poseidon asked as he sat down on the damp grass by the river.

Leaning on a pine tree, Alec crossed his tan arms and replied slowly, "Back home, there were certain people called the Warriors whose main job was to find and kill any monster that came too close to the base camp. I was just starting out as a Warrior-in-training, so, yes, this was the first time I've actually been outside the camp and encountered a monster up close and personal. My father and I saw a few more from a distance on the way here, but we managed to stay away from them."

Poseidon nodded, but he quickly followed up with another question, "Do a lot of people get killed in your area? Because every human from the town who comes into this forest ends up dead. We were actually the first to survive, but we know now that we're gods, not humans." When Zeus nudged him in the side, Poseidon added, "Sorry about your dad, by the way. Too bad we couldn't get there sooner."

But Alec didn't seem to hear the apology. "That's strange," he mused. "Monsters are usually attracted only to people with the Sight, or people who know the truth about the Greek myths and who can see monsters for what they really are—that includes young children who don't know about the myths but believe in monsters. So I guess there aren't *too* many deaths where I live, especially since no one goes outside of the Knowing base camp very often."

He paused, and I thought back to when the Monster Watch and I went into the woods for the first time. Personally, I was betting the monsters attacked all the humans who came into the forest because they felt that their home and maybe even Hades, their leader, were being threatened. I certainly couldn't think of any other reason.

"Why?" Apollo cut in. "What do people without the Sight see when they look at a monster?"

Alec shrugged and said honestly, "I have no idea what people without the Sight see. But I do know that normal teens and adults don't even notice monsters because they have been blocking them out of their minds for thousands of years now, ever since humans chose to stop believing in the Greek gods. I'm surprised you do not know this."

We all lapsed into a state of awkward silence, digesting this information. Even Ares was tapping his chin, thinking—that was something he didn't do very often—and then he inquired, "How many people are in the Knowing? You know, just in case we need extra soldiers."

I should have guessed that would have been what Ares was going to ask. All he thought about was war.

Alec frowned thoughtfully, then answered, "A couple hundred, give or take a few." Ares nodded, and I knew all the other gods were doing the math in their minds and realizing that Alec's Knowing camp had almost twice the number of people who lived in our hometown.

A few minutes later, after the ongoing flow of questions had finally stopped and Alec had settled in a little bit, the rest of us gathered our weapons and started to head out. I was about to begin walking back with the rest of the gods, but I heard Alec softly whisper to me in Greek, "Lady Athena, I wanted to thank you for killing the Minotaur." I just turned around and nodded at him in acknowledgment.

Then, taking advantage of the opportunity, I asked, "You are feeling guilty. Why?"

Alec only raised his dark eyebrows, not looking very surprised that I had figured him out. "You read people well. My father used to tell me that," he said wistfully.

I gave him a dubious look. "That didn't answer my question."

He gave me a weak smile in return, then sighed and finally answered me, "The Oracle told me to come alone. But my father . . . he always wanted to meet the gods more than anything, and he insisted that he would go, that everything would be fine. He thought we might even be able to have one of you bless the family after all our troubles . . ." His voice slowly trailed off, and he shook his head before finishing, "It's all my fault. I shouldn't have let him come. This was my quest, not his."

Then he began staring at the ground, and I felt terrible for him, so I awkwardly put my hand on his warm shoulder. Perhaps that was an action too forward, too inappropriate for me to have done, but it was too late to take it back. He looked back up and his blue eyes met my gray ones, but this time they looked fierce, not sad. I could tell he was a fighter.

"Will you train me, Lady Athena? I need to know how to defend myself," he asked, his tone flat.

I frowned, but reluctantly nodded after he gave me his most pleading look. I couldn't help it. Aphrodite was right; he was cute, for a human.

At last, I turned around to leave him, but acting on reflex he grabbed my arm to stop me. Blushing with embarrassment, he pulled his hand away and whispered, "Wait. Can I ask you one last thing?" When I nodded, he continued seriously, "You said you think I'm dangerous. Why? I've done absolutely nothing to earn your distrust."

After hesitating a moment, I answered him cryptically. "That is a story which I believe should be told at a later time."

I left Alec behind with a very confused expression on his face and set off toward my home, though I heard his voice echo once again through my mind.

*Please.* It was a prayer, the first I had ever received from a human. But I did not send him anything in reply.

I sighed as I lazily kicked my way through the forest undergrowth, not bothering to try to be quiet to avoid any monsters. Anything that came my way would be a welcome distraction that would only delay my arrival at home even further. Unfortunately for me, I didn't run into any more monsters. Because it was well known throughout the forest that my friends and I were gods, we weren't bothered by monsters as much as when we were younger, though that didn't stop us from making a sport out of fighting them. Even so, I didn't run into any nymphs or satyrs or any of the rest of the gods, which meant that my friends were probably farther ahead of me and on their way to the Fire Pit for lunch. Feeling slightly lonely, I sighed as I hid my spear, shield, and armor in a hollow log at the edge of the trees.

I sighed once again as I stepped out into the bright sunlight and walked across the street toward my gray house, its paint just starting to peel near the roof. Looking at the unkempt yard full of weeds in front of it reminded me that I needed to mow the lawn, a task that I usually tried to ignore. Then again, I thought the house's dilapidated appearance matched what usually went on inside perfectly. Maybe I just didn't want another façade in my life.

As I walked through the front door, I could hear voices coming from the kitchen. All talking stopped immediately as I strode into the kitchen, and I found five different sets of eyes staring at me. Finally, my mother put her hand to her head and spoke in a raised voice. "Where have you been? It's almost one, and I told you to be here at eleven thirty! The one time I ask you to be on time for something, you're late. Why is that?" But I just smoothed back my hair and tugged impatiently at my long side ponytail, waiting for my mom to stop yelling at me. If only she knew the things I went through every day . . .

Eventually, everyone else left the room to talk some more, and I had the chance to make myself a grilled-cheese sandwich and eat in peace. Needless to say, I savored every second of the silence. I would probably be forced to socialize with my cousin Katie for the rest of the day, after all.

When I finished my lunch, I sneaked upstairs easily, without anyone noticing, and sat down on my bed to read a book. I was in the middle of a chapter when

I heard the door creak open, and my cousin walked into the room. I just kept reading and tried not to look too disappointed.

Katie shot me a fake smile and tied her blonde hair up in a ponytail as she said perkily, "So what are we going to do today? I think we should go see that new movie. You know, the one with Selena Gomez."

I only groaned, thinking, *Why stay inside on a beautiful sunny day like this?* If it was my choice, the rest of the Monster Watch and I still would have been in the woods, playing reverse hide-and-seek.

When I didn't answer her right away, Katie yanked the book out of my hands and teased, "I don't get it. How can you read so much and still be in tenth grade?"

I only glared at her. Apparently, she didn't realize that some of the most valuable lessons are the ones learned on the street (or in the forest), not in classrooms.

"I'll have you know that I *chose* to stay behind in school to be with my friends. And anyway, I'm taking college classes online," I snapped at her. But even college classes were no match for someone who knew almost everything.

"Fine. You can work on your stupid homework for physics or art history or whatever the hell you're taking later, but right now, my mom's driving us to see that movie." Katie had to literally drag me out of the room, and I sighed, realizing that I didn't have much of a choice. I would have to finish that book later.

## Chapter 7:

# THE FOURTH OF JULY

I woke up the next morning bright and early at six-thirty. Quickly and quietly, I sneaked downstairs, careful not to wake up Katie, who was fast asleep on an air mattress in the corner of my room, by the cluttered bookcases. Not a soul was awake yet in my house, and it was so serene and quiet that I could hear the surprisingly comforting sound of Connor playing his guitar from his house next door. I sighed and wished it were a normal summer day, one filled with rounds of reverse hide-and-seek from dawn until dusk. But it wasn't, and so I knew that Zach and Luke were probably sleeping in, leaving me to tackle my own problems.

I was outside in my backyard shooting at an empty Coca-Cola can with my BB gun when my cousin walked out of the house about a half hour later, but I ignored her as I concentrated on my sights. *Ping!* A BB pellet hit the can and sent it flying a few feet backward in the grass.

Katie sighed from behind me, smoothing out her blonde hair, and asked, "Why are you up so early?"

"Did I wake you up? Oh, I'm so sorry," I replied sarcastically. I fired another shot. *Ping!* The can flew backward another five feet. The shiny can now lay more than fifty feet away. *Ping!* Sixty. *Ping!* Seventy.

Katie looked impressed. "You're a good shot," she stated, and I just shrugged because I'd had lots of practice, and I'd hit targets a lot farther away before. Then, without saying another word, Katie sat down on the back porch steps and watched me shoot for a while. For once, I actually managed to tolerate her presence quite easily, and she didn't seem too annoyed with me either.

About an hour later, my mom called from the kitchen, "Breakfast!" And together, Katie and I raced back inside. While we ate, I tried to engage in polite conversation with my aunt and uncle, but my mind was elsewhere. Looking out the window, I watched with jealousy as Connor, Zach, and Luke headed into the forest together, probably on their way to check in with Pan, Alec, and Persephone. Zach saw me looking at them from across the street and waved at me with a smile, which only made me feel even worse.

Sighing to myself, I looked down at my plate and hoped Alec would forgive me for not training with him for the next few days, because I realized that I had forgotten to tell him about my other plans. Then I tried to tell myself not to feel guilty, that I didn't care if Alec was mad at me or not, but it didn't work, which was strange because I hardly knew the boy at all, and I had never felt that way about anyone before. So I simply stabbed my fork into my pancake in anguish, feeling conflicted and itching to get my hands on a monster, just so I could have the satisfaction of sending it down to Hades.

Of course, no one else in the room noticed my violent assault on the pancake. Instead, they continued to talk about the best tourist attractions in Paris. Suddenly, Katie's cell phone rang, and she ran upstairs to answer it while I wondered why she would have her phone on during breakfast anyway. It was considered rude in my house. Luckily my mother excused me from the table around the same time, so I went outside to sit in the antique rocking chair on the front porch.

I sat quietly there on the porch, listening to the birds sing joyfully in the warm summer heat of the Woods. If I listened very closely, I could just barely hear Pan screaming from inside the forest, trying to scare the living daylights out of whatever god, nymph, satyr, or monster was nearby. I smiled. Who knew such a terrible shriek could be so comforting?

I was just wondering how long Katie was going to talk on the phone when Josh and Cole ran by Zach and Luke's house next door. They grinned and waved when they saw me, and then they quickly jogged their way up the street to meet me.

"Where's the rest of the Monster Watch?" Cole asked, his caramel-colored hair shining in the sunlight. Still angry that I wasn't allowed to go into the forest, I just pointed across the street toward the edge of the trees, not saying anything, but Cole nodded in understanding.

Josh ran one hand through his short, curly brown hair and grinned. "So where's your cousin? I heard she's hot. But not as hot as you or Alicia or Becca, of course." I frowned and stuck my leg out, playfully kicking Josh in the shin. "Hey!" he exclaimed, and Cole laughed, his brown eyes twinkling.

Then I heard the screen door creak open behind me, and I swiveled my head to see Katie walk out confidently, smoothing down her black miniskirt. Intrigued, Cole and Josh raised their eyebrows, but I just rolled my eyes. "Oh, Ashley, are these your friends? I didn't know you had any," she joked, but I chose not to answer her, so she introduced herself to the two boys, flipping her hair flirtatiously all the while. I, on the other hand, closed my eyes to block out the rest of the conversation and opened them only when I heard Katie say goodbye. Unfortunately, it was just in time to see Cole wink at me as he and Josh trotted away, and after that, he kept taking glances over his shoulder at me every few strides. I sighed, thinking that boys just complicated life.

"I think that one guy, Cole, likes you," Katie stated the obvious, leaning up against the front of the house as she watched the two friends disappear down the road again.

I frowned. "Yeah, so what?"

When she turned to face me, she looked like I had just slapped her in the face or something. "So what? What do you mean 'so what'?! You need to go for it, girl!" she exclaimed, playfully punching me in the shoulder, and I rolled my eyes again, knowing that Katie would never understand my reasons against dating and love in general. I was Athena, after all. I was supposed to be a virgin goddess and never marry, just like Artemis and Hestia. Therefore, I saw absolutely no point in dating, especially not Cole. Don't get me wrong, he was a nice guy, but as the years had passed, I realized he could never know the other half of my life.

Katie shook her head and tied her silky hair up into a ponytail as she changed the subject and ordered, "Come on, we're going shopping." I only groaned, staying in the chair, but Katie took my hand and yanked me out of my seat. "Ugh, you're just like my friend from school," she complained, and I bit my lip to keep myself from smirking as we headed for her mother's car in the driveway.

Three hours later, we had finished shopping for the day, and Katie's mother had just dropped us off at the Fire Pit for lunch. I was desperately hoping none of my friends would be there, but when there is only one restaurant in the entire town and it happens to have the best lemonade in the world, it's a guarantee that you are going to know everyone in there. Sure enough, I glanced over and saw Zach, Luke, and Connor sipping lemonade in our usual booth. Luke saw me too, but he didn't wave. Not really wanting Katie to embarrass me in front of any other friends, we sat down at a two-person table near the front of the restaurant.

Meanwhile, Zach and Luke's mother, Martha, walked up to take our orders, holding a small black notebook and brushing off her left hand on the dark red apron she was wearing. "Hello, Ashley. What can I get you today?" she asked, smiling at me.

"Two lemonades and two turkey sandwiches, please," I replied after checking with Katie. Then my second mother nodded before disappearing through a wooden door that led to the kitchen, and she came back only a few minutes later, lemonades in hand. "Thanks, Mom," I told her, and Katie gave me a strange look. Again, this was something that she would never understand.

Katie and I had barely even touched our food when I heard the familiar voice of Josh come from right in front of me, saying, "Hey, Ash. What's up?" Immediately, I looked up to answer him, but in shock, I started choking on the big gulp of lemonade that I had just taken. My mind was already bursting with a thousand different thoughts at once.

Standing in front of me next to Josh was none other than Alec, who happened to be wearing an old blue shirt that I instantly recognized as one of Zach's. I figured that Zach must have lent it to Alec, since Alec's only other shirt was currently covered in his dead father's blood. This reminded me that we still had to give his father a proper funeral ceremony. All we had done was bury him under a pile of rocks deep in the forest, so the sight of him wouldn't scare anyone.

Anyway, Alec was grinning, his bright blue eyes shining because he knew he had one up on me by surprising me there. I quickly wiped my mouth, blushing and realizing that I had a few drops of lemonade dribbling down my chin. Katie was correct in that I didn't always need her to embarrass me; sometimes I embarrassed myself.

"I just wanted to introduce my own cousin to Katie. Ash, I think you already know him," Josh explained, sharing a goofy grin with Alec. Wondering if those two realized how dangerous it was for Alec to be out here in the town, I just frowned. It was obviously not the reaction that the two of them had been expecting, however, as the smiles quickly disappeared from their own faces. They knew they were in for a lecture.

Still frowning, I got up out of my chair and grabbed Josh's arm. "Excuse us for a moment," I said to Katie with a tight smile. Alec followed obediently. As soon as we were outside and away from anyone who could overhear us, I quickly turned to Josh but squinted because I found myself staring right into the sun. Although I loved warm weather, sometimes clouds were a good thing.

"What do you think you're doing?" I demanded.

Josh simply shrugged. "No one here will know that he's not my cousin, except for the gods. So what's the harm? It's only for today."

"You're just lucky your parents didn't come here for lunch," I hissed back at him irritably. With that, I turned on my heel and walked back inside the restaurant to finish my lunch with Katie.

Josh and Alec also went back inside, but the two of them sat at the back table with the rest of the Monster Watch. The daring Alec winked at me as he walked by, still laughing to himself, and it was enough to make any other girl faint in delight. I just rolled my eyes, however, because I couldn't help but think I had just been introduced to a side of Alec that I was sure no one on Earth had seen in a very long time—a happier side, that is. In just one day, he had gone from being quiet, submissive, and nervous to being confident, proud, and playful. If he wasn't proof of the effect that the gods had on people, I didn't know what was.

As soon as I looked back over at Katie, she raised her perfectly plucked eyebrows at me in an unreadable expression. "What?" I asked her, annoyed.

"Nothing. Nothing at all," she whispered mischievously, and I glared at my lemonade, suddenly wishing we had never come to the Fire Pit for lunch and worried that I had accidentally given Alec the wrong impression. I purposely avoided looking at the Monster Watch's table for the rest of our meal.

---

The next few days went by slowly and uneventfully, but I cannot even put into words how happy I was when Katie left to go back home. But I didn't stop to think about that, because I had way better things to do. It was the Fourth of July, after all, and decorations were going up like crazy.

Every house and shop had an American flag hung outside a window, and sparkly red and blue stars completely covered the few old-fashioned street lamps that were lined up along Main Street. As you could probably guess, the Fourth of July was one of the most popular holidays in the Woods, if only because it had the biggest celebration. For the entire day, the Fire Pit gave out free glasses of lemonade (of course, that didn't really make much of a difference to the rest of the Monster Watch and me, since we got free food all the time), and our county prided itself with having the most spectacular fireworks show in the entire state. The houses on Maple Street, such as mine, had the best views of the show, if you sat on the roof, like I always did.

The Monster Watch and I had been helping out with the decorations all morning, but we were also itching to get into the forest to play a good round of reverse hide-and-seek. After all, I hadn't played a round since before Alec arrived. So, weapons in hand, Apollo, Poseidon, and I raced deep into the darkness of the forest and split up to find Zeus, who had run off to hide. Apollo had started jogging in the direction of the meadow, and I was making my way toward Pan's hideout. I was feeling a little lazy that day, so I decided to take my sword, which was much easier to carry than the long metallic spear I usually used. (A word of advice: It's good to be versatile with weapons because you never know who or what you might run into.)

Within half an hour, I had found Zeus hiding in the bushes and the two of us had met up with Poseidon and Apollo. (While silently cowering in the foliage, Zeus had almost been trampled by a giant wild boar, but I had chucked my sword at it and thus killed it.) It was almost dinnertime, however, so we headed home right away. "Your house?" I suggested to Luke and Zach, but they only exchanged uneasy glances.

"Um, Ash," Zach started as he hid his weapons and armor in a hollow log. "I'm supposed to tell you that Maddie and Alicia are throwing a barbecue and a watch party for the fireworks, and, um, you're kind of . . . not invited."

I sighed, shaking my head. "That's not really surprising," I told him with a small smile. I tried to be nice to Alicia, but she was so jealous of me and Zach all the time that she didn't really care what I did. However, I had gotten used to her rude actions over the years, so they no longer bothered me very much. A little company would have been nice, though.

"Well, bye, guys." They waved and headed off, while I went into my house. Neither my father nor my mother was home, so I went straight upstairs to work on an essay for one of my online college classes.

A few hours later, I checked the time, finally realizing how late it was and then cursing aloud. My parents still hadn't come home, and the fireworks were about to start. Remembering that I hadn't had any dinner yet, I raced downstairs and popped a bag of microwave popcorn. Then I went back up to my room and, from my tiny balcony, I climbed up the trellis and rain gutters to the roof of my house, where I situated myself comfortably at the highest point. Silently, I stared out into the dark night sky, which was lit up by glittering stars as far as the eye could see. It was a beautiful sight, as usual, and it completely lived up to my high expectations.

I was just thinking that the night would be perfect if only I wasn't alone when I heard a rustling from the rose bushes down on the ground, under my balcony. I froze, my hand still in the popcorn bag, wondering what it was and realizing that I probably should have brought my pocketknife up to the roof with me. Reluctantly, I peered over at the edge of the roof and saw an arm reach up, and—you guessed it—Alec pulled himself up and sat down next to me.

"Hey," he said casually, as if he did this sort of thing every day. But now that I was thinking about it, I thought that it wouldn't be surprising if he did. You might have guessed that he would be breathless after climbing up all the way to my roof, but you would have been wrong. That boy had skills. I felt my heartbeat flutter a tiny bit, but I tried to ignore it. The gods were much more handsome and completed much more difficult tasks every day, after all. I shouldn't have been so amazed by Alec.

"Why are you here?" I asked slowly, in English, not even bothering to say hello back to him. Instead, I studied him closely as he sat down next to me. It seemed that over the course of the three days I had been banned from the forest, Alec had *very* eagerly followed Zeus's orders and had all too quickly trained himself to stop referring to us gods as "sir," "lady," or "lord." Because we gods were the same age as him, I knew Alec found us to be a lot more relatable and open-minded than he had originally expected, thus he was starting to become much more comfortable around us. Maybe a little *too* comfortable.

Alec simply sent me a sideways glance and shrugged. "The same reason you are," he answered blandly, running his fingers through his dark hair. "I wanted to watch the fireworks. And of course I wasn't invited to the party, since I'm not even supposed to exist here, so Zeus just told me where you lived. He said you would probably be home and that you'd most likely be up on the roof, and apparently he was right."

I smiled, suddenly thankful that I wasn't alone anymore. "Popcorn?" I offered, holding out the bag to him. He nodded and grabbed a handful, and loud booms filled our ears as the sky was lit up with red and white explosions. I wondered what was happening at Alicia's party.

For a second, we sat silently, only eating our popcorn, until Alec leaned over and whispered in my ear, "So what's your human name again? Ashley, is it?"

I frowned, thinking for a moment, and then admitted, "I like Athena better." Ashley was cool, I supposed. She was a tomboy, smart, and somewhat popular, but her parents had no trust in her whatsoever. Basically, her life at home sucked, for lack of a better word. In truth, Ashley just couldn't compare with Athena, who knew everything, could do whatever the hell she wanted, and was praised for almost everything she did.

After a long pause, Alec switched from English to Greek and reluctantly confessed, "Me too. But I suppose I don't even know Ashley, really."

My heart fluttered again, and I bit my lip, hoping he couldn't see straight through me and reminding myself how dangerous he was. He had only met me a few days ago, yet he totally understood me! No one but Zeus had ever gotten to know me so quickly and completely. But I cursed myself again and again, knowing I wasn't supposed to be thinking about this or letting my heart run off without my brain, my logic. I was Athena, after all. Besides, no dating equals less drama.

Just as another firework exploded into balls of color, Alec changed the subject and asked, with a sly smirk on his face, "When will you train me to fight? You promised me, remember? And you owe me for forgetting to tell me that you would be busy dealing with your cousin for three whole days."

Sensing his eagerness and playfulness, I looked him right in the eye and challenged, also in Greek, "How about after the fireworks? Or is that too late for you?"

"Bring it on," Alec answered immediately, and I saw him grin as yet another red firework lit up the night. "But before we do this, you have to tell me why you think I'm so dangerous."

I sighed. "You really are impatient, aren't you?" I muttered, not really wanting to have this discussion, but Alec just waited expectantly for me to continue.

"You said you would tell me at a later time, and now is a later time," Alec pointed out in annoyance.

"Fine," I grumbled, tugging at the end of my ponytail in anguish. He only tapped the rooftop with his fingers incessantly, until I finally continued, "The first reason why you're dangerous is that you are probably the only living human who knows where this current generation of Greek gods lives. Knowledge is power, after all."

Alec nodded thoughtfully. "That makes sense," he murmured as he watched another explosion of color light up the sky. "And the second reason?"

"The second reason is that you've been lying about your amount of training," I accused, studying his arms a little more closely. "You say you've had none, but I can see you have toned muscles from some kind of workout.

Granted, they'll be at least twice as big once *I'm* done training you, but they're muscles nonetheless."

"Fair enough," he solemnly whispered under his breath as he closed his eyes. His voice had gotten softer and softer. I noticed that he didn't ask me for any more reasons why I thought he was dangerous (and I did have a couple more), but I guessed I had hit a sore spot on his character, something that related to his past with the Knowing. I let him be.

For a few more long minutes, we lay on the roof together, staring quietly at the colorful sky over the forest. The Woods actually seemed quite calm for once, although I could hear excited shouts coming from Alicia and Maddie's house party across the street, shouts that were interrupting the rhythmic booms of the fireworks show. I found myself starting to think about what my life would have been like if I wasn't a god, but then I quickly decided that I liked this life just fine. Without my other identity and monsters to fight and forests to explore, I figured that my life in such a small, isolated town would have been quite boring. Maybe I really was just an adrenaline junkie at heart.

Suddenly, my thoughts were interrupted when I heard someone else down on the ground. This time, however, the voice belonged to Cole. "Hey, Ashley, is that you up there?" he yelled, and I cursed under my breath in almost perfect unison with Alec. Now what were we supposed to do?

## Chapter 8:

# A FLASH

"Can I come up there?" Cole shouted at me from somewhere down below.

"Sure," I yelled back reluctantly, knowing Cole probably wouldn't leave me alone. Then turning to Alec, I whispered, "Hide." With that, the dark-haired boy disappeared over the peak of the roof and into the darkness.

Meanwhile, Cole climbed his way up the side of my house, though he was much less graceful and agile than Alec. By the time Cole sat down next to me, he was breathless, and I was certain that Alec was snickering at him from the other side of the roof. When he finally regained the ability to speak, nodding to the colorful sky, Cole said, "Great fireworks, huh?"

"Yeah," I agreed, tugging at the end of my ponytail in thought. "The colors remind me of when you pulled that prank on Matt six years ago."

We both started chuckling at the memory of an angry Matt covered in paint. "That was a good one, wasn't it?" Cole remarked, running his fingers through his caramel-colored hair, and I just smiled.

After a long pause, I offered, "Popcorn?" for the second time that night. Like Alec had done only a few minutes earlier, Cole nodded and took a handful. Our conversation turned back into awkward silence, and again I pictured Alec laughing hysterically at Cole and me. Then I shook my head and closed my eyes, trying to get him out of my head. I found the fact that Alec was listening to every word we said kind of unnerving, and I wondered what he was thinking about Cole.

After fidgeting for a while, Cole finally whispered, "What's really in there?" I didn't have to open my eyes and look at him to know he was talking about the woods. That was the question everyone around the county wanted to ask the Monster Watch. And really, who could blame them?

But sometimes, the truth is so outrageous that it's better to actually tell a piece of it than to lie. So, in the spookiest voice I could muster, I told him, "Monsters."

"Ha, ha," he laughed sarcastically. "No, just tell me. Ever since that day Josh and I pulled that prank, I've been thinking I made a mistake by not going in there. Is that crazy?"

Trapped in an awkward moment and not exactly sure what to say, I sighed and said, shrugging, "Well, everything happens for a reason." Even if it really is the Fates who control everyone's destinies.

Cole and I sat quietly for a few more minutes, watching the fireworks burst in the night sky, but I couldn't sit still at all. As the seconds ticked by, I became more and more restless, silently wondering what time it was because I had promised to start training Alec after the show. Over the past six years, my life as a god had slowly become my first priority over school and home life, and I knew the same could have been said for the rest of the gods too. We couldn't exactly prevent it from happening, however, because we had so much to keep track of, not just in the Woods, but also around the world, a duty we often neglected.

Eventually, Cole broke the silence and asked me, his gentle brown eyes looking straight into my stormy gray ones, "Can you take me into the forest someday?"

I froze in place and chewed my lip. *What am I supposed to say to that?* I thought to myself, slightly surprised by Cole's question, although I always knew he would ask it one day. Even if I wanted to give Cole a short tour of my second home (and I'll admit I was tempted to), the decision of whether or not to allow people into the forest wasn't really mine to make. The majority of the Olympian Council had to agree on what was best.

Just then, I heard the familiar sound of my father's old pickup truck driving up to the house. "We'll see," I told Cole honestly, considering the timely arrival of my father to be very lucky. "But right now, you have to go." I practically shoved him off the roof, and he obediently took off running down the road. Cole didn't need to be told twice in this case; the entire town knew my father wasn't the nicest guy, let alone the fact that he was one of the few non-native, virtually untrustworthy citizens of the town.

When I was sure that Cole was gone, I turned around to call Alec back over, but he was already sitting next to me. "Boo," he whispered right into my ear, smiling in spite of himself. But before he could even blink, I slapped him hard across the face. Not *too* hard, though.

"First lesson," I started in Greek, "don't mess with Athena. She hits back. Harder."

Alec just grinned back at me, looking unfazed. "Good to know," he whispered brightly, and I rolled my eyes at him as I jumped off the roof onto the balcony and then to the ground, carefully rolling when I hit the ground so I didn't hurt myself. Alec did the same, and we sprinted down the road and into the forest when my father was looking the other way. After all, my father probably would have yelled at me for going in so late at night, and the same could have been said for my mother, wherever she was.

When we stopped a few feet inside the tree line, I quickly pulled out my armor and a sword from a hollow log and started to strap on my bronze and silver breastplate, pausing to run my finger over the familiar picture of a gold owl carrying Medusa's head carved on the front. Not bothering to grab my helmet, I looked up and was surprised to see Alec pull out his own armor, sword, and round shield out of a different tree. These pieces were also bronze and very well made, although they did not look quite as fancy or intricate as mine.

"Where did you get those?" I asked in Greek, remembering that he had come here with only a sword. I had just assumed he would borrow Ares's stuff.

"Hephaestus made them for me," Alec explained with a shrug, his voice strangely tight. "You were with your cousin."

I nodded silently, feeling a bit out of the loop, and Alec followed me toward the meadow, which was a nice open place to train. As we trudged through the undergrowth, we could still hear the thunderous booms from the fireworks high in the sky above our heads. They blocked out all the other noises that we usually heard in the forest, such as the birds and the wind whistling through the trees. However, we could not see the bright bursts of light anymore because we were under the thick cover of the tall treetops, traveling through murky darkness.

We then stepped out under the fiery sky into the empty field of long grass that brushed up against our shins as we walked to the center of the meadow. Without saying a single word, I turned around to face Alec, pointing my sword directly at his chest. He did the same to me, and for a second it was like the world was frozen in time, our eyes locked and our silver swords shone in the surprisingly bright moonlight.

"The second lesson," I began in a serious whisper, "is that if you're going to fight a monster, you fight to kill, or you don't fight at all. Commit to your plan. Your whole head and your whole heart have to be in it together, if you want to keep from going crazy with post-traumatic stress."

Alec nodded, eagerly absorbing the tips, and from the way his stance kept shifting slightly, I could tell he was ready to start practicing. "Now, show me everything you've learned. Pretend I'm a monster," I ordered firmly, knowing it wouldn't be too hard for him to imagine; during the days I spent with Katie, I was sure he had observed the rest of the Monster Watch acting less than noble on multiple occasions. Humans and gods can be monsters too, after all.

And then Alec lunged at me, his cool blue eyes suddenly seeming angry. I quickly blocked the thrust of his sword, and it hit my shield with a loud clang. I swung my own sword down to the left, just barely missing the skin on his side, and I heard his sword slice through the air by my ear. Thus, my theory that Alec had been properly trained, contrary to what he had told the rest of the gods and me earlier, was confirmed. And he was good, really good—about a million times better than I thought he would be. To be honest, I began to think that he was almost as good as Ares in some aspects. But unfortunately for Alec, I was better than Ares in *all* aspects.

Without stopping to think about his training anymore, I let my instincts take over and slammed my shield into his body, throwing him way off balance, even though I hadn't hit him too hard. However, the blows and the falls from the sky that the rest of the gods and I took during battle practices would certainly injure or kill any normal human, so I had to admit that Alec was doing pretty well.

But he could have been doing even better. Every time he met my gaze, he would let down his guard just a little bit, a very slight hesitation that only the most experienced fighters would notice. I couldn't tell if he was worried about hurting me or simply distracted by the overwhelming beauty of a goddess.

"The third lesson is about focus, Alec," I muttered to him under my breath as we kept fighting. "Don't fight your instincts, and don't let yourself get distracted by your opponent or anything else. If you're trying to guess my next move, watch my body, not my face." He smirked at that last part and eagerly obeyed, and I vowed to myself that that would be the last time I ever asked him to purposely avoid my eye contact.

I went easy on Alec to start with, letting him hit me a couple of times. But when he realized I wasn't really trying at all, we began exchanging more blows, harder and harder each time. Eventually, I noticed him getting tired. Taking advantage of his sudden fatigue and the hole in his defense, I slammed my shield into him once again, this time even harder than before, so he almost fell. That was when I swung my sword right, and the sharp blade seared through his blue shirt and the skin on his left side, making a clean and shallow gash. But he was not going to give in easily. Staggering and gasping for breath, he raised his shield just in time to block my next swing, though I used one of my legs to knock his feet out from under him and he fell back into the long grass, clutching his bleeding side.

"Lesson four: always remember where your armor is."

I pointed my sword down at him, the tip of the blade just barely touching his Adam's apple as I looked into his shining blue eyes. Yes, even though he was breathing hard, sweating a lot, and bleeding from several shallow cuts, he still managed to keep smiling, and so I simply shook my head in bewilderment, impressed by his attitude. I, on the other hand, wasn't even starting to breathe harder, but because I was a goddess, this wasn't really a fair fight to begin with.

He pushed himself up off the ground and said breathlessly, "Good practice." Those were probably the only two words he could muster at the moment. I didn't answer him, but led him over to a hollow tree on the edge of the meadow, where Apollo kept hidden emergency medical supplies. Even gods get hurt every once in a while, after all, and one can never be too careful with injuries.

As Alec and I sat down on a log and took off our armor, I started to wipe off my arm, where Alec had managed to make a single shallow cut. He was in the middle of pulling off his bloody shirt when he started squinting at my arm. "Is your blood gold?" he asked, looking shocked. I nodded, forcing myself to tear my eyes away from his six-pack abs as I flashed back to when the other gods and I had first discovered the unusual color of our blood.

---

It was in the middle of our very first battle practice after finding the rest of the gods, and I had been battling with Ares in the meadow. I had just made a cut on his triceps when I noticed that his blood was an odd color. I stopped fighting in midstep and called out to the others immediately. "I think your blood is . . . gold," I said, pointing to Ares's wound. We all stood staring at the blood in silence, too shocked and confused to speak.

"It's never done that before," Ares told us, obviously mystified.

Poseidon and the other gods walked over to join Ares and me. "I think you've finally lost your marbles, Ares."

Ares threatened to punch the god of the sea, but Aphrodite intervened and got Ares to calm down and cooperate. He slowly turned his arm to the right and to the left, and we discovered that his blood wasn't totally golden yet. The color just depended on the way the light hit the wound.

The rest of the gods and I soon realized that all of our blood was beginning to change from red to gold, which we assumed was because we had found out our true identities as gods, and we didn't worry about it anymore. It was just a side effect. However, ever since the day of our first battle practice, our blood had slowly turned more golden and less red. Six years later, our blood really was the color of pure gold, and so we all had to live in fear of blood tests whenever we visited the doctor's office. The doctor's office had become like prison to us; no one wanted to end up in there for fear of becoming a human lab rat.

---

Facing Alec again, I helped him bandage the slice I had made in his side, and he grimaced as the medicine stung his open wound. Luckily, the cut was shallow, but it was still very long. "I bet this scar will be permanent," Alec mused in Greek, more to himself than to me, as I wrapped the bandage around his shirtless chest.

"That's okay," I told him with a smirk, avoiding eye contact as I somewhat nervously tucked a stray piece of hair behind my ear. "Scars are hot. Ask any normal girl."

"You really think so? I mean, I didn't realize you were a normal girl," Alec responded just as playfully, and I paused in the middle of dressing his wound to look up at him and raise my eyebrows.

I shook my head and argued, "I never said *that*. I'm just saying I did you a favor. You'll have plenty of girls fighting for your attention now, though I'm sure there were some before you came here too."

At this, Alec laughed out loud, which just brought a smile to my own face. He had one of those good, contagious laughs. "Oh yes, you *obviously* did me a favor by almost killing me. Forgive me if I forget to thank you," he said sarcastically, ignoring my other statement about girls, and I smirked again.

Once we had finally stopped chuckling, I returned to being more serious in nature and started to dab at the bloody flesh wound in Alec's side again. Part of it cut all the way around to his back, and as I carefully turned his body around, my eyes grew wide when I caught sight of a tattoo at the base of his neck. It was a small sword in a black circle, which was about two inches wide. "What is it?" I whispered to him in Greek as I slowly traced the circle imprinted on his skin.

He let me continue to trace his tattoo as he spoke, his voice suddenly seeming frigid. "It's the symbol of the Warriors, the protectors of the Knowing camp. Every occupation has a symbol, which each person is required to wear as a tattoo. We get it when we start training. I just got it a little early."

I frowned, not sure I liked the idea of tattooing an identification on somebody. Too permanent, I supposed. Even if he really wanted to, Alec (or any other Knowing member, for that matter) could never truly leave that part of his life behind.

I stopped studying his tattoo and faced him once again, meeting his icy blue gaze. "Aren't you finished training? You're the best person I've ever fought using swords, besides Ares, of course," I pointed out to him.

"I trained myself," he stated dryly, dropping his head to stare at the ground. "Technically, you're not supposed to start training until you turn sixteen. Even when I had the vision that led me here, the leaders wouldn't prepare me for anything."

His voice was angry now, and I could understand why. The Knowing had basically thrown him to the monsters and left him for dead, not even bothering to help prepare him for his mission to find us. The more I heard about the Knowing, the less I liked them, though I was also impressed by Alec even more. Training yourself was hard—all the gods knew that—but Alec was really, really good, and I couldn't help but think that the rest of the Knowing had seriously underestimated him.

"What are the Knowing people like?" I asked him, wanting to learn more about the people I would probably meet someday in the future.

Alec frowned. "To be honest, they're all cowards," he informed me bluntly, and I raised my eyebrows in surprise.

"What do you mean?" I questioned, chewing on my lower lip in thought.

"I'm the first person in ages to have left the base camp. The Knowing people complain that the gods have turned their backs on them, but the Knowing haven't even made themselves known to any of you. Even the Warriors hardly ever venture out of the camp because they're too afraid of monsters and the fact that the gods might be mad at them for some of the things they've done. To put it simply, the Knowing are pretty much untouchable inside the camp, so no one wants to leave it," Alec explained to me, an anxious edge to his voice. "I think almost all of the Knowing camps have lost contact with each other as a result. The base camp in Kentucky used to keep in contact with the smaller camps around the United States, but I can't remember the last time we even spoke with one of the other leaders. Even my leader, who was originally from the New York camp, has given up."

"Then we'll have to change that, create a new era of cooperation or something," I said lightly, meeting Alec's gaze with raised eyebrows, and he quietly nodded in agreement. I couldn't help but notice how his expressions became darker when he was talking about the Knowing than when he was talking about anything else, which made me infer that there was a lot more to the story. I didn't have the heart to press him, however.

"We can call it the Golden Age of the Forest Gods," Alec whispered with a small, somewhat hopeless chuckle, but I smirked at his suggestion anyway. I thought it suited my generation of gods quite well.

In silence, we stared out at the beautiful meadow. At the moment, the moon was illuminating a thick, silver mist that was settling right above the lush green grass, covering the soft ground like a blanket. The fireworks show was over, but we still stared up at the twinkling sky and stars anyway. Alec put his hand over mine for a split second, and I felt my heart flutter again. I hated him for being brave enough to touch me like that. I hated it more than anything.

*No,* I told myself. *What are you doing? Don't let this happen! It's only been a few days, for gods' sakes!*

Which also meant the fulfillment of the prophecy was growing nearer and nearer. The rest of the gods and I seemed to be careening toward our destinies at top speed, and I didn't know how to slow this train down.

"Thanks for helping me," he whispered, looking deeply into my eyes. My mind whirling, I just smiled weakly at him before moving my hand away from his, and he sighed.

"So how do you like living with Pan and Persephone?" I asked, changing the subject.

Alec frowned to himself, then confessed, "It's great. It really is. They're very accommodating. My only complaint is not getting any sleep, with the nymphs and satyrs coming and going from the hideout all through the night."

I smirked. "You'll get used to it. The rest of the Monster Watch and I did. We still like to camp out there every once in a while. Then again, it usually just turns into a party."

A dark brown flash caught my eye, and I watched a deer run through the meadow, cutting right through the blanket of mist. Suddenly, an arrow pierced its skull, and the deer crumpled to the ground before it could even take another step. It was dead.

Instead of feeling sorry for the deer, I just grinned and quickly pulled out my walkie-talkie from a belt loop. "Artemis, was that you?" I asked, knowing that the goddess of the hunt would have her walkie-talkie on and with her just in case anything bad happened while she was alone. From afar, I watched her step out into the meadow next to the deer, accompanied by two tree nymphs that served as a couple of her virgin huntresses. When she heard my voice call out to her, she looked wildly around her murky surroundings, trying to catch sight of me in the darkness. I waved, and then Alec and I walked toward her.

"What happened to you two?" she asked in Greek, studying the bandage that covered Alec's entire midsection.

"Alec wanted me to train him," I informed Artemis, placing my hands on my hips.

The blonde only smirked as she yanked the arrow out of the deer's forehead and pulled out a burlap sack from behind her. Alec and I helped her stuff the dead deer into the sack, and then we tied it tight. Next, Alec lifted the sack up onto his shoulders, but his wound started to gush even more blood, and I could see his fresh bandage already turning red. "I'll do it," I told him, shaking my head, and he nodded reluctantly.

Together, the three of us made our way to Pan's hideout, leaving the two green-skinned tree nymphs to go back to their own neck of the woods. When we finally reached the hideout, Pan was still swimming in the river with some water nymphs and Persephone sat on his throne, leaning forward and braiding the long hair of a young tree nymph. Meanwhile, Artemis and Alec took the deer out of the big brown sack and started to skin it and cut it in half using swords and pocketknives. Persephone only frowned and turned away, not wanting to look at the poor dead animal and all of its sticky blood, but I did not have any sympathy for her. After all, without Artemis hunting for them every once in a while, the nymphs and satyrs would be forced to consume nothing but berries. Monsters tended to gravitate toward the deer as well, since tasty, unarmed humans no longer strutted foolishly through the forbidden woods. There were always smaller rodents running around the forest floor at night, of course, but natural predators like owls tended to pick those up.

Leaving Alec and Artemis to finish slicing the deer, I walked over and sat down in the grass beside Persephone, who had been stealing glances at me suspiciously. "You're hiding something, aren't you?" she whispered, tucking a piece of light brown hair behind her ear, but not meeting my gaze. "Every time you look at Alec . . . it's like you know something about him that no one else does."

"So what if I do?" I challenged with a shrug, pretending it wasn't a big deal and glaring at Alec's back as he helped Artemis hand out slices of deer meat.

Persephone was looking at me now, raising her eyebrows expectantly. "Don't you think you should tell the rest of us gods?"

I shook my head. "Not yet."

"When?"

I sighed irritably. In my mind, I flashed back to when I was nine, sprinting alone through the forest one day, a particularly frightening moment only two others knew about. My dignity had depended on me escaping that godforsaken arrow—and I had, in fact, escaped—but upon reflection, I was sure that arrow would have led to a better fate than what awaited me now. So, when an image of the Oracle placing a finger to her lips flashed through my brain, all I could say to Persephone was, "When the prophecy comes true." I couldn't even bring myself to specify the part of the prophecy to which I was referring, the part of the prophecy that no one really understood yet.

"Why not now?" she questioned, shrugging. "Won't you feel guilty keeping secrets from all of us? At least from Zeus, you must."

"I would feel even guiltier if I did let them know. Right now, Alec's my problem, not theirs," I explained, frowning at the ground and picking at the incredibly long blades of grass around my legs.

Shaking her head at me, Persephone only sighed and admitted, "I'm not sure if I'll ever completely understand you."

"Maybe it's better if you don't," I replied shortly. Then I pushed myself off the ground and followed Artemis and Alec away from the hideout to deliver the other half of the deer to the Oracle of Delphi.

We all still wore our armor, knowing that this northwest area was where most of the monsters lived, and that they would be attracted to us for two reasons: one, we had a bloody deer with us, which would be some excellent free food for them. And two, monsters tried to track and kill every person who knew about the Greek myths, which was the whole reason the Knowing had Warriors. Even though he was with two powerful gods, Alec was still a prime target. Hopefully, we would be lucky and not run into any monsters, but all three of us knew that it was probably not going to happen. We gods had learned early on in our exploration of the forest that luck was almost never on our side.

Slowly, we wove our way through the maze of spider webs and pine trees, toward where we thought the Oracle's camp was. However, even for us, this part of the woods was still not fully explored, and so we ended up taking two wrong turns. On the bright side, Artemis managed to shoot a harpy in the process, before it got too close to us.

Eventually, we stepped into a very tiny clearing, with a small fire raging outside a tiny camouflaged tent. The Oracle sat by the flames, braiding her black hair with purple ribbons, and turned to face us as she said, "You brought food?" We nodded silently, and I threw down the burlap sack, which landed with a loud thump next to her. All of a sudden, she started to shake, as if the sound had caused a reaction, and her eyes glowed bright green. Artemis and I had seen her do this before, and we knew she was about to tell a prophecy. Her mouth opened, and more green light flowed out as mist started to cloud around her. She finally spoke,

"In six years' time will come one god's prime,
And he will be tired of being under fire.
He will fight for what he thinks is his right,
But it could tear apart the balance that's fair,
And the duty will fall upon you all,
In order to save the world."

Alec stood very still, his mouth wide open, as he heard the prophecy for the first time. Artemis and I, however, just waited for the Oracle to return to her normal self so we could leave. I was not too shy to admit that being around the Oracle was not very comfortable. To put it simply, she was not very sociable, and the gods thought the fact that she fainted every time after she spouted out a prophecy was kind of creepy and unnerving. She had never even told us gods where she was born or where she had originally come from—only that she had been reared by nymphs here in the forest.

Suddenly, we heard a huge roll of thunder, and a white-hot flash of lightning lit up the entire forest. It started to pour within mere seconds, and a few drops of rain were already starting to leak through the thick cover of the trees, splashing onto our confused faces at random intervals. As you could probably guess, such a storm was very unusual. Even during battle practices, when all the gods' powers clashed at once, the sky wasn't *this* unpredictable.

*Zeus, what have you done?* I thought to myself worriedly. It had to be him, even though he was at Hera's party. It had to be. He was the only god I knew of who could have made a huge storm like this within a few short seconds. But why? Something had made Zeus so upset that he could accidentally cause a deadly flood, and I knew we had to stop him.

The Oracle, who had regained consciousness by then, quickly stamped out the fire and dove into her tent for cover. "You must save us!" she exclaimed to us over her shoulder, sounding quite panicked.

We didn't need to be told twice. Without another word, Alec, Artemis, and I took off in the direction we thought was toward our houses, though there was no way for us to be sure. As branches slapped and stung our fatigued bodies, I couldn't help but think that the prophecy was finally coming true, and by the looks on Alec's and Artemis's faces, I could tell they were thinking the exact same thing. I could only hope we would get there in time to prevent any further damage from being done . . .

# Chapter 9:

# TROUBLE

"Go back to Pan's hideout and round up all of Artemis's huntresses in case we need help!" I shouted to Alec in Greek as he, Artemis, and I raced through the woods in the pouring rain.

Between the branches slapping my face as we ran along, I could just barely see Alec shaking his head. "No! You might need help!" he yelled back, and I exchanged a quick, distressed glance with Artemis, wishing he would just listen for a minute.

Looking forward just in time, I jumped sideways to avoid crashing into a huge tree and replied as we continued to run, "Then who will protect the others if Pan's hideout is attacked?"

No answer.

I looked him in the eyes seriously and pleaded, "Alec, please, don't worry about me. I'll be fine. Artemis will be fine too. It takes a god to bring down another god, and I don't want you caught in the crossfire."

Alec frowned, obviously not happy with my request, but he did cut right and disappeared into the trees after a minute of thought.

Artemis and I picked up our pace, and within fifteen minutes, we reached the edge of the forest. We tore off our armor and threw the pieces, along with our weapons, into a hollow log before we ran out onto the street and sprinted toward Alicia and Madison's house. Out in the open there were no trees, so we got even more soaked than we did in the woods. Through the pouring rain and the randomly flashing lightning, we ran almost blindly for what seemed like forever before we finally got to the house.

The rest of the gods were standing out in the front yard, forming a large circle, and Zach and Alicia were screaming at each other, but I couldn't make out what they were saying over the deafening thunder. Madison stepped between the two of them, trying to calm them down, but she was pushed to the ground by Alicia and fell on her beautiful garden, crushing half of the colorful flowers. Mud splattered all over her cute summer dress, and her lower lip started to quiver. I was pretty sure she was about to cry, if she wasn't already; it was hard to tell through the rain.

*"Stop it!"* I screamed at them, worrying that my voice would be lost in the thunder as I broke into the center of the circle. The rest of the gods turned to look at me in shock, and most of them also looked grateful that Camille and I had come. The silence didn't last for long, however, and within a few seconds, Zach and Alicia were yelling at each other again. Then Alicia slapped him hard across the face, and all the gods joined in with Zach to start screaming at Alicia in a loud chorus.

With a cry of anger, I tackled Zach, pinning him to the ground before he could even think about doing anything to Alicia. He roared with anger, and another bright white flash of lightning lit up the stormy sky above us. I cursed at him in frustration. Not only was he causing what could end up being the worst flood in Washington state's history, but he could have ended up causing the end of the world if we didn't stop him.

Suddenly, I was yanked up off of Zach and the fabric of my shirt pressed into the skin on my neck, beginning to choke me. I ducked my head instinctively, but was unfortunately not able to avoid a hard punch from Matt. *Ouch.* I was quite sure that punch would have broken any normal person's jaw, and that I was going to have a horrible, ugly bruise by the morning.

Frowning, I desperately wormed my way out of his grasp, and Matt tried to punch me again, but this time I caught his fist and twisted his arm behind him. Out of the corner of my eye, I saw Camille grab Luke by the collar of his shirt to prevent him from intervening as well. Still holding Matt hostage, I pointed up at the sky with my free hand and yelled at the rest of the gods, "What the hell is going on here? Look at what you did!" I peered through the pouring rain, specifically looking at Zach, who was still sitting on the ground, partly covered in mud. I couldn't believe it—we were already falling apart!

When our leader didn't speak, Haley explained quickly, without even pausing to take a breath, "Zach was kissing Madison and then Alicia got jealous and there was a huge fight and . . ." She trailed off, clearly unsure of what to do.

"I was not jealous!" Alicia exclaimed, glaring at Haley and crossing her arms. "I was just mad."

"Yeah, you were mad because you were jealous," Luke told her off, not helping the situation at all. Now Alicia looked like she wanted to punch Luke as well.

Meanwhile, Zach's little raindrops, like thousands of arrows from his army of clouds, continued to pelt us. I couldn't even think straight. "Stop this," I told Zach, waving my free arm in the air. He didn't even bother to move a muscle and just mindlessly picked at the grass he was sitting on. "NOW," I shouted. He shot me a glare, but slowly the rain lightened up and the rest of the gods began to regroup and calm down.

However, now that the truth was out, I was starting to think that this wasn't the problem the prophecy spoke of after all. A fight over a boy didn't really seem like a big deal to me, but then again I wasn't into drama (or boys) like Alicia was. On the other hand, I also knew that if we didn't solve this issue right away, Alicia would turn on all of us, which really could cause the end of the world.

Finally, the rain slowed to a stop, though it was still very cloudy and dark since it was now almost midnight. All of a sudden, we heard a door open behind us, so we all turned to face the house as Alicia and Madison's father, the police officer, poked his head out. "What are you kids still doing out here?" he said gruffly, a touch of annoyance in his deep voice. I couldn't blame him for being suspicious of us; we were standing out in the front yard late at night, soaked all the way through to our skin, after all.

Quickly, after I forced Zach to apologize to Alicia, we all dispersed and returned to our respective houses. Only Josh remained, and since he was the messenger, he reluctantly agreed to go tell everyone in the forest about what had happened. Because Zach was in no position to lead us at the time, I was the one who sat up on the roof waiting for Josh to come out of the forest and give a full report, so I didn't actually get to fall asleep until two a.m. Needless to say, I slept in late that morning.

When I woke up, the first thing I did was walk over to my mirror and look at my jaw where Matt had punched me the night before. There was an ugly purple and yellow bruise about the size of fist throbbing incessantly, and simply brushing a finger over it hurt like crazy. *Oh well,* I thought. It just made me look tougher.

Frowning, I walked over to my window and peeked outside. None of the Monster Watch was out there, which was kind of surprising. I assumed Zach wouldn't want to go into the woods today anyway, and since I didn't know where anyone else was, I took my old blue bike out from the garage and biked down Main Street, grabbing my leather jacket on the way out. It was cold, and the sky was still dark and cloudy, but at least Zach wasn't making it rain anymore. The streets were still flooded in some parts, and the smooth pavement was slippery.

Outside of the Fire Pit, I threw down the bike on the slick sidewalk and stepped inside. I then sat down by myself at our usual table in the back of the room as Martha came over and handed me a glass of lemonade. She looked like she was going to ask about the horrible bruise on my face, but then thought better of it. I was grateful; my own human mother would have pestered me nonstop.

When I asked where the boys were, she told me that Zach wasn't feeling well (like I believed that! He was probably still storming around his room—literally), and Luke was on a date with Christina, a pretty blonde from the neighboring town of Pine Grove. I had seen them walking around together once or twice before, but I really didn't know much about her. I just knew that she loved the beach almost as much as Luke did, and I was pretty sure that was all they talked about, although even Camille and I admitted that they made a cute couple appearance-wise. Becca had started a rumor that Christina was really the goddess Amphitrite, the wife of Poseidon, but I didn't want to test Christina until the prophecy was a thing of the past.

Speaking of Luke and Christina, they walked into the restaurant right at that moment. Luke glanced at me for only a second and Christina waved, but then they sat down together at a table for two. All of a sudden, I felt very alone. I had no idea where Connor or anyone else was, which probably meant they were all cooped up in their houses for one reason or another. Sighing sadly to myself, I left the restaurant and walked across the street into the forest, leaving my bike on the sidewalk. It wouldn't help me much in the woods anyway.

"Hey, wait up!" I heard Cole say to me from across the street.

I plastered a smile on my face and turned around, trying to be friendly even though I wasn't in the mood. "Hi, Cole. What's up?" I asked politely as he jogged up to me.

He took a deep breath before his soft brown eyes met my cold gray ones with a sense of urgency. I gulped and closed my eyes, knowing exactly what he was going to say next and dreading it. This exact moment had been in the making for a very long time. Sure enough, he pointed toward the trees and told me firmly, "I'm ready. To go in, I mean. Are you coming?" I thought he was trying to convince himself more than me.

I chewed my lip, thinking quietly for a minute, and Cole ruffled his caramel-colored hair nervously. "All right, fine. Just wait one minute," I said to him as I stepped a few yards into the forest, making sure there weren't any stray pieces of armor lying about. Then I pulled the walkie-talkie off my belt loop and, desperately hoping one of the other gods had theirs on, I said in Greek, "This is Athena, calling in an emergency situation. I'm taking Cole into the forest. I need help keeping the monsters away so he doesn't see anything."

It was dead silent for a moment as I waited for someone to answer my urgent plea. What was really only a few seconds seemed like ages before the walkie-talkie crackled to life and I heard Zeus's voice say gruffly, "Why the hell are you doing that?" I could tell he was still angry from the night before.

"If I don't take him in now, I think he'll go in on his own to try to impress me or something," I explained in annoyance.

"But if he lives, other people will want to go in too," he argued, and I had to admit to myself that Zeus really did have a good point. The last thing we wanted was to become tour guides.

I was tugging at my side ponytail in deep thought when I heard Alec's voice come on the line, and I knew he was using Pan's walkie-talkie until we could get him one of his own. "Well, are we doing this or not?" Alec asked unhappily, and I was kind of surprised to hear that he was on board with my plan.

Zeus groaned. "Fine. But I won't be able to get there very fast. Alec, what about you?"

"I'm at the meadow with Persephone and a few nymphs. I can get over there right now and follow you, I guess," Alec agreed, but he still sounded unhappy. Once I told him where to find us, I walked back into the sunlight to meet Cole again, apologized for the wait, and led him into the forest, where it was almost dark enough to need a flashlight.

The two of us were silent for a while, and the only things we could hear were the birds calling to each other and the slight breeze whistling through the trees. I wondered if Alec had run into any monsters yet and if he was having any trouble fighting them on his own, because it would have been a real problem if he ended up dying. He was supposed to become our hero, after all. According to the Oracle, we couldn't save the world without him.

After walking for a few minutes longer, I realized just how loud Cole was being. I supposed I had been tuning out his crunching footsteps subconsciously. The rest of the gods and I had learned when we were much younger to be as quiet as possible to avoid any monsters whatsoever, and Alec had also caught on to this idea very quickly, but I wasn't sure Cole was even trying. I desperately wanted to check in with Alec, who was probably very annoyed and angry at the moment, since Cole was making his lookout job twice as difficult. The poor Sightless guy was probably attracting every single monster in the forest by making all that noise.

I stopped for a minute, ready to give Cole a lecture on taking quieter footsteps, but then my walkie-talkie crackled to life. Luckily, it was on a low volume, but I could still hear Alec's troubled voice ask quietly in Greek, "Why are you *really* doing this for him?" My breath caught in my throat, and I bit my lip, suddenly wondering the same thing. "Don't lie to me, Athena. And don't lie to yourself either." I found myself hating how his words sounded so much like something I would have said.

"What was that?" Cole asked loudly, interrupting my train of thought.

"Just static," I answered dryly, turning away from him. My jaw was starting to throb again, and I was really wishing it would stop. Meanwhile, Cole frowned, probably deciding whether to believe me or not.

We were silent and unmoving, frozen in time, until he said, "Well, are we going yet?"

But I didn't answer him; I was too busy thinking about what Alec had said to me. Why was I doing this for Cole anyway? Was it just because he was my friend and I felt pressured to do him a favor? Or was there another, more personal reason I didn't even want to consider? Admittedly, Alec's arrival in the forest seemed to have a very troubling effect on my love life, or lack thereof. More often than not I found myself wishing I had sent him away from the forest like Hera suggested.

However, my confused thoughts were interrupted yet again when Cole put his hand on my shoulder, slowly turning me around to face him. "Are you okay?" he whispered, his brown eyes full of concern, and I simply nodded, deciding that I never should have brought Cole here in the first place. I had caused too much trouble already.

All of a sudden, he leaned in to kiss me, gently placing his warm hands on my hips, the skin on which suddenly felt like it was burning. He closed his eyes and slipped his fingers through the belt loops on my jeans, pulling me closer. *This cannot be happening,* I thought. *I am* so *not ready for this.* As fast as I could, I pushed back before he got the chance to kiss me, turning my head away from him. I was hyperventilating and my mind was reeling.

"I'm sorry, Cole. I shouldn't have brought you here," I said quickly, eager to get him out of my second home.

Cole opened his mouth to speak, but he never got the chance. The sound of rustling branches distracted him, and he turned to face whatever had made the sound. Then Alec, who happened to be wearing his armor and holding a sword covered in monster blood, stumbled out from behind a large pine tree. His piercing blue eyes widened as they met mine, and it was as if we were tied together in a single moment of fear. Alec, a person unknown to the town, had been seen in the forbidden forest, a place where dozens of people were rumored to have been murdered, and there was no taking it back now. Needless to say, this meeting was not good for anyone in the little clearing. So, acting on the spur of the moment, I did the only thing I could think of.

I punched Cole. Hard enough to knock him out. His black pupils dilated as his eyes rolled back in his head, and then he slowly fell backward, crashing to the ground with a loud thump. "Sorry again," I muttered to an unconscious Cole before I looked up to see Alec's jaw drop in shock.

"That was so awesome," Alec said, his eyes full of wonder, but he didn't mention anything he had told me via walkie-talkie. I only hoped Cole wouldn't remember any of this when he awoke. After all, I guessed that the only reason Alec appeared so happy was because he now knew that I didn't really have any romantic feelings toward Cole. It was becoming plainly obvious that Alec was interested in me as well.

"What happened here?" Zeus asked in Greek as he walked up behind us. Alec just smirked at me, and with enthusiasm, he filled Zeus in as the three of us dragged Cole's limp body back to the edge of the forest.

"He's heavier than he looks," Zeus grumbled as we dropped Cole on the ground, and I nodded in agreement. Although the scrawny, Sightless boy was still unconscious, none of us—especially not Alec—was willing to wait for him to wake up. Yes, it was probably kind of cruel, but Zeus and I left him sleeping peacefully next to Main Street and immediately headed back into the forest. Even though the entire town had almost been flooded by Zeus's storm, the gods still had battle practice scheduled for that day. So to the meadow we went, leaving Alec to wander back toward Pan's hideout alone, as he didn't particularly want to be killed by our superhuman powers.

---

The ground shook hard beneath me, knocking me off balance, and I fell into the long grass before I could even take another step forward. I got up just in time to see Poseidon raise his golden trident again, ready to bring it down and cause another earthquake. So I dropped to the ground once more, using the grass as a cover while I surveyed the entire situation. Then Aphrodite, who was wearing a bright pink-and-black workout outfit, suddenly dove down to rest beside me. "Hey," she whispered. I simply rolled my eyes at her, thinking she was about to give away my position.

But just then, a piercing scream cut through the air like a knife. All of the gods immediately stopped what they were doing and instinctively looked toward where the sound had come from. At the edge of the meadow, Hera was still screaming, hanging from a tree, wrapped in thick vines that looked as if they were squeezing her to death. Panic emanated from her like heat from a heater. Zeus did not hesitate to run toward her, ignoring everything that had happened between them the night before. Demeter, however, was standing right next to the suffocating Hera, with hers fists balled and a bloodthirsty look in her usually calm brown eyes.

"Let her go!" Zeus demanded at the top of his voice, but Demeter didn't even cast a glance in our direction. She was too busy torturing Hera.

I waited for Zeus to tackle Demeter, to do *something*, but he only stopped in his tracks, seemingly hypnotized. I was preparing to throw my spear at the goddess of the harvest, but then Hera seemed to regain her senses, realizing she was about to die. I saw her face suddenly relax, and she closed her eyes, her muscles rippling. The next thing I knew, I was blinded by a flash of purple light, and I felt as if I were being blown to bits. I couldn't even walk, let alone see straight.

Struggling to remain standing and trying to regain my vision, I blinked furiously, but there was only endless purple light. Seconds passed, seeming like ages, and I was beginning to worry that none of us would ever be able to see again, that this had been Hera's plan all along—to make sure we couldn't fight back against whatever she was going to do to us. But soon, I could make out blurs, which eventually became shapes that looked like the rest of the gods again.

Rubbing my eyes in disbelief, I stomped over to join the rest of the gods standing over Demeter and Hera, who was now free of the vines and just beginning to breathe regularly again. Demeter's face was equally red, and she began sobbing, which confused me even more. The other gods, too, exchanged wary glances.

"I'm sorry. I—I don't know what came over me," Demeter gasped between sobs, with her head in her hands and strands of blonde hair sticking to her wet face. "I'm so, so sorry. Will you forgive me?" She looked to Hera for an answer.

And after debating with herself for a while, Hera answered cryptically, "Yes. Eventually."

I decided that "eventually" was better than "never" in my book. Trust didn't come easily to us.

---

Unsurprisingly, Zeus ended battle practice right after that terrifying ordeal, and all of us gods split up for the rest of the afternoon. The rest of the Monster Watch and I headed deeper into the forest to see if Alec wanted to join us in a round of reverse hide-and-seek, while the other gods headed back to Main Street. Certain things looked as if they were starting to get back to normal again.

Poseidon, Zeus, and Apollo took off in different directions, ready to start our game. I was given the job of picking up Alec, who had been introduced to reverse hide-and-seek during the days I had spent with Katie. The Monster Watch had made the executive decision that Alec, as the newest player in the game, would be hiding first that day.

After walking for a while, I finally reached Pan's hideout, where I patiently waited for Alec to put on his armor. We then strode away, leaving Pan to swim with some water nymphs in bikinis and Persephone and Artemis's huntresses to collect berries for a daytime snack.

"It's kind of hard to believe a cheating scandal almost caused the end of the world last night," Alec chuckled to himself as he took one last look over his shoulder at Pan's hideout before it disappeared from view.

I smirked. "I think you're exaggerating a little bit about the end of the world, but I definitely agree with you," I told him, absentmindedly fingering the walkie-talkie on my hip. "Some of the gods take these things a little too personally."

Alec laughed again. "If Aphrodite and Hera were here, I bet they would be complaining about how painfully obvious it is that I've never had a girlfriend, and that you've never had a boyfriend."

"And I don't plan on getting one," I retorted seriously, hoping that Alec was getting the message. I didn't need to cause any more trouble among the gods, and I definitely didn't need those wretched feelings of non-familial love seeping into my mind like poison, interrupting my train of thought and slowly killing me.

"Really? You could've fooled me," Alec scoffed, his voice tight as he glared down at the lush ferns his shoes were crushing. "I don't know why else you would have brought Cole in here."

"Because Cole's my friend," I hissed defensively. "I don't expect you to understand."

"You're right. I don't understand. And I don't believe that's the real reason you brought him in here. I don't even think *you* know why you brought him in here."

"If you felt so strongly about this, why didn't you try harder to stop me?" I argued, raising my voice, crossing my arms, and stepping in front of him to block his path.

"Because I'm not a god," Alec reminded me, his voice equally cold and unforgiving. "And you're the goddess of wisdom. It's nearly impossible to convince you *not* to do something you've set your mind to."

I shut my eyes, taking deep breaths in and out, in and out. "My mind was never made up, Alec," I whispered, opening my eyes but avoiding eye contact. "*You* were right. But still, you shouldn't have given up on me. I would have listened to you. I don't care that you're not a god."

Alec didn't say anything more. He only looked down at the uneven ground, mulling over what I had just said and lazily kicking at a small rock. I wasn't sure what he expected me to say, but it definitely wasn't something so radical.

Suddenly, Alec surprised me by placing a hand on my left shoulder, his face now mere inches from mine. I was having a hard time trying to predict what he was thinking, what his next move would be, and that was perturbing to me. He carefully reached out to touch the huge, ugly bruise on the side of my face before he asked in a worried whisper, "Is your jaw okay?"

Maybe it was crazy, but I felt my jaw immediately stop throbbing at his warm touch. Half of my body was telling me to slap his hand away from my face, but the other half wanted Alec to stay right where he was. I could do nothing but force myself to stand firmly in place and to ignore the fact that my muscles were beginning to cramp up with stress.

Finally, I managed to raise my shoulders in a shrug. "I've been hit harder."

"I'm not surprised," he said, his face still close to mine. "You are Athena, after all."

He was grinning now, actually grinning. I assumed he was trying to cover up how he was really feeling after our first argument, but I didn't want to confront him about it again because I knew it would probably lead to another fight. Two could play at this treacherous game.

"Yes, I am," I stated simply, unsure of what else there was to say on the matter. After pausing for a moment, I continued, flashing back to when I knocked out Cole for trying to kiss me, "And *you* obviously didn't learn anything from what happened with Cole earlier."

While slowly, romantically slipping one of his strong arms around my shoulders, Alec smirked and said, "Oh yes, I did. I learned that I shouldn't flirt with you unless I want some serious damage to various parts of my body."

I played along with his outrageous antics, permitting myself to lean into him for just a second, and raised my eyebrows at him as I asked, "Then why are you flirting with me now?" He only grinned, still tightly holding onto me, and I hated myself for thinking that being with him felt so natural.

"Babe, I've been flirting with you ever since last night, and I'm lucky I'm not dead yet. But I just realized that I'm okay with earning a few more permanent scars, if it means I get to spend more time with you." He laughed lightly as he said this, but at the same time he somehow sounded much more serious than before—*too* serious, if there was such a thing.

Eager to change the subject, I pushed Alec away. "It's your turn to hide," I informed him matter-of-factly. This time he did not argue, and I smiled to myself when I heard the crackling of branches behind me, meaning that Alec was running away. Finally.

# Chapter 10:

# MISSING

After I found Alec hiding up in a tall tree, I radioed Zeus, Poseidon, and Apollo so we could meet up. The five of us headed over to Pan's hideout to drop Alec off after finishing our round of reverse hide-and-seek. We were about a few yards away when we heard Pan and Persephone bickering, and Alec groaned, looking annoyed. He probably wished he were somewhere else, but he didn't have any other place to be and knew that he should take advantage of spending as much time with the gods as possible, especially because Persephone had to go back to the Underworld at the end of the summer. That was only a short time away, and we still had to save the world at sometime or another.

Stepping out next to the river pool, we saw Pan sitting on his rock throne, brushing moss off his furry goat legs, and Persephone sitting on a blanket with some nymphs. The nymphs were urging Persephone to divulge information about her relationship with Hades, but the brunette was blushing, shaking her head no. I knew he was a sore subject for her, since she didn't even like talking to Demeter about him, so I wondered how much she had told them already.

Finally, she admitted, her voice hushed, "We were just friends, really. Then puberty came along, and things got really bad between us. Bad and awkward. I needed a girl to talk with down there, but he couldn't give me that. So things fell apart. Honestly, there's not much to tell."

Here, Persephone turned her head and noticed us standing behind her. Suddenly embarrassed in the presence of Zeus, Poseidon, Apollo, and Alec, she shut her mouth and blushed an even deeper red. The nymphs had enough sense to refrain from pressing her any further, and Persephone quickly shooed us away so she could make some dinner alone. The rest of the Monster Watch and I only exchanged confused shrugs and made our way back to our homes, as it was already getting dark. Where had the day gone?

We were passing through the meadow when Zeus, who was leading our single-file line, pointed out something on the other side of the meadow. It was a hooded figure dressed all in black, riding on the back of a huge, well-muscled black horse. The person, whoever it was, was heading our way, and I was pretty sure that he hadn't noticed us yet. When he looked up, however, we caught a glimpse of his pale face, and I immediately knew who it was. One fleeting moment was all it took to recognize the lord of the dead.

"What the hell is he doing here?" Poseidon muttered angrily in Greek, and I frowned, knowing full well that Hades was supposed to be in the Underworld. Technically, he was allowed into our realm only if he had an invitation from Zeus, or if he was delivering Persephone.

"Let's find out," Apollo whispered back to us. He followed Zeus and took another few steps toward Hades, who sat frozen on his horse. His dark, creepy eyes narrowed and locked on us.

"Hello," Zeus said, raising his voice so Hades could hear. "What are you doing up here on this lovely evening?" I could tell that Zeus was trying to sound as friendly as possible, so he wouldn't send Hades running in the other direction.

But it didn't work.

Hades slammed his heels into the horse's belly, and it turned around on a dime, quickly bolting in the other direction, back under the trees. Without stopping to think about what we were doing, the rest of the Monster Watch and I started racing across the meadow after him. He was obviously avoiding us for a good reason, and we had to know what it was.

Sprinting as fast as we could, we jumped over logs and large tree roots and ducked to avoid low-hanging branches, but even when you're a god in the best shape you could ever be in, you can't quite outrun a galloping horse (especially when you're wearing heavy armor). Unless you're Hermes.

Still running, I yanked the walkie-talkie off one of my belt loops and yelled into it. "Hermes! If you're listening, we spotted Hades in the woods. He's on horseback, heading east toward Main Street. You need to cut him off now before he gets away!"

After almost falling on my face from tripping, I heard a reply from the walkie-talkie: "On it."

The four of us ran through the dark forest, following the trail of broken branches left by Hades's horse. Branches whipped our reddening faces as we carried on, unsure when Hades would stop. The Monster Watch and I could only hope that Hermes could find Hades and cut him off in time . . . and that we weren't running through poison oak. We were following the trail uphill as fast as we could, but by now the four of us had fallen far behind Hades and his horse, and we still hadn't heard another word from Hermes.

Eventually we rounded a bend and came up at the top of the small hill, where the trail ended at a small cave just large enough for one person to fit into. The Greek symbol cut into the stone marked the cave as an entrance to Hades's realm. Unfortunately, Hermes and Persephone were the only other gods besides Hades allowed into the Underworld.

I sat on the grass, defeated, tugging at my ponytail and trying to catch my breath. Poseidon, clutching at a stitch in his side, slammed his golden trident into the ground in frustration, creating a slight tremor in the earth, and Zeus just frowned at him.

"Now what?" Apollo asked once he had caught his breath. Sighing, he used his dirty red shirt to wipe the beaded sweat off his brow.

Zeus ruffled his dirty-blond hair and continued to pace in a small circle as he answered, "Well, Hades is obviously not allowed to be up here on Earth, so we have to know what he was doing." He paused for a moment to think, but he must not have come up with anything because he looked to me almost right away. "Any ideas, Athena?"

I stopped tugging at my hair and leaned back against a tree. "Before we do anything else, we need to talk to Herm—"

I stopped mid-sentence, as I heard a loud noise that sounded like rock grinding against rock come from the tiny cave, and the boys and I turned around to see Hermes appear in front of us, as if on cue. He was barely even breaking out in sweat, even though we knew he had just sprinted all the way from his house to the Underworld and back.

"Give me a full report," Zeus ordered immediately.

Hermes nodded. "I got here just in time to see Hades enter the Underworld through the cave, so I followed him," he explained. "I tried to get him to tell me why he was up here in our realm, but he didn't answer. Basically, Hades told me to buzz off and then threw me out of there, except he was cursing a lot more."

The five of us stood in silence while Zeus tried to figure out what to do about our new dilemma. For all we knew, this could be a random event that wasn't significant at all, or it could lead to the start of a huge war, which could then lead to the end of the world. We really had no idea, but due to the voicing of the prophecy, I guessed the latter was more likely.

At last, Zeus stopped pacing and stood up straighter, glancing at each of us in turn, the way he did every time he was about to say something important. "We need to inform the rest of the gods about what happened today, and from now on we'll keep an eye out for anything unusual in the forest. Report everything suspicious to me," Zeus finished, looking pointedly at Hermes.

"I'll tell everyone," Hermes confirmed, and then he shot off like a bullet, going east toward Main Street. Even though it was late and he should have been home already, delivering this message was way more important. Saving the world comes before dinner, after all.

Still trying not to worry about Hades, the rest of the Monster Watch and I headed back to our own houses. We had just stepped out of the quiet forest when I heard the familiar sound of yelling come from my house. I sighed glumly, knowing that my parents were fighting again, and that my dad was probably drunk.

Zach squeezed my shoulder and whispered, "Hey, Ash? You can come over to our house anytime, you know." Luke nodded in agreement, although he was frowning in deep thought.

"Yeah, mine too," Connor offered sweetly, like any good friend would do.

"Thanks, guys, but I'm fine for tonight," I assured them. The three of them exchanged dubious glances, not totally believing me, but they didn't say any more. They knew it was better not to press me.

I reluctantly waved goodbye and then stood there quietly for a minute, just staring at the yellow light emanating from inside the house. I could see the shadows of my parents projected on the wall, waving their arms around crazily, like the vicious monsters I fought fearlessly every day. But now I just felt alone, debating whether or not to go inside the house. After all, I could always just turn around and go back into the forest to find Alec. I knew he would welcome my company anytime.

I must have stood there, in the dark across the street from my house, for five whole minutes before I finally decided to climb up to my balcony and into my room, so that I could avoid my parents' wrath. When I reached my dark room, I lay back on my bed to try to rest, but instead I found myself listening to my parents screaming at each other from downstairs. It was awfully hard to sleep when they were being so loud. They usually started fighting about money, even though I was pretty sure we had plenty, but their arguing always wound up being about the fact that my father was constantly drunk. Today their fight was different; they were fighting about me, specifically about why I had been staying out so late recently.

"Ashley can do whatever she wants to! She's been doing that since the day she was born!" my father slurred angrily as I frowned and closed my eyes.

"But she could be killed! No one even knows what's in that terrible forest," my mother told him. She usually tried to keep her cool during these fights, but I could tell she was way past that point. I wondered how long they had been at it so far.

"Well, the Monster Watch knows, and they're obviously fine," my father retorted in a raised voice.

I raised my eyebrows, not believing what I was hearing. For possibly the first time in my life, I was agreeing with my drunken father. He continued, "Ashley can take care of herself! Hell, she's probably the smartest kid her age in the entire world! She doesn't need us! She never did!" Now my father's voice broke, and there was a long pause before my mother spoke again.

I felt horrible, thinking that my father was right. I never really did need my parents, except for the use of their money and when I was a baby, of course. I had been making my own meals, walking to school, and spending as much time out of the house as I could since I was five or six. Frowning to myself, I wondered what my life would have been like if I were a normal girl, since the forest really was the reason my friends and I found out at such a young age that we were gods. Would my parents have formed a closer bond if they had had to take greater care of me and give me more guidance throughout my life?

"It's all because you're such a bad father! Always drinking and disappearing, she never would have gone into that wretched forest with those . . . those silly *boys* if it weren't for you!" my mother screamed. At this, my jaw dropped, and I glared at my ceiling.

Now my mother was ragging on my father about the fact that my best friends were guys? I was partly the goddess of war, for crying out loud! Of course some of my friends were guys! And I had to prove myself to every single one of them, or else they would still be sexist jerks like half of the other guys from outside the Woods that Katie described to me. Hell no, I didn't go into the forest because my parents didn't give me the care I wanted. I had first gone in to save my friends, and if given the chance, I wouldn't have changed anything I had done.

Not in the mood to listen to any more of my parents' fight, I silently stepped out into the hallway, then walked to the end of it and climbed up into the attic, where I often hid from my arguing parents when I was little. I could always think better up there, without all the noise from my parents' shouting.

Standing quietly for a minute, I breathed in the musty smell of the attic and frowned at the rafters draped in silver cobwebs. I saw nothing but old, beige bed sheets on the floor, and I figured that no one had been up there in years, until something in the corner of the room caught my eye. It was a shiny golden picture frame that had obviously been dusted off recently, but I couldn't see what the painting was because it was facing the dark wall. Feeling curious and knowing it was probably one of the many antiques my dad had bought for my mother, I walked over to it and picked it up carefully.

Staring back at me was an old painting of my mother and father standing under clear blue skies in front of the Eiffel Tower in Paris. Minus the beer belly, my father looked pretty much the same—grumpy expression, thinning hair—but my mother was wearing a fancy black dress, and she looked much younger, wearing a big smile, her brown eyes shining. I hadn't seen her smile like that in years, which led me to believe that my father was the one who had been looking at the old memory.

Suddenly feeling as if I had intruded on my father's personal thoughts, I quickly put the picture back exactly how I had found it, then started to return to my room. While I was in the hallway, I narrowly avoided running into my father, but he was so drunk that he hardly noticed. He just grunted something unintelligible, and I nervously inched around him, making a beeline for my room, where I collapsed on my bed, ready to get some sleep.

---

I woke up and quickly got dressed in jeans and a simple teal V-neck, eager to get into the forest. The appearance of Hades the day before had completely changed the equation, and I still wanted to find out why he had been up in our realm. Therefore, I met up with the rest of the Monster Watch in the meadow, where we all sat on a red-and-white-checkered picnic blanket, to discuss a new plan. Alec, Pan, and Persephone arrived a few minutes later, and we started eating our breakfast of berries and granola bars. It wasn't much, but it was better than eating with our parents inside on a nice, sunny day like this.

"So," Zeus started, munching on some blackberries, "what was up with your parents last night?" He was trying hard not to express his deeper worries.

"Yeah, that sounded horrible," Apollo chimed in.

I shrugged, not really wanting to talk about the whole thing, and answered blandly, "Just my mom complaining about how I'm always in the woods, and how my dad's always drunk." Alec shot me a concerned look, as this was the first time he had heard about my parents' less-than-perfect marriage, but I just bit my lip and looked down at the lush, green grass to avoid his gaze.

I continued eating my granola bar, and thankfully, we switched topics and started discussing what to do about Hades. The rest of the gods were going to sneak into the woods later to meet up with us so we could talk about separating into groups to patrol the forest every day. We knew we had to do something to stop whatever Hades was doing.

After we ate, we all tossed around a volleyball for a while and chatted about different monsters. Eventually, the other gods showed up one by one, and our volleyball circle got bigger and bigger until Hera and Demeter, the last two gods, finally arrived.

Zeus clapped his hands together to get everyone's attention and waited for Pan to catch the volleyball. When we were all silent, Zeus ordered, "All right, we're splitting into patrols. Patrol one will be me, Hestia, and Hera. Athena will be leading patrol two, along with Artemis and Apollo." He paused to let us take in the information, but I was happy with my team; for the most part, we all worked well together.

"What about me?" Ares questioned impatiently.

"Ares will be leading patrol three, with Aphrodite and Dionysus," Zeus continued as Ares gave a nod of approval, "and patrol four will be led by Poseidon, with Demeter and Hermes. Hephaestus is at home working on . . . well, whatever he's working on, and Alec, you can pick whatever patrol you want. Persephone and Pan are heading back to their hideout."

Alec nodded and, not unexpectedly, walked over to join my team, high-fiving Apollo on the way. "Yes!" Apollo grinned and exclaimed enthusiastically, "We can call ourselves the A Team. Athena, Apollo, Artemis, and Alec—mighty protectors of the forest!" I simply rolled my eyes as some of the other gods chuckled, and then we split up, my patrol heading north.

---

My walkie-talkie crackled to life and Zeus's voice said, "A Team, have you seen anything yet?"

I sighed. We had been searching for almost two hours already, and no one from any patrol had seen anything suspicious. Honestly, the most interesting thing that happened to my patrol was Apollo tripping over a large tree root and falling flat on his face. "That's a negative," I replied into the walkie-talkie.

"Patrols three and four?" Zeus asked.

"Nothing here," Ares grumbled unhappily. I guessed there wasn't enough action for him so far.

"Hey, how come my patrol doesn't get a cool nickname?" Poseidon complained. Artemis and I only exchanged disapproving glances.

"Just answer the question!" Zeus told him over the radio.

"You're no fun," Poseidon stated bluntly. "But no, we haven't seen anything."

Another two hours passed with no better results. We had scoured the entire forest, including around the Oracle's camp, but none of the patrols had even seen a monster, which was also suspicious. It was as if they were all missing or had disappeared from our forest. Until then, there hadn't been a single day I spent in the woods when I hadn't run into a monster. Maybe this too had something to do with Hades. All the monsters did come from the Underworld, after all.

Eventually, the rest of the patrols met back up with mine in the meadow. Since no one had found anything, it seemed absurd to stick around for the entire day. Everyone except the rest of the Monster Watch, Alec, and I went back to their houses to relax, but we agreed to keep our walkie-talkies on at all times, just in case something terrible happened. Long-term emergency protocol, as Poseidon called it.

---

Alec, Zeus, Apollo, and I had just found Poseidon hiding by the river in yet another round of reverse hide-and-seek when our walkie-talkies came alive with Hermes speaking in Greek. His deep voice was low and quiet, so I knew he was probably out in public, and he sounded more than a little worried as he informed me, "Athena, I'm here at the Fire Pit for lunch, and apparently your father's missing. Your mom is really freaking out."

"Yeah, so?" I said, not really caring. I automatically assumed that my father had just left the Woods again, like he usually did after having a huge fight with my mother. He always came back after a few days.

But I was wrong this time.

"No, I don't think so. I mean, he packed up all of his clothes and things . . . and just left," Hermes restated. "He's gone, Athena. And I'm not so sure he's coming back."

## Chapter 11:

# RETURN OF THE MONSTERS

When I finally reached the Fire Pit, I saw my mother sitting outside, alone at a round table set for two. I sighed and sat across from her, then pushed my bangs out of my eyes and asked cautiously, "Are you okay, Mom?"

She dabbed her big brown eyes with a napkin before looking into my narrowed gray ones. "I'll be fine, sweetie."

I gritted my teeth and leaned back in my chair, slightly annoyed. Anyone could clearly see that she was not fine at all.

"Don't give me that. Just go home, and I'll close up the antique store today," I told her, hoping she would do what I asked and feeling even more like a parent than usual, as I often did when I had to keep the gods from doing something stupid. My mother shook her head and opened her mouth to respond, but I interrupted, "Mom, just go home. Please."

"Oh, I guess I can go." She nodded reluctantly, slowly got up off the chair, and started the short walk home. I stood up when she left and was about to walk next door to close the antique shop for the day when my other mother popped her head out of the Fire Pit.

"Will Catherine be okay?" Martha asked me, her eyebrows knit together with worry. Not really wanting to talk to anyone, I simply nodded and bid her a polite farewell.

I walked into the antique shop next door, ignoring the ring of the tiny bell, and turned around to flip the sign in the display window so that it read CLOSED instead of OPEN. Then I weaved my way through the maze of antique chairs, tables, and miscellaneous items and sat down at my mother's cluttered desk in the back of the store, facing the quiet entrance. I flipped through the many papers on the desk, but I didn't find anything interesting or worth reading, so I just leaned back in the chair and allowed myself to drift, deep in thought.

Eventually, after spending quite a long time staring blankly off into space, I picked up the phone on the desk and dialed my father's cell phone number automatically, almost like a robot. I wasn't sure why or how I had memorized it, since I had never bothered to call him before, so I figured it was one of those unexplained, godly things that came with being Athena and therefore knowing almost everything.

I waited while the phone rang, and rang, and rang, until a monotone voice told me to leave a message, so I barked angrily, "Where the hell are you? And why did you just leave without warning? I can't believe you're giving up on Mom! She needs you. Can't you see that? I'm not even sure why she cares about you, but she does. So call me back when you get this message." I didn't even bother to leave my name or number.

After that, I went outside and locked the wooden door behind me before heading home, mindlessly kicking tiny rocks as I strutted along, bored out of my mind. Within a few minutes, I reached my empty house, which, due to the lazy summer heat, seemed to sag slightly in its foundation, like most of the others in town, but its gray color just made the house look sad. Shaking off my depressed thoughts, I went straight up to my room and did nothing but homework for my online art history class the entire afternoon. I didn't even care that I had not eaten lunch yet. I wasn't particularly hungry, to be honest.

Around six o'clock, I realized that my mother was probably going to stay in her room crying the whole night unless I made some dinner, so I lazily stumbled down the stairs and cooked some mac 'n' cheese. I sat at the kitchen table alone, finishing up my dinner while staring at the phone on the granite countertop, waiting for my father to call. He certainly had some explaining to do.

After another couple of hours of staring at the phone some more and reading my newest book, I determined that my father was going to keep being a jerk and not even bother to call. Sighing, I got up off the chair and started my way up the stairs. "Mom! Dinner is in the kitchen," I yelled toward her bedroom door before I walked through mine.

By then it was around ten, so the sun had set and most of the stars were out shining through the black night. Eager to get some fresh air, I climbed up to the roof and sat on the rough surface, staring randomly at the sky out over the woods and thinking quietly to myself. The view seemed especially spectacular that night.

I hugged my knees, wishing my father would just call me already. He at least owed my mom and me that, I thought. After fifteen years of marriage, you would have hoped that they had learned to compromise and work together, but apparently not. Having a child probably made their lives worse, even if I didn't bother them very much. It was for this reason I often wondered what my parents' lives would be like if my mother had never given birth to me, since I couldn't even remember a time when their marriage wasn't on the rocks due to their ongoing arguments.

The maladaptive daydream faded quickly, however, when a rustling noise made its way up to me from down on the ground. I knew it had to be Alec. He was the only person who never asked for my permission to come up to my thinking place, and I realized his visits were probably going to become more regular over the course of the summer. When he easily pulled himself up onto the rough roof, I purposely avoided his enchanting gaze and continued to glare out at the sky, still angry with my father. That night, I was not in the mood to socialize, so I hoped Alec would realize this and leave quickly.

I expected Alec to try to get me to talk to him, but he seemed to know me well—apparently better than either of us had originally thought—even though we hadn't known each other long. He silently but nervously sat down next to me and watched the stars with me, not making any move to speak at all. But I was grateful; I hadn't realized his company would be so quiet and refreshing.

About half an hour later, still neither one of us had said anything, and it was quite late. "I should probably go inside now," I whispered awkwardly in English, pausing to fix my ponytail.

I started to stand up, and Alec did the same. With a sly smirk on his handsome face, he offered jokingly, "Let me walk you home."

"Thanks a bunch," I replied sarcastically, and Alec let out a soft chuckle. It made me smile, even though I was trying hard not to.

We had returned to a state of silence, my stormy eyes locked with his dazzling blue ones. As he held out his hand for me, Alec softened his voice and said in Greek, "Are you sure you can't stay out here just a little longer? It's beautiful."

I knew he was using Greek to his advantage. After all, Alec was the only one of us Sighted beings who spoke in Greek outside the forest, except for me when I was speaking to him, because we had agreed to it. Speaking in Greek helped me to forget whatever drama was going on in my regular life, and Alec didn't know me as Ashley anyway. To be honest, I didn't think he needed to know Ashley. I didn't really want him to.

For a split second, I stood there on the roof like a statue, silently debating my options. I finally sighed, trying to sound as annoyed as possible, and sat back down again on the roof, avoiding taking his hand. Alec smiled, though, and he sat next to me before looking back out at the sparkling sky, listening to the crickets chirp softly below.

"So, how is Cole?" Alec asked me hesitantly after a minute of silence, and I thought I caught a hint of jealousy in his tone while he twiddled his thumbs nonchalantly. "That was a nice punch, by the way." His face brightened as he recalled a couple of days ago, when I had knocked out Cole to keep him from seeing Alec in the forest.

I frowned at the sky, then cleared my throat and answered honestly, "I wouldn't know. I haven't seen him since we left him lying unconscious by Main Street." I turned to look Alec in the eye and confessed glumly, "I keep thinking that I should stop by his house, but I wouldn't know what to say. I don't know what he remembers . . . and what he doesn't, if you know what I mean."

I bit my lip and put my head in my hands as my mind flashed back to when Cole had tried to kiss me, and the burning feeling on my hips returned for a split second. Alec tried to look concerned, but at the back of his mind, I knew he was secretly happy that I hadn't talked to Cole yet.

"Who cares what Cole thinks anyway?" he asked, trying to cheer me up.

"Alec, he's my friend," I tried to explain, like I had the day before, but I wasn't sure what else to say. Honestly, there wasn't much to say about Cole and me to begin with.

"Yeah, well, Poseidon's your friend too, and you don't care what *he* thinks," Alec argued, playfully nudging me in the side with his elbow. I rolled my eyes, and he grinned at me. "Babe, you're too good for Cole." He paused to think for a moment, then added, "Poseidon too, actually."

I rolled my eyes yet again and watched Alec chuckle to himself, but we were suddenly interrupted by Artemis's panicked voice coming from the walkie-talkie on Alec's belt loop. "This is Artemis, calling in an emergency. I'm being attacked by a group of monsters by the north edge of the meadow. Help!"

And then she was cut off, but Alec and I didn't waste another second. We leaped off the roof and onto my balcony, where I quickly grabbed my own walkie-talkie and my trusty pocketknife before jumping to the ground. We raced into the forest and threw on our shiny bronze armor, tightening the straps the best we could as we sprinted through the thick brush and tall pine trees. It seemed like ages had passed before we reached the meadow, but this was probably due to the fact that we were worried and impatient. As soon as we broke out of the trees, however, we caught sight of the blonde Artemis shooting arrows right and left as fast as she could, and a monstrous golden lion was crouched a few feet in front of her, threatening to tackle her and rip her to pieces. The way her arrows bounced off its shiny hide could only mean that this was the Nemean lion, a beast with invincible skin.

Alec and I were still racing across the open meadow when a black shape flying low in the sky caught my eye, and I could tell immediately that it was a harpy—the very same pale harpy that had been the Monster Watch's first kill. I guessed she had finally been sent back from the dead, like most monsters were. Some came back to life sooner than others, however.

Meanwhile, the oblivious Artemis was still sending arrows aimlessly at the Nemean lion, which was about twice the size of a regular lion and still looked ready to pounce. Nevertheless, I knew the harpy was the bigger danger to her at the moment, so I yelled at the top of my lungs, "*Artemis!* Heads up!"

Having heard my abrupt warning, Artemis's head snapped up, and she sent an arrow flying into the dark sky. After soaring in a perfect arc, the arrow pierced the black-haired harpy squarely in the chest, and the harpy seemed to hang in midair for a moment. Then she gasped for air one more time, flapping her wings uselessly as she fell and crumbled to dust. She had been sent back to the Underworld once again.

But the battle wasn't over yet, because the giant lion suddenly lunged at Artemis, although, luckily, Alec and I reached them just in time. Without bothering to stab the lion, since his sword would have only been deflected off its hide, Alec did a full-body slam into its thick neck. The huge cat stumbled and shook his head, giving Artemis just enough time to dive out of the way of the lion's powerful jaws.

I saw Artemis pull out another arrow from her worn leather quiver, ready to shoot the Nemean lion again, but I shook my head and told her with a sigh, "It's no use."

Alec, Artemis, and I slowly backed away from the lion, but it just followed us, stalking us like prey, with a terrible gleam in its huge brown eyes. Normally we gods would simply laugh and eagerly toy around with monsters for fun before we killed them, but we wanted to kill this particular beast as quickly as possible in order to start discussing why the monsters had suddenly decided to team up against a god.

"How did Heracles defeat the Nemean lion again?" Artemis asked me, her voice shaking slightly as she recalled the legend of the twelve labors of Heracles.

"He strangled it," I said, just before Alec could respond. Of course, I knew all the Greek myths by heart, and it seemed as if Alec knew all the myths pretty well too. I was betting that the children at the Knowing camps studied a lot of mythology, which would definitely come in handy for strategies to defeat specific monsters.

Frowning thoughtfully, Alec tightened his grip on his shiny sword, which he kept pointed at the lion's head. "No offense to you ladies, but I'm not sure any of us are strong enough to strangle that thing," he stated worriedly.

I smirked and informed him, "You don't know everything about us gods. There's a reason you don't get to take part in battle practices."

And it was true. Although we gods weren't immortal because we were reincarnations, we still had the ability to jump higher, run faster, withstand more force, and become a lot stronger than a regular human, as well as being much better-looking than the average person. Most of those qualities came in awfully handy during battle practice, when more often than not we were struck by lightning or pounded by ocean waves spurting up from a crack in the earth, and would definitely come in handy during a war. But Alec didn't know a lot about that because he was forced to sit out of our battle practices, lest he be seriously injured or even killed. And to be perfectly honest, we didn't *want* him to know every single thing about us.

"Distract the lion. I have an idea," I whispered to Alec and Artemis.

Alec nodded obediently before darting to our right, and the Nemean lion turned on its heels to face Alec again, ready to pounce at any second. Taking the opportunity while the lion was looking away, I ran a couple steps before taking a giant leap into the air and landing firmly on the lion's wide back, straddling it like a horse. I smiled when I saw the surprised look on Alec's handsome face, but I became momentarily distracted when the lion reared up in the air, throwing its head and letting out a huge roar, so I grabbed its thick, curly golden mane.

The lion reared up again on its powerful hind legs, desperately trying to throw me off, though I was determined to stay on. Artemis shot an arrow at the lion, hitting it on its lower left hind leg, but of course it didn't even leave a mark; I knew this was meant only to distract the lion with the unbreakable skin. As planned, the Nemean lion whirled around again, this time to face Artemis, but simultaneously gave a huge shake in another effort to throw me off. I twisted my fingers in its mane to get an even tighter grip, and when the lion had calmed down slightly, I stretched my arms lower, sliding them around its thick neck to form a chokehold. I quickly closed my eyes and took a deep breath, then yanked back on the lion's neck as hard as I possibly could.

The magnificent beast let out a low moan and tried to open its jaws to take in more air, but it was much too late. Alec saw a brilliant opportunity for him to take, and so he ran straight toward the lion at full speed before kicking it in the throat, hard enough to collapse its esophagus. Finally, after the skin on its neck folded inwardly, the golden monster stumbled and fell to its knees, and I hopped off it, landing firmly on solid ground.

Wordlessly, the three of us faced the giant lion, which was now lying in a humongous heap in the tall grass, and watched with wide eyes as it took its last painful gasps of air. A few long minutes later, the huge animal broke into tiny pieces and crumbled to a mere pile of dust, which then disappeared into the soft soil. The Nemean lion had been killed once again.

Alec ran one hand slowly through his dark hair and cleared his throat. "Well, since no one else is saying it, I guess I will . . . nice job, A Team." I only smiled along with Artemis. "Hey, why does something like this always seem to happen to the three of us?" Alec wondered aloud.

I simply ignored his question, since this was only the second time a weird event had occurred when the three of us were alone—not quite enough to support a pattern, in my opinion. Then I turned to Artemis, who was straightening her loose bun, and asked her gravely, "How many monsters did you kill before we got here?"

Artemis frowned. "The Minotaur and another harpy."

Alec gulped, obviously thinking the same thing as Artemis and I. There was no reason for four monsters to attack a single god in one day, especially not at the same time. As of late, it was a rare occurrence for even one monster to actively try to kill one of us (except for Alec). Which meant that Hades had to have sent the monsters here himself, I realized. But why? Just the day before, there were no monsters to be found anywhere in the forest, although now it looked like they had returned in full force.

"You need to get back to Pan and Persephone. They might get attacked too, and they don't really have any weapons," I ordered to Alec, and suddenly we all became more serious. Without another word, Alec nodded in agreement and turned on his heel, racing northwest toward the hideout. Artemis and I followed slowly behind; we had decided to stay in the forest for a while, just to make sure everyone was completely safe.

Around midnight, Artemis and I decided it would be fine to leave Alec, Pan, and Persephone alone with a couple of extra weapons, and the two of us headed home right after a few more nymphs and satyrs stopped by to see what was going on. We ran into a small, green, leathery-skinned dragon called the Python, which was about twice the size of the Nemean lion, but Artemis shot it with a few arrows and I threw my spear into its gut for good measure. The poor dragon was dead before it even got close enough to spit fire onto us.

---

The next morning I woke up only a little later than normal and had a nice breakfast at Luke and Zach's house, along with Connor, before we headed into the woods for a patrol meet, where all four of the patrols were going to discuss the events that had happened the previous night. By then, Hermes had informed all the gods about the return of the monsters to the forest.

As soon as we reached the meadow, the rest of the Monster Watch and I sat down in the long grass, talking about monsters and the weather, while the rest of the gods started showing up one by one. We did have to wait quite a long time, since the rest of the gods had to sneak out of their houses at non-suspicious intervals to meet. If people knew that a bunch of kids besides the Monster Watch had survived a trip into the treacherous forest, our town would have had to suffer through yet another epidemic of regular, Sightless people going in and never coming back out.

Eventually, most of the gods showed up, and we were just waiting for Alec, Pan, and Persephone to arrive, assuming they had survived the night. But as the minutes passed and still none of them had appeared in the meadow, we were all getting more and more worried.

"Maybe we should go check—" Hera started, but suddenly Alec, sweating and fully clad in his armor, burst out alone into the open meadow. This was a very bad sign.

Sure enough, with panic in his bright blue eyes, Alec continued to sprint toward us as he yelled breathlessly in Greek something not one of us expected: "Persephone's gone!"

And then all hell broke loose.

## Chapter 12:

# THE LITTLE HERO EMERGES

All of the gods' jaws dropped as they stared at the hyperventilating Alec, and Zeus demanded instantly, "Tell me what happened."

Alec put both of his hands on top of his dark hair, taking deep breaths and trying to slow his heart rate down again. "Persephone went out to collect some berries about half an hour ago, and she hasn't come back," Alec managed to gasp between deep breaths, his eyebrows knit together with worry. "She was only supposed to be gone for a couple of minutes. There aren't any signs of her anywhere."

"I'm going to *kill* Hades," Demeter growled, anger clouding her normally cheerful mind.

"We don't even know for sure if it was him," Hestia began calmly, placing her hand lightly on Demeter's tan arm.

"Well, who else would it be?! All signs point to him," Demeter exclaimed, exasperated, shaking off Hestia's comforting touch. "Hermes, get down to the Underworld right now," Demeter ordered, even though she didn't have the authority to do so.

But Hermes knew this well, so he didn't move a muscle, and only looked Demeter squarely in the eyes. Demeter let out a frustrated yelp and yanked at her long blonde ponytail, but Zeus just frowned and told her to calm down while he thought. Meanwhile, the other gods whispered worriedly among themselves, discussing what should be done next.

After a few minutes, Zeus agreed to let Hermes go down into the Underworld to try to reason with Hades. Hermes shot off like a rocket toward the east, heading to one of the tiny cave entrances to the Underworld, but the rest of us stayed right where we were to wait for our leader's next orders. Most of the gods restlessly paced around in circles and exchanged some stressed shouting matches as Alec groaned guiltily and collapsed on the grass; tension was obviously running very high.

Eventually, we all came to a decision. Zeus sighed a bit forlornly, then demanded, "Split into patrols. Kill any monsters you see, and warn all nymphs and satyrs of what has happened today. We don't need anyone else to be killed."

We all nodded in agreement and immediately split up. Zeus, Hera, and Hestia headed north, while my A Team, minus Apollo, trudged south. Apollo had agreed to protect Pan and the nymphs and satyrs who couldn't protect themselves back at the river hideout, as it would be much easier for him than for Alec because the god was armed with a bow instead of a sword. Poseidon and Demeter went east, and Ares, Aphrodite, and Dionysus took off to the west.

Artemis, Alec, and I walked through the forest on high alert, taking the time to scope out every bush. We didn't dare to speak; we only listened for the tiniest rustle of brush. We were ready for whatever monster wanted to attack us that day, even though we were still tired from fighting the Nemean lion the night before. However, the three of us had yet to come across anything remotely unusual or out of place. We even stopped to talk to a few nymphs to ask them if they had any information, but they had none to share and hurried off to meet with a few satyrs.

We had almost reached the loud, rushing river when I spotted something glint in a rare spot of sunlight shining down through the thick tree cover. I wordlessly pointed it out to the others, who only nodded in acknowledgment, and in a single-file line led by me, we silently made our way toward whatever it was.

A golden substance was slowly trickling down the rough branch, leaving a thin trail of liquid beads behind. I hesitantly dabbed my index finger in the substance and held it up to my nose, sniffing it. Blood. And it didn't have the greenish tinge that monster blood had, so I knew it had to be from a god, satyr, or nymph. But considering the circumstances, the blood was most likely, unfortunately, from a god.

"Are you thinking what I'm thinking?" I whispered over my shoulder to Alec and Artemis.

"Persephone," they replied together in unison, their voices flat.

I nodded, and we all turned around to look for any more blood or another sign of Persephone having been there. Suddenly, Artemis snapped her fingers, and I looked up to see her pointing a few feet in front of us, where another tiny pool of golden blood lay on the ground, slowly being absorbed by the soft soil. Needless to say, this was definitely not a good sign.

We cautiously approached the pool of blood, but saw a few more tiny drops ahead of us on another branch. Brows furrowing, the three of us continued to slowly follow the thin trail of blood through the trees and branches that clawed like cats at our tanned skin, which was tough after having spent so much time in the forest and, therefore, did not break under the pricks.

Finally, the trail ended at a small boulder about fifty feet southwest of the original bloody branch we had found. The three of us stopped in our tracks, staring silently at the rock for a minute and studying the last part of the trail. There were very shallow—almost invisible to people who weren't looking closely—marks in the ground, which implied that someone had been dragged right up to the large rock, but unfortunately for us, the tracks ended there.

I exchanged solemn glances with Artemis as she paused to redo the bun in her wavy, blonde hair, which had been pulled apart by the branches we had just walked through. "You don't think . . . ?" Alec stopped mid-sentence in amazement, bowing his head in deep thought.

But I knew what he was thinking anyway. "Yes, I do think that," I told him grimly. I met Artemis's hazel eyes again to be sure she agreed, and she obviously did.

"Well, let's give it a go," she huffed unhappily.

Wordlessly, Alec, Artemis, and I walked up to the rock and placed our hands on its rough surface as I counted off, "One, two, and three!"

We all pushed on it as hard as we possibly could. The large rock rolled over in what seemed like slow motion, and we were instantly blasted with a rush of cold air. Left in place of the small boulder was a gaping hole, just wide enough for a person to fit through, and right at the edge were a few more drops of golden blood. The hole was so deep that we couldn't even see the bottom—only steps made of hard earth that descended as far as we could see into the darkness. I took a quick glance back at the overturned rock, and sure enough, on the side of the small boulder that had been buried in the dirt was a Greek symbol, marking it as yet another entrance to the infamous Underworld.

My breath caught in my throat; this was the closest any of the gods besides Hermes would ever be able to come to the Underworld, and probably to Hades. I wasn't quite sure if that was a bad thing or a good thing, but like anything else, I supposed it depended on the situation.

"I'm going in," Alec proclaimed suddenly, straightening up to his full height and checking to make sure his bronze armor was secure.

Artemis and I looked at him in shock. "No," I refused immediately, shaking my head. I wasn't going to let him go down there alone, where Hades could easily kill him without any of us knowing. Not one of us besides Hermes even knew what was down there, and losing the Knowing boy would have been awful for more than one reason.

Alec's eyes met mine, and he continued calmly, "Athena, I need to do this. I'll be fine."

I shook my head again, not giving up. "No, you don't. Hermes is already down there. Wait for the report so we know what the deal is." Alec only narrowed his eyes at me, mulling over what I said. "Please, Alec," I pleaded with him. "We can't save the world if you're dead."

Alec continued to hold my gaze, but our staring contest was interrupted by Poseidon's voice coming from each of our walkie-talkies. "This is patrol four. Hermes has returned from Hades. Here's the report."

The walkie-talkies went silent for a moment before Hermes's voice came on the line and informed us of what he had seen. "You probably guessed it, but Hades wasn't talking. I barely even made it past Cerberus today," he said, referring to Hades's giant three-headed guard dog. "But I am pretty sure he has Persephone down there, even though I didn't see her. There were extra guards patrolling the hallways."

"Thanks for the info, Hermes. Any updates from the rest of the patrols?" we heard Zeus ask.

Taking my cue, I pressed the TALK button on my walkie-talkie. "Yes, A Team found a trail of blood leading to a new entrance to the Underworld," I informed everyone listening.

"Lord Zeus, I volunteer to go down and talk to Hades," Alec added into his own device, referring to Zeus formally—a sign that the dark-haired boy was dead serious. I frowned, noticing Artemis do the same, but deep down I knew there would be no stopping Alec on a mission. He had already made it this far, after all. And he had learned from me.

There was a long pause before Zeus finally responded, "What makes you think you'll be able to get him to talk, when Hermes couldn't?"

Alec must have been thinking about what to say before Zeus even asked, because he answered firmly, "I'm not a god."

I didn't need to hear Zeus's reply; sometimes four little words were enough to win an argument. They could mean so much, could change an entire equation in the blink of an eye.

And Alec was smart; if he played the right angle, I knew he would be able to get Hades to talk. However, I also knew that his plan was really risky. Alec wouldn't have any of us to help protect him, since there was no way that Hades would let Hermes back down there again, so it would be a miracle if Alec made it out of the Underworld completely unharmed. Not to mention that if he took even one tiny step down the earthy stairs, there was no going back; he would have to go all the way down and finish what he started, whether he liked it or not. He would have to be brave. He would have to be strong. But most importantly, he would have to survive.

And if he survived, he would have to be a hero. There was no question about it.

"All right," Zeus answered slowly, still pondering the idea. "Let's meet and figure out the details."

"Everybody, wait," I said into the walkie-talkie, a light bulb flashing on in my brain. "I have an idea."

"Of course you do," I just barely heard Ares's voice mutter ungratefully, and I simply ignored him, ready to tell the rest of the gods my ingenious plan.

---

Two hours later, the rest of the gods and I were back in the forest, all standing around the entrance to the Underworld that we had found earlier in the morning. While the other gods nervously murmured among themselves, Alec closed his eyes and started taking deep breaths to calm himself down. I kept one eye on him as I checked to make sure his armor was on tight, and then I adjusted the tiny camera and microphone (which was about the size of a button) that I had placed on his bronze chest plate a few minutes earlier. Next, I turned to face my shiny black laptop, which sat atop a fallen log beside us, and checked the wirelessly transmitted camera feed to make sure the image was clear–it was.

Alec started fidgeting with the minuscule camera, but I only sighed, reminded of the long spy phase I had gone through when I was younger. I used to use those little electronic toys to keep an eye on my drunken father, just in case he ever tried to abuse my mother again. And he did, on more than one occasion. I had enough evidence to have him sent to prison for at least a few months, but, of course, no one else knew about it. I didn't feel inclined to betray him anyway, since he hadn't touched my mom so brashly in a long while now.

"Everything looks good," I informed everyone a minute later, pushing my father to the back of my mind, and the rest of the gods only stayed silent. Alec gave a short nod, but he was busy having a staring contest with the dark entrance to Hades's realm. I wondered who was winning.

"Are you ready?" Zeus asked Alec, slowly running his fingers through his dirty-blond hair. "Are you sure you still want to do this?"

Alec nodded again, his dark hair shaking with his head, and started to say, "If I don't come out—"

I slapped him hard across the face before he could even finish his sentence. When Alec's bright eyes widened and his handsome jaw dropped in shock and confusion, I smirked and placed my hands on his shoulders, looking him right in the eye. "You're coming back out," I told him seriously, knowing that if he started to doubt himself then, he *definitely* wouldn't come back.

And with that, I shoved Alec into the deep hole and down the first few steps made of reddish-brown earth. The steel-gray rock magically rolled over by itself, tightly sealing the secret entrance to the Underworld before Alec even had the chance to look back. I let out a sigh of relief, and then the rest of the gods and I turned to face the screen of my sleek laptop.

The camera view shifted slightly as Alec took a deep breath and another hesitant step down the stairs to Hades. "It's kind of cold in here," Alec whispered lightly as he continued his walk, but then he grew quiet. In fact, it was pitch black until Alec flicked on his flashlight, lighting up the narrow stairwell that appeared to descend forever.

---

Alec had been making his way down the seemingly endless stairs for about fifteen minutes when the tiny microphone started to pick up noises coming from farther along in the black tunnel. At first, it sounded like a dog barking, and even though I hadn't been into the Underworld, I knew it was Cerberus. However, there was also another noise that sounded almost like singing, although I couldn't tell for sure. Maybe I was just imagining things.

Alec rounded a bend in the tunnel, and he continued to walk down more stairs for another two minutes or so, until the rest of the gods and I could see a bit of light on the laptop screen emanating from farther down in the Underworld. Suddenly, the dark tunnel opened up into a gigantic cavern, where the stairs continued to descend along the cold rock wall until they reached the bottom of the Underworld, which appeared to be entirely blanketed in a thick mist, except over the infamous River Styx. The only light in the whole cavern came from a small, candlelit lantern hanging from the bow of a small black gondola, which was waiting patiently on the wide river.

The cavern was divided into two parts by the River Styx, a huge, bluish-black channel of calm water. I could see that it was littered with the ghostly souls of people who had either died trying to enter the next realm or had been trapped in the water forever after trying to swim across instead of paying the fare to take the gondola driven by Charon, a servant to the lord of the Underworld himself. As long as Alec could avoid falling into the treacherous waters, he would make it to Hades's palace perfectly fine.

As Alec carefully stepped off the earthen stairs, I realized that it wasn't mist that covered the entire riverbank; in fact, it was a huge mass of the ghosts of dead people—the ones who hadn't been buried with money under their tongues in the ancient Greek tradition and therefore weren't able to pay Charon's fare to get across the River Styx into the true Underworld.

Slowly, Alec pushed his way through the thousands of eerily quiet misty white ghosts that almost looked transparent, and he stopped right at the dark rocky edge of the River Styx, where the black gondola sat waiting for him. On the boat, a tall hooded figure we could only assume to be Charon stood hunched over and leaning on the long pole he used to steer the boat. He was facing Alec, but still we could not see his face—just a black shadow. Charon simply, silently held out a frail, ugly gray hand to Alec, waiting to be paid.

The camera on Alec's armor shook for a minute while he pulled two golden drachmas, the currency of the ancient Greeks (I supposed the Knowing societies still used them), from his pockets. When he placed them in Charon's bony hand, Charon slowly lifted them up closer to his face, as if studying them to see whether or not they were real. It had probably been decades, even centuries, since a live person who knew about the Greek myths (besides Hermes, of course) had tried to come down to the Underworld.

Eventually, Charon placed the money in a pocket in his long black robes and turned around to face the other side of the quiet river, standing still while he waited for Alec to climb onto the boat and sit down. Once Alec had situated himself relatively comfortably, the two of them slowly made their way across the calm waters, ignoring the ghosts in the river as they unsuccessfully tried to grab at the boat with their transparent hands.

When the two of them reached the other side, Alec eagerly clambered out of the boat and onto the rocky shore, where even more ghosts—ones who had actually been able to pay Charon's fare—stood in a long line, waiting to be evaluated and sent into the three different parts of the Underworld. At the front of the line stood Cerberus, who was almost as tall as the cavern itself, looking down with wild eyes and barking angrily at all the ghosts that passed under his thick, meaty legs. Simply ignoring the long line of waiting souls, Alec took a shaky breath and started making his way to the front.

"Just like I told you," Hermes muttered at the laptop screen next to me, although he knew Alec wouldn't be able to hear him. Even though the microphone worked only one way, I wished we had tried putting a camera on Hermes before then. Then I shrugged and turned my attention back to Alec and the giant three-headed dog, desperately hoping everything would go as planned.

Alec stepped in front of the first ghost in line and stopped in his tracks, waiting to be evaluated. Realizing that he wasn't actually dead, the monstrous black dog glared menacingly at Alec, and all three of Cerberus's heads started growling, but Alec just stayed as still and calm as possible while they leaned in closer and closer to him. I was almost surprised Alec didn't pass out from the horrible stench of dog breath that fogged up the camera lens.

"Hey there," Alec began in Greek, his voice shaking slightly. "Easy, little Cerberus. That's a good dog," he murmured as he slowly reached out his hand to pat the giant guard dog, but Cerberus started growling again. Immediately, Alec placed his hand back at his side and continued, "It's okay, boy. I'm just going to see Lord Hades, all right? Trust me; we're friends." Cerberus stopped growling and perked up as soon as he heard his master's name. "That's right, going to see Lord Hades now," Alec told the dog and carefully took a tiny step forward. When Cerberus didn't do anything, Alec took another couple of hesitant steps forward.

Cerberus continued to growl off and on until Alec had slowly made his way all around the huge animal. In one last swift, graceful movement, Alec reached behind him and pulled out a huge bone, which he had hidden under his chest plate earlier, and quickly threw it over Cerberus's heads. Eagerly, Cerberus barked and spun around to retrieve the bone, and Alec took off in the other direction before the guard dog could turn back, heading toward the menacing castle in the distance.

As fast as he could, Alec raced across the Fields of Asphodel, rolling hills of an unnatural, grayish-colored grass, toward the looming palace, past the confused-looking ghosts of hundreds of both animals and people. Although I knew it was impossible, every footstep closer to the black palace made it seem as if the palace and its Corinthian columns were growing larger and larger. It was probably just some trick of the light, but then again, I had learned many years earlier that anything was possible in our world.

"I'm coming, Persephone," Alec whispered as he stopped in front of the palace at scary-looking iron gates that must have been at least twenty feet tall. It was hard to tell from the camera's viewpoint, but it looked to me like the points were topped with human skulls. For a moment, Alec paused at the closed gates, wondering what to do next, but then, as if by magic, the iron gates instantly swung open toward him, almost hitting him smack in the face.

Alec took another few deep breaths, then made his way up to the tall double doors of the palace, which were also made of iron and swung open automatically as Alec walked up the concrete steps. I heard Alec gasp as he took a few steps into the palace to see a totally different interior than one might have expected. Although the entire exterior was black with decorative skulls and terrifying statues of monsters, the entrance hall he had just walked into housed ceilings almost as tall as Cerberus, and beautiful paintings decorated the cream-and-white-striped walls all around him. Not sure where to go, Alec just stepped onto a long red carpet and followed it around two corners, until he suddenly found himself face-to-face with the lord of the dead.

"Who the hell are you?" the powerful god spat angrily in Greek as he studied Alec with his frightening black eyes, clearly upset that some stranger had interrupted his pleasant evening. Nervously shifting in place, Alec took a daring glance up at the very pale-skinned Hades, who was dressed all in black and sat upon a tall, looming throne made of crystal skulls at the far end of the rectangular room. Hades was also clutching the staff in his right hand like his life depended on it.

Alec quickly gulped and sank down on one knee to bow in respect to the handsome god. He took another deep breath and began, "I'm—"

"Alec?!" Persephone's surprised and panicked voice cut through the air like a knife, a cry that I knew would only endanger Alec further. Nevertheless, he immediately looked up to see the beautiful daughter of Demeter being dragged into the large throne room by two of Hades's ugly monster servants. Her light brown hair was messy and her short, white summer dress was ripped to shreds, revealing parts of her undergarments, but she looked okay to me otherwise. The frightened and confused Persephone had reddish rope burns on her arms and legs, and although someone had bandaged them with gauze, he or she had obviously done a poor job of it.

"You two know each other?" Hades asked gruffly, pure hatred in his eyes, and Alec looked back up to the angry god, nodding silently. Hades's gaze locked with Alec's, and without taking his eyes off the Knowing boy, Hades ordered to his servants, "Take her away."

Alec instantly opened his mouth to object, but thought better of it and stayed silent. In the background, Persephone disappeared again, though I could hear her fighting every step. Then a heavy door slammed closed, leaving the two teenage boys completely alone. "Now, tell me why you are here, *little hero*," Hades sneered at Alec, who was still kneeling on the ground.

"I came here to check on Persephone, my lord. The rest of the gods and I were worried about her," Alec said truthfully, gripping the handle of his sword tightly, just in case he needed it.

Hades raised his dark eyebrows and clicked his tongue in thought. "Ah, you know the Olympian Council," he mused, lazily twirling his black staff around. I was pretty sure Alec nodded again from the way the camera was shifting around. Hades continued, "Well, as you can see, I'm attending to Lady Persephone, so you can just go home and—"

I frowned as Alec stood up and interrupted the god of the dead angrily. "Pardon me, Lord Hades, but it seems to me that Lady Persephone still has more than four weeks left of freedom from you."

Hades narrowed his eyes, clearly very unhappy with the feisty Alec. With a ferocious glare in his eyes and a tight grip on his deadly staff, Hades only continued what he was saying before Alec had interrupted him, "As I was saying, you can just go home and tell your stupid Council that Persephone is staying here *with me* and that I will be granted the freedom to do *whatever I want* up in your realm, unless they want an all-out war for the ages. I really don't care for the way your beloved Council parades about the forest and kills even the monsters that try to steer clear of them. And you expect me to believe that the other gods have Persephone's best interest in mind, when they had never even met her in god form before the start of summer? They are clearly too ignorant to reign very well."

I knew what Alec's response was going to be before the words were even out of his mouth. With a quick glance around me and at the laptop, I could tell by the determined looks on their faces that a few of the other gods with similar hot-headed temperaments, namely Ares, Poseidon, Dionysus, and Zeus, were in agreement with his idea. I, however, only shook my head in disagreement, knowing that if I had been in Alec's position, I would have had a much better chance of preventing what was about to happen and creating an alternative option for the future.

*Maybe this new era of cooperation will have to be renamed the Not-So-Golden Age of the Forest Gods*, I thought to myself darkly. And with a gulp, I turned back to watch the screen again.

"Then there will be a war," Alec proclaimed fearlessly, his voice harsh. "The gods may be ruthless and a bit ignorant, but they know how to protect and care for their people much better than you *ever* will."

Still keeping a tight hold on the butt of his sword, Alec gave one last small bow before he abruptly turned on his heel to stride out of Hades's menacing palace with a swagger in his step and without being formally excused. Then my little hero sprinted all the way back out of the Underworld before anything could stop him.

---

I heard the sound of a heavy rock rolling over, and the rest of the gods and I whirled around to see Alec's face emerge from the darkness as he heaved himself up and out of the small entrance to the Underworld. When the sweaty Alec stood all the way up to his full height, the boulder magically, of its own accord, sealed the never-ending hole once again.

Grinning proudly, I walked over to him and started to take the hidden camera and microphone off his shiny chest plate. "See? I told you that you would come back out," I whispered into his ear.

Alec smiled, looking more than relieved, but Zeus pulled us right off of our high horse again when he said loudly, "Our problems aren't over yet, you know. We can't fight this war on our own, not if Hades is going to use every single monster that's under his control."

Then Zeus's blue eyes met Alec's, and they finished in perfect unison, "We need the Knowing."

It looked as if we were going to have to carry out Alec's hero ceremony some other time.

# Chapter 13:

# LEAVING THE WOODS

Zach, Connor, Luke, and I were biking down Main Street toward the Fire Pit, eager for delicious lemonade to help cool us down on the sweltering summer day. It had been only one week since Alec had gone down into the Underworld, but it felt like much longer. Most of my days had been filled with playing reverse hide-and-seek with the rest of the Monster Watch, and I spent long nights training with Alec and sometimes hunting with Artemis. Hades had made no other threats so far, although there were a few more monsters roaming the forest than normal.

When the four of us reached the restaurant, we lazily dropped our bikes on the burning sidewalk and walked into the Fire Pit, where old electric fans were humming, plugged into every available outlet in the entire building. Not many of the old buildings in our town had air-conditioning, after all, and just sitting outside in the summer could make you break out in a sweat.

Martha looked up to see us walk through the swinging door, and her blue eyes immediately brightened. We sat down at the bar seats, since we weren't planning on staying for long, and waited while she happily made us four fresh lemonades. While Zach and Luke were bickering about what to do after lunch, I glanced around the room to see who else had stopped in for a bite to eat.

First I saw Becca sitting at a small table across from Matt. She was flipping her golden hair, obviously flirting, while Matt was gazing at her in some sort of dreamlike state with his big brown eyes. It looked kind of funny, since Matt, who dressed like a stereotypical buff guy from a biker gang and happened to be the complete opposite of the gorgeous Becca, was totally falling for her, nodding his head like he was in love with everything she said.

I rolled my eyes in amusement and continued to look around the room, noticing Shane and Jack chatting at the Monster Watch's usual booth in the back. Perhaps they had been waiting for us to join their party of two, because no one ever dared to steal our table; ever since the Monster Watch had come out of the forest unscathed for the first time, we were considered almost untouchable by the townsfolk. Confirming my suspicions, Shane saw me looking over and waved, eagerly offering to make room at the booth, but Jack was too busy gulping down an entire glass of lemonade in just three huge sips to notice me.

However, Josh and his best friend, Cole, happened to walk into the restaurant at exactly that moment. Cole's soft brown eyes locked onto me, and hoping to avoid an awkward conversation, I quickly turned away from him to pretend that I was actually paying attention to what Connor was saying. Unfortunately, my plan didn't work out as well as I hoped.

I felt a tap on my shoulder and hid a grimace as I reluctantly swiveled around on the bar stool to face Cole. "Um, hi," he said awkwardly, scratching his head. "Can I talk to you for a minute? In private."

Part of me wanted to say no and run into the woods as fast as I could, but the guiltier half got the better of me. I just glanced at Zach for permission to leave the Watch discussion, and he nodded curiously. Sighing, I walked with Cole out of the restaurant and onto the street. "What is it?" I asked him, with more of an edge to my voice than I meant to have.

"What happened in the forest two weeks ago?" he whispered to me, sounding quite frightened. "The only thing I remember is waking up by the side of the road. And you never came to talk to me about it."

I bit my lip, rapidly trying to think of what to say. There was no way I was going to tell him what had really happened. He never would have forgiven me. Not that I would ever forgive myself, either.

"We walked about twenty yards in before you just blacked out. It was weird. I thought you were seriously ill or something, so Zach helped me drag you out here," I lied fluently, keeping my expression calm. "Zach and I didn't want to get in trouble by telling someone you had been in the woods, so we just . . . ran back in."

Cole frowned, scratching his head as if deciding whether to believe me or not. Eventually he just shrugged it off and started to ask, "Um, okay. Anyway, I was wondering if you wanted to go to the movies or—"

"Look, dude, I have to go. I think my lemonade's ready," I told him apologetically, and I brushed past him and headed back into the Fire Pit without another word, my heart racing nervously. Cole was a great guy, but I couldn't date him in this universe, and I definitely did not want to make things any more awkward and tenser than they already were. Even if Alec really did like me, he knew that he couldn't have me, so I was sure he would eventually get over it. He had to.

Martha had just delivered the lemonades when I reached the bar stools. The rest of the Monster Watch and I said a quick goodbye as we grabbed our drinks, plus an extra one. We told Martha that it was for my mother, but it was really for Alec. Then, waving to Josh and Cole, the four of us finally left the restaurant and picked up our bikes off the scorching hot pavement, ready to go home.

A few long minutes later, Connor and I were drinking our lemonades and sitting in ancient wooden rocking chairs next to Zach and Luke on their large porch overlooking our quiet street and Main Street. On the other side of Main Street, just inside the forest, Alec slurped his own lemonade in a safe spot where he could see us but no one could see him. We were chatting with him in low voices through our walkie-talkies, mostly about monsters and whatnot. Luckily, Zach and Luke's parents were still working at the busy restaurant. It didn't close until late at night.

"So what did Cole want?" Poseidon asked me in Greek. "It was kind of weird how he, like, dragged you away from us."

I shrugged indifferently. "He doesn't remember what happened that day I took him into the woods, and he wanted to know," I told the boys. "I lied, of course." Poseidon nodded in approval and satisfaction, and then he took a long, slow sip of lemonade.

Silence took over the lull in our conversation for a few seconds as we all paused to catch our breaths in the tiring heat, and I wished Zeus would send a couple of clouds to hide the hot sun for a while. We had powers for a reason, after all, and they were meant to be used in one way or another. Therefore, I could only shake my head in amazement when I noticed that the ice in our lemonades had already almost melted completely, even though it had only been a couple of minutes since we got them. But Zeus was seemingly oblivious to this fact, and he actually appeared quite comfortable with the abnormally high temperature.

Frowning, I swatted away a small fly that seemed to have no sense of direction whatsoever, and I automatically looked over at the edge of the trees when Alec's voice crackled through the walkie-talkie. "What are we going to do about getting help from the Knowing?" he asked no one in particular. "There is no address for the camp, so I'm not sure how to send them a message. It's pretty much in the middle of nowhere. I think I'll have to go all the way back."

Zeus sighed and answered him, "Well, we obviously can't send you all the way back to Kentucky alone. Hades probably has a price on your head already, and half of the Knowing might not even believe you when you tell them everything that's happened so far." Apollo, Poseidon, and I nodded in agreement before taking another sip of cold lemonade in unison.

"No, I don't think *anyone* in the Knowing will believe me, let alone half of them," Alec muttered darkly, more to himself than to the rest of us, and I raised my eyebrows.

"What did you just say?" Zeus asked in surprise and confusion.

"Nothing," Alec recovered, and I frowned dubiously. "Forget I said anything."

"Okay, so who's going with Alec and how are they getting all the way out to Kentucky?" Apollo wondered aloud, running his fingers through his golden hair.

"They'll have to take a plane at least part of the way, if we have any hope of finishing this war before the end of summer. And for that, we need a cover story . . . and money. A lot of it," I added, still keeping an eye out for that perseverant fly that kept coming back to annoy me.

Zeus leaned back in his rocking chair in thought, and the porch floorboards creaked under him as he took another sip of lemonade. "Well, which one of the gods might actually be allowed to travel almost all the way across the country without warning?" he asked all of us.

I sighed as I ran through all the gods in my head. Zeus and Poseidon were a definite no; same with Apollo, as they were needed here in the Woods. Aphrodite would never agree to do something like this, not even for Alec, since there was no telling when she would be able to stop for a shower or a change of clothes. The unforgiving Ares probably wouldn't even care about helping to protect Alec, and Hera and Demeter were out, as their policeman father would be too suspicious of them. The quiet Hestia's parents were way too overprotective, and Hephaestus wouldn't be much of a help to Alec anyway. Dionysus just wasn't the best god for the job. Hermes might have been okay, but he would be needed in the Woods as well, since he was the only other one of us besides Alec who could go down to the Underworld to talk to Hades. That left only two gods.

"It has to be me or Camille," I told them, switching back to English. "Whichever one of us can come up with a good enough cover story so that our parents will agree to it."

Zach, Connor, and Luke nodded in agreement with my conclusion, but Alec's confused voice asked, "Camille?"

"Artemis," I translated for him, since Alec didn't know all of our human names. I was about to add something else, but my cell phone suddenly rang from inside my jeans pocket, and I frowned in confusion because no one ever called me. There was never any real reason to, since house calls were more common in small towns like mine.

I pulled out the old black flip phone and squinted at the small screen, reading the caller ID. Shaking my head, I cursed under my breath and forced myself up out of the chair. When Zach, Luke, and Connor looked at me questioningly, I explained simply, "It's my dad." I walked into their house, where I could speak to my father privately, and answered the phone rather harshly, "What do you want now?"

I heard my father sigh, and he said, "I'm sorry, Ashley. I should've left a note or something—" Surprisingly, he didn't even sound drunk, yet his voice seemed to cut off all of a sudden, and as he cleared his throat, I could have sworn that I heard him frowning. "It just wasn't working—things between your mother and I, that is. I don't know if you knew."

"Of course I knew!" I interrupted loudly as I paced back and forth through Zach and Luke's kitchen, walking in circles around their dining room table and chairs. "How could I not know, after so many years?" I paused to think for a moment and asked suddenly, "Wait, where are you anyway?"

"Paris," he responded blandly, and I sighed, thinking about the painting of my parents in front of the Eiffel Tower that I had found a few weeks earlier.

"Are you ever coming back?" I asked quietly.

But he only ignored my question and continued, "Just tell your mother that I'm sorry, because she won't pick up my calls, but she probably should've known this was coming. Oh, and if she really doesn't want all of those paintings I got her over the years, just send them back to me."

"No, she wants them," I said quickly, thinking they could probably be sold at the antique shop for a fair amount of money, if my mom was willing to selling them. But I also knew there was no way all that would happen in just a few days. I would have to find money for plane tickets another way.

Fortunately for me, I was still on the phone with a disinterested man who trusted me enough and felt guilty enough that he almost never asked questions.

"Hey, Dad, you wouldn't mind buying two plane tickets for a flight from here to Kentucky, would you?" I chewed my lip as I waited for his reply.

He let out another exasperated sigh, and I envisioned him furrowing his brow, scrunching up his hooked nose, and scratching his head, the way he always did when something was bothering him. "Why can't your mother do it? She knows about this trip, right?"

"Of course," I lied. She would know within a few hours, at least. "Mom's just really stressed out right now, and I thought you could do it for her. I need the tickets as soon as possible. And you should put them under my name somehow, because Mom won't be taking me to the airport."

"Wait—what?" My father sounded like he was getting angrier. "What do you mean Catherine isn't going? Ashley, what the hell are you trying to pull? I want an explanation. *Now.*"

Suddenly, I heard the screen door creak open and slam shut, and then Luke, Zach, and Connor poked their heads around the corner of the wall, looking at me questioningly. They wanted to know what was taking so long. I motioned for them to leave the room again, but they only ignored me and sat down at the kitchen table to listen in on the conversation.

"I'm feeling very left out right now," Alec grumbled through the black walkie-talkie on my belt loop from outside in the woods, but Zach just told him to shut up and let me think.

I pressed the phone harder against my ear. "Remember that college camp I wanted to go to?"

"No," my father grumbled, and I smirked.

"Well, I'm signed up for the summer program at the University of Kentucky. Mom said she needs to stay here and take care of the antique shop, so Martha offered to fly there with me, as long as we paid for her," I informed him, making the story up as I continued, though I hated how easy it was becoming for me to make up lies spontaneously and worried about the all-too-likely possibility of getting caught. If my father had actually remembered the camp I had wanted to go to, he would have known it was in New York, not Kentucky. Still, it was a plausible story, and I knew Martha, the most loving second mother I could ever hope for, definitely would have gone with me if she were needed.

"All right, I'll buy two round-trip tickets and email the link to you. But you have to promise me that you won't do anything stupid in Kentucky and that you'll remember to tell your mother I'm sorry. I don't know when I'll call again or if she even wants me to," my father reluctantly agreed, and I gave the boys at the table a thumbs-up. They exchanged high-fives as I said goodbye to my dad, and after I hung up the phone, we raced back out to the front porch.

When we all finished our lemonades and told Alec about what my dad was doing for me, the rest of the Monster Watch and I grabbed our bikes again and slowly pedaled back to the restaurant, trying but failing to ignore the sticky heat. We threw our bikes down on the sidewalk almost exactly like before, not caring that they were blocking the path. The boys followed me as I opened the Fire Pit's door with a loud creak, and I looked inside to see everything almost exactly like the four of us had left it only an hour earlier. Becca was still sitting with Matt, but Jack and Shane had joined Josh and Cole at a different table, nearer to the front of the restaurant.

Our messenger, Josh, turned around in his chair to see who had walked in, and I quickly met his brown eyes and gave him a look that read, *Get over here now.* Nodding in understanding, Josh slowly got up out of his chair and started to make his way over to the Monster Watch and me. The rest of the gods in the restaurant noticed this too and followed Josh outside, where we could all talk without being overheard.

"What's going on?" Jack asked, squinting his dark eyes against the burning sun as he stepped around our bicycles.

"I can get us the tickets to fly to Kentucky. If Camille is okay with it, I should probably be the one to go with Alec," I informed Becca, Shane, Josh, Jack, and Matt, who looked very upset that we had interrupted his lovely date.

Shane frowned, narrowing his eyes at me. "May I ask how you managed to procure these tickets? Or do I even want to know?"

I smirked and replied, "Believe it or not, all I had to do was beg my dad. I think he feels bad about leaving my mom like this, so he was moderately open to the idea of helping out."

The others nodded, and Josh clarified, "So do you want me to go tell Camille now, or can I finish eating first?"

Zach was about to reply aloud, but then he caught sight of Cole, who had obviously gotten curious as to why all of us were outside talking in low voices, so Zach just nodded silently instead. Pushing open the wooden door and sticking his caramel-colored head out, Cole asked innocently, "What's going on?"

We all glanced at each other, even nudged one another, quickly trying to figure out who would answer him. Finally, Josh nervously pushed his curly hair out of his eyes and spoke up apologetically, "I have to go. Sorry, man, but I'll catch up with you later." He took off down the dusty road to go talk to the other gods, leaving Cole looking confused and hurt. When Cole looked to me for an explanation, I just shrugged, not meeting his eye. He would never understand the fact that we gods had to (and would willingly) drop everything if some ungodly trouble suddenly arose.

Then the rest of the Monster Watch and I bid farewell to everyone else, and we turned around to head into the woods for a game of reverse hide-and-seek with Alec. Since it was my turn to hide, it took two long hours before the boys finally gave up on trying to find me, and they were obviously tired of trying to fight monsters at the same time. Poseidon, Zeus, and Apollo had fared perfectly fine, but Alec gave us quite a scare when he finally met up with us, limping badly and bleeding from a nasty, bloody gash on his right forearm. Fortunately, upon closer inspection, the wound didn't appear nearly as bad as we thought. I, on the other hand, was left undefeated, even after narrowly avoiding being trampled by the prancing Pegasus while I was hiding in a bush.

About an hour later, Zeus, Apollo, Alec, and I were sitting down with Pan on a log by his hideout, and Poseidon was happily swimming in the small pool with two nymphs who were a few years older than us. Alec winced as I bandaged his injured arm, and I looked up at him with great concern, pulling my hand back from his wound in surprise. I knew we couldn't have him too seriously in pain at a tense time like this, when we would need every last fighter at a moment's notice.

"I'm fine," Alec whispered to me with a forced smile, and I returned to my work even though I didn't quite believe him.

Suddenly, our walkie-talkies erupted with the unmistakable voice of Hermes. Apparently, he had finished delivering the message to the rest of the gods. Poseidon and the nymphs immediately stopped swimming, and Apollo, Pan, and Zeus looked up from eating berries to listen in as he said in Greek, "Artemis says the plan sounds good. She can't go to Kentucky anyway, since her aunt is visiting this week. It's all on you, Athena."

I honestly wasn't surprised, so I just sighed and replied shortly, "Okay, thanks for letting me know." I finished wrapping the bandage on Alec's strong arm and stood up. "I'm going to go home and sort everything out." Next, facing Alec, I told him seriously, "We leave in three days. Don't get killed while I'm gone."

Alec only smirked as I started walking south toward my house, leaving the others behind. "I'll try not to!" he yelled after me flirtatiously, as I disappeared into the foliage.

---

I ran up the rickety steps to my front porch and entered my house, noticing that my mother wasn't home from the antique shop yet. After I had printed out the plane ticket information, I used the format from my invitation to the prestigious New York summer camp to type a fake acceptance letter from the University of Kentucky. I had always wanted to go to the program in New York, but I never actually applied to it, even though I was certain they would have accepted me. Knowing everything did have its perks.

The next day I showed my mother the fake acceptance letter, much to her surprise, and she told me that she didn't even realize I had applied this year (or any year, for that matter). She did, in fact, allow me to go after some thought, although I could tell that she didn't really want to be alone after what had happened with my dad. But what else was I supposed to do? I had a much more important mission. And when my mother offered to go online and buy the plane ticket to Kentucky, I quickly intervened and told her Dad already did.

For the next two days, I went into the forest only at night, to train with Alec. I was too busy during the day trying to work out the travel details and to pack as lightly as I could, with only the necessities that could fit in a backpack: two changes of clothes, a toothbrush and toothpaste, and a few snacks. Unfortunately, Alec and I would look awfully strange walking around in Grecian armor, and our usual weapons would never make it through airport security, so we would just have to be extra careful when we were fighting whatever monsters that were bound to chase after us.

While I was busy arranging the plans, however, somehow Hephaestus managed to make Alec and me special swords that could easily go through security and were concealed as round rocks, small enough to fit in our pockets. With one squeeze, the long sharp metal blade of a sword would shoot out of one end of the rock, and another squeeze of the hilt would turn it back into an ordinary rock. Alec and I just had to make sure we didn't accidentally lose the tiny, inconspicuous objects.

On the night before Alec and I were going to leave the Woods, I sneaked out of my bedroom around eleven to head into the forest, grabbing my armor, spear, and shield on the way. Because Artemis and I reckoned that there would be some archers at the Knowing base camp (which was confirmed by Alec), we had agreed to go hunting for Stymphalian birds that night so she could teach Alec and me a few tips about archery, which the two of us could then pass on to the archers at the camp. Therefore, as soon as Artemis arrived at Pan's hideout, she, Alec, and I started to head toward the Oracle's region of the forest, where the greatest concentration of the metallic birds lived.

For the first hour or so, Alec and I took turns practicing our shots with Artemis's bow, aiming at certain trees or branches while staying hidden in the bushes. I supposed we could have kept shooting at unmoving targets, but Alec and I found that to be quite dull. Frankly, killing monsters, especially without good reason, was much more fun. Henceforth, when Artemis thought we had enough experience, we stopped trying to be quiet and waited patiently.

The giant birds appeared right away, disturbed by our presence in their territory. Three of them flitted nervously from branch to branch, and their razor-sharp metal feathers made terrible grinding sounds every time they moved. Nevertheless, I managed to hit my mark on the first try, and the bird disappeared in a puff of ashes. This caused the two remaining birds to screech and circle higher in the trees, sensing immediate danger.

I passed the bow and arrows to Alec so he could have his turn, and he rolled his sparkling blue eyes at me, as if to sarcastically thank me for making his job a lot harder. Indeed, he missed the anxious Stymphalian birds, which were even bigger and taller than us, on the first two tries, but his third time was the charm. As soon as the second bird had disappeared, however, five more immediately joined the one remaining, apparently angered by our unwarranted assault on their population. Although these birds usually only harmed other beings by destroying crops with their toxic droppings, they were known to turn into hungry killers when provoked.

"I think they've declared war," Alec announced with a smirk, passing the bow and quiver full of arrows back to Artemis in exchange for his sword.

I grinned at my friends confidently. "Apparently they haven't learned the most important lesson of war: never start battles you can't win."

And the battle began. A steel-gray Stymphalian bird swooped down from the trees, metal wings and sharp talons outstretched, but Artemis shot it immediately. Another flew toward me, and I dove out of the way but rolled over on the ground just in time to throw my spear into its belly. I was showered with dark ash as the smooth spear fell back into my hands, and I raised my silver shield just in time for a second bird to crash into it with the force of a high-speed train.

Behind me, Alec was slicing and stabbing at the underside of the mechanical bird hovering above him, blocking the acidic yellow droppings and the snapping of the bird's bronze beak with his own shield. Meanwhile, Artemis was hiding in a bush, not wasting any arrows and patiently waiting for the perfect moment to shoot at the humongous birds flapping around her, the moment when the silver light from her bright moon glinted at just the right position off of their wings, which seemed to be covered with what looked more like flattened tips of spears than real feathers. Artemis was on a hot streak and had killed her third by the time Alec had finally killed his second.

The terrific battle came to a conclusion when I quickly unbuckled the straps that held *aegis* on my left arm and hurled the heavy shield like a discus at the last Stymphalian bird, which then slammed against the trunk of a pine tree and fell to the grass, heaving for air. Fearlessly, Alec raced up from behind it and jumped on its back just as it began to take off again. The brave young hero didn't even shout for help as the bird screeched and twisted around twenty feet up in the air, struggling to throw off its determined rider. Finally, he managed to stab the bird's back with his sword, and I dropped my weapons to catch him with my superhuman strength as he plummeted back down to earth, followed by a small cloud of gray monster dust.

"Thanks," Alec told me with a weak smile as he wiped off the bright red blood from his hands, which had been cut on the gigantic bird's bladelike feathers. "Riding a Stymphalian bird wasn't quite as much fun as I thought it would be."

Artemis and I simply rolled our eyes at him in response, and then we headed back to Pan's home to drop Alec off. I was eager to get some rest.

---

Finally the day Alec and I would leave for Kentucky arrived. First, I got up early and took a shower before putting on some jeans, a red T-shirt, and my leather jacket. Then I grabbed my black backpack and the ticket information I had printed out and quickly headed downstairs.

To my surprise, my mom was already in the kitchen, preparing a bowl of cereal for me. "I'm going to drive you to the airport in half an hour," she said, not even looking up at me.

"Oh no, that's okay. I called for a taxi last night, and it should be here soon. I didn't want you to take off from work just for me," I told her. Alec had to get to the airport as well, and since he wasn't even supposed to exist, there was no way my mom could ever find out about him.

"Okay then. Give me a hug before you leave, sweetie," she told me, and I clenched my teeth but obeyed anyway.

She sighed, and I thought I caught her wiping her eyes with her delicate hand, but I didn't say anything besides, "Bye, Mom." And then I walked out of the door and into the woods to meet Alec. If she even noticed that I only had one small backpack for two weeks' worth of traveling, she didn't say anything.

When I finally reached the meadow, our usual meeting place, the rest of the gods and Alec were already there waiting for me. "Ready?" I asked Alec. He was the only person there, besides me and Pan, who wasn't wearing armor.

Alec simply nodded and walked over to stand next to me, now facing the rest of the gods. "Well," Zeus spoke up, looking me in the eye, "give me a hug, and don't get killed."

Grinning, I walked over to him, gave him a hug, and replied, "Just keep the skies clear for us, Father Zeus." He smiled, his blue eyes twinkling, and nodded, while Hera just glared at me from behind him.

"Don't be thinking that I'm going to give you a hug too, Athena. Because I definitely won't," Poseidon said, stepping up behind Zeus and winking.

I just shook my head as Hephaestus stood up awkwardly with his wooden cane next to Poseidon and held out his rough hand, on which sat the two rocks that could turn into swords. He handed the larger one to Alec, since he was slightly taller than me, and the smaller rock to me. "These should work just fine. I laced them with magic, so if you drop them or they get lost, they should return to your pockets within five minutes, give or take a few. You know how these things work," he instructed us with a wave of his hand. "Oh, and good luck."

Alec and I nodded in unison, and I was about to respond to the smith god when I was suddenly pulled away by Aphrodite. I just let out an exasperated sigh, knowing full well what was coming. Frowning, she quickly reached behind my head to fix my ponytail and then placed her perfectly manicured hands on my shoulders. "Okay, by now I'm assuming you know that Alec likes you—"

"I know everything," I told her bluntly, crossing my arms.

Starting to remind me of Katie, she sighed and explained, "Well, yes, but let's just say that love is definitely *not* your area of expertise. I mean, you haven't said anything to Cole or Alec on the subject yet." Fixing her own hair and clasping her hands together dramatically, Aphrodite continued, "I just wanted to tell you that you shouldn't be afraid to fall in love."

I only raised my eyebrows in silence. "I'm not supposed to fall in love," I reminded her matter-of-factly.

Aphrodite shook her head and argued, "No, you're just supposed to be a *virgin*. You of all people should know about loopholes. Don't you have a law degree or something?"

I looked her in the eye. "Forget it, Aphrodite. It's not happening. And I have to go now, so—" I was interrupted when she suddenly hugged me tightly, and I was all too aware of her curvy body and breasts pressing against mine. Her voluminous blonde hair was strewn over my face, and the fruity scent of perfume was overwhelming. She couldn't help it, though. Her aura and good looks were more than enough to evoke powerful feelings of desire or to send one's senses spiraling out of control—but always in a good way.

Reluctantly giving in to her charms for a moment, I sighed and hugged her back, but then I pushed away again. "Bye," I told her softly, tucking a stray piece of hair behind my ear. Even though we had our differences, I had to admit Aphrodite was a pretty good friend, like most of the gods.

I turned back to face the rest of the gods one last time before saying farewell. "Well, happy hunting, Artemis, and to everyone else, please stay alive," I said with a nod toward my good friend, the goddess of the moon.

When they all smiled back, Alec knelt down on one knee, giving one last bow to his gods and best friends, the determined look of a hero now permanently written across his face. Without another word, we slowly headed north to meet our taxi, leaving the other gods behind to go kill some of the monsters Hades had sent. I hated to admit it, but I was going to miss them.

# Chapter 14:

# THE JOURNEY

Alec and I carefully made our way out of the sprawling forest, walking as quietly as possible to avoid all monsters. When we finally reached the empty street, a small green taxicab was parked by the Fire Pit, patiently waiting for us. The driver, a tall black man with a receding hairline, saw us and stepped out of the car. With a smile, he offered to take our backpacks and put them in the trunk, but we declined. (Backpacks don't take up that much space, after all.) Alec and I just buckled ourselves in and stared unblinkingly at the backs of the car seats in front of us. After a moment, Alec leaned over to whisper something in my ear, but I only shied away from his hot breath.

The cab driver looked at us in the rearview mirror, grinning. "I hope you two young lovebirds have permission to be taking such a long trip," he remarked jokingly, but I turned bright red, just then realizing what Alec and I must look like together, with our only luggage being the backpack, and feeling slightly angry at what the man was implying. Frowning and beginning to sweat nervously, I only glared in silence out the window at the lush green meadows we were driving through.

Alec sensed that I had taken offense and glanced at me uncomfortably, color rising to his cheeks. Scratching the Knowing brand on the back of his neck, Alec explained, "We're not dating."

"Ah, my mistake," the cab driver responded with a wink, though I wasn't sure if he believed Alec or not. "I'm Larry, by the way." Both Alec and I flashed Larry fake smiles, then returned to staring out our windows, hoping to avoid any more awkward conversations with him. Or each other.

---

About two hours later, we finally reached the airport in Seattle. Larry got out of the taxi first and politely opened the car doors for us, and I paid him in cash, plus a fair tip. Quickly, Alec and I walked through the shiny steel and white airport up to the check-in stand, where we received our boarding passes from a smiling lady who looked like she had gotten too much plastic surgery in her life. When we made it through security without any issues, Alec and I agreed to get some lunch at one of the tiny, bustling fast food stands.

As we stepped over to the McDonald's, I quietly chewed my lip, trying not to think about what the other people in the airport thought about Alec and me. To make things worse, we were getting into the short line to order when Alec carefully but all too eagerly shifted his stance and slid his other arm up around my shoulders, as if to protect me from something. I sighed; he was not helping our image at all.

"Alec, what are you doing?" I warned, tensing up. I felt lightheaded and hyper-alert, much too aware of every ridge in his abs and arm muscles pressing against my side.

"Shh," he hissed angrily through gritted teeth. "Those guys at our three o'clock are staring at you like you're a piece of fresh kill."

I was already frowning to myself in annoyance, but as casually as possible, I glanced in the direction he was talking about. Sure enough, four guys about our age were standing by a wide column, lust and greed gleaming in their eyes as they looked me over, *all* over. I couldn't help but notice that Alec was glaring at them like he wanted to stab them or something . . . which he probably did.

But Alec managed to restrain himself from attacking and only pulled me closer. "Hey, it's fine," I whispered to him, allowing myself to play along for just a minute. "Let's just buy some food now." Alec nodded reluctantly and stepped forward in line with me, his well-muscled arm still wrapped tightly around my shoulders.

We had ordered our food and were waiting to pick it up when I started to think that Alec was enjoying our charade a little too much. I had just pulled away from him when a low voice coming from behind us said, "How are you doing, little lady?"

Slowly Alec and I turned around, knowing full well what was coming, and we found ourselves face-to-face with the four guys who had been staring at me not five minutes earlier. Next to me, Alec's muscles grew taut as he studied the boys. The speaker, a tough, overconfident blond guy with gleaming brown eyes, grinned at me in a flirty manner and carefully reached around me to grab the food that the McDonald's worker had just set down for Alec and me, pausing to get a better look at my breasts. Apparently, he liked what he saw, because a sly smile crept onto his face. Anger rolling off him in powerful waves, Alec yanked the white paper bag away from the blond and growled, "Thanks, man, but I got it."

The boy narrowed his dark eyes at Alec, studying him closely. "You got a problem with me, pretty boy?" the blond sneered. He probably thought a guy as good-looking as Alec would be afraid to get his face messed up, but he was dead wrong.

Alec handed the food to me and clenched his fists, looking as if he were ready to strike, and silently I prayed for him to restrain himself. *Please don't do it, Alec. Please don't punch him right now, right here.* We really did not need to draw any more attention to ourselves at the moment.

The hero stood up a little straighter, sizing up the tough blond boy, a flicker of hatred in his blue eyes. I was watching the two of them very closely, along with the members of the other boy's posse, who were getting agitated and appearing as if they too were ready to jump in to join the fight. Only they didn't know that Alec, trained by the best, could probably take all four of them down by himself in little more than a minute. Normal humans just couldn't compare to monsters or gods.

Suddenly, something making its way toward us caught my eye in the small crowds milling about the airport. I gulped and nudged Alec nervously. "Alec," I whispered, "we need to go. Like, now."

But Alec just frowned, not moving a muscle or taking his eyes off of the annoying blond boy. Starting to feel the slightest bit of panic, I whispered again in frustration, this time in Greek, "You'll be killed by the Minotaur in less than thirty seconds if we don't move now."

Now *that* got his attention. Immediately, Alec's eyes flicked in the direction that I had motioned to, where the meaty Minotaur was pushing its way through the crowds toward the two of us, its furry black hands clenched in tight fists. I couldn't help but wonder what the regular humans without the Sight in the airport saw the Minotaur as, since they obviously didn't look twice at the bloodthirsty monster. But even though the rest of the gods and I had killed the beast every single time we ran into it, for some reason that hungry beast never seemed to stay dead for very long.

Alec cursed under his breath, and we took off toward the gate where we were supposed to wait for our flight. The blond boy and his posse just stared at us in confusion, and we ran as quickly as we could through the thick crowds of people, determined to avoid the monster.

When something occurred to me, like a light bulb flicking on in my brain, I pushed my way more toward Alec.

"Hey," I whispered in Greek, "what if the Minotaur is on the same flight?"

Alec's eyebrows knit together in confusion, as he was still struggling to comprehend what I had said. "How would the Minotaur get a plane ticket?"

I shook my head and replied grimly, "I don't know—maybe Hades, but I wouldn't put it past a monster. We need to kill it before we get on the plane."

Alec nodded in agreement. I handed him the food. Grunting, I ran in a U-turn, now going head-on toward the Minotaur, whose unblinking red eyes instantly locked onto me. Then I jumped sideways, narrowly avoiding crashing into an elderly couple, but I quickly apologized and continued on my course.

The Minotaur and I were getting closer and closer, until we were only a few feet apart. My hand moved to my pocket, from which I pulled out the small round rock. With a tiny squeeze, the sharp, shiny sword blade popped out, and it pierced the Minotaur's gut right as I stepped sideways to avoid crashing into its thick body, although one of its muscular arms slammed into my neck. The Minotaur gasped and groaned, trying to pull out the sword as I twisted the blade in its midsection, squeezing the hilt of the sword at the same time. When I finally pulled the blade all the way out, it had returned to its rock state.

Surprisingly, no one in the airport had even given us a second look, but I turned around, running and pushing my way through the crowds as I tried to return to Alec, just in case he had come face-to-face with another monster in my absence. I then took a glance behind me and sighed in relief when I saw a pile of dust on the cheap, navy-blue airport carpet where the Minotaur had been standing not a minute before. Thankfully, it was dead.

Only a minute later, I caught up to Alec, who was sitting in a small leather seat at the gate, by a tall window overlooking the runway. When he caught my eye, he gave a helpless shrug. "What do we do now? We have a while until the flight leaves," Alec complained.

"Stay alive" was my only reply as I watched him stuff a Chicken McNugget into his mouth. Then I just watched the planes outside roll in and out of the gates and waited until Alec finished his food and passed the rest to me. Eventually, a flight attendant called for us to board the plane, and we hurried on board.

Sighing in relief, I sat down by the window seat, and Alec took the one on the aisle. "How long is the flight?" I asked him. I had only been on a plane once or twice before, and I had never been to Kentucky.

Alec just shrugged and answered, "Maybe about four or five hours. Did you bring a book?" I shook my head, suddenly wishing I had. "Me neither," he said.

"You don't even own a book!" I reminded him.

Grinning, he replied, "Not in the Woods anyway, but it's a good thing they have *Sky Mall* magazine. You know, the one with all of those crazy inventions and stuff?"

I nodded and told him, "Oh, please. I could invent something better in my sleep."

"I bet you could," he agreed, still smiling. Then I smirked and rested my head against the back of the seat, closing my eyes in preparation to catch up on lost sleep and perhaps even invent something while I was dreaming.

---

Suddenly I was jolted awake, and the loud voice of a female flight attendant sounded over the intercom while the button telling me to buckle my seat belt clicked on. "Please put your seat belts on and return your seats to their upright positions. We will be landing in approximately twenty minutes. The current temperature outside the airport is seventy degrees, and it is partly cloudy."

I shook my head and rubbed my eyes to help wake myself up a little quicker. Sighing, I stared out the window at the large, open fields and rolling hills—almost the complete opposite of the forest at home. We were getting closer and closer to the ground as we circled the airport, waiting for our plane's turn to land, and the sky slowly grew darker with each passing minute. It was nearly eight o'clock in Kentucky.

"Hey, you're awake," Alec noticed, nudging me playfully. "Did you invent anything while you were sleeping?"

I paused to think for a moment, trying to remember my dream. When I couldn't, I just replied slyly, "Not this time." Alec laughed, and I smiled back at him as I returned the seat to its upright position in accordance with the flight attendant's orders. "And how are you? Did you get any sleep?" I asked, studying him closely.

Alec shrugged. "Not really. But don't look so worried; I'll be fine," he answered, and I nodded as the plane touched down on the runway and started to taxi toward the gate. As soon as the flight attendants opened up the door, Alec and I jumped off, eager to get out of the airport as quickly as possible. There were too many people in one place for our liking; it didn't matter to us if they were Knowing or not.

Because we only had our backpacks, we didn't have to wait at the baggage claim, and so we simply walked out the front entrance of the airport right away.

"How far is the camp from here?" I wondered aloud as we strode confidently through the sliding doors out into the cool night air.

He shrugged again. "About a hundred miles, give or take a few. I was thinking about taking another taxi most of the way there. There aren't any roads leading to the camp."

I gave a short nod, and together we waited on the sidewalk for a taxi to pull up. The driver smiled at us and asked if we wanted to put our bags in the trunk, but just like the previous time with Larry, we declined. Close to two hours later, Alec and I were dropped off at an empty bus stop in the middle of the countryside, no questions asked. Our surroundings were almost pitch black, except for one street lamp illuminating the covered black bench with a dull orange glow.

"Which way?" I looked to Alec, and he pointed north before he started walking without saying another word. For another hour, we walked over the rolling hills in silence, keeping an ear out for anything suspicious, but we could hear absolutely nothing, other than the sound of squishing grass from under our worn-out boots. We really were in the middle of nowhere, I noticed, though I supposed it was quite a logical place for the secret Knowing base camp.

However, for the very first time, our prolonged state of silence seemed awkward. Usually, I welcomed the peaceful quietness as, together, we strode confidently through the dark forest and listened for any sign of a monster we could brutally beat to death. But there in the open fields of Kentucky, I felt kind of clueless and strangely exposed in more than one way, and I was sure that Alec would have agreed if I had asked him about it. His footsteps seemed much more like a march to me now, and he stood up straight and rigid, obviously on high alert. Alec was acting as if he were trying to fit himself into a mold that didn't suit his personality or his naturally rugged appearance very well, and the way his fists were clenched by his sides only highlighted his great agitation. To be honest, the young hero seemed uncomfortable in his own skin, and I was sure it had something to do with the Knowing.

A couple minutes later, I stopped to give my aching feet a short break, and Alec halted next to me. "We could sleep here for the night, if you want," he offered sweetly, but I noticed that Alec seemed to be getting more agitated as we got closer to the camp, so he probably just wanted to delay his arrival even more. Again, I wondered why, although still I didn't say anything to him about it.

So I shook my head and said firmly, "I'm not tired. Let's get as close as we can to the Knowing camp tonight." Reluctantly, Alec nodded in agreement and continued to walk, picking up the pace. We jogged for another forty-five minutes before we reached the bottom of a steep hill, where Alec stopped nervously in his tracks once more.

"Let's stop here for tonight," he announced. "We can sleep under this tree." We then threw our backpacks down on the grass, and Alec carefully leaned against the tree, crossing his arms over his chest for warmth.

"We should probably take turns on guard duty, watching out for monsters," I suggested, brushing a stray piece of hair out of my face.

"I'll take the first shift," Alec said, and I agreed reluctantly, lying down on the grass and using my backpack as a pillow. It was warm enough that I didn't need a blanket, and even though I had slept on the plane for a couple of hours, I still fell asleep almost right away. (If I had the chance to get extra rest, I *always* took it.)

---

A bird cawed from somewhere above me, and I woke with a start. Adjusting my lopsided ponytail, I looked through the darkness of the night over at Alec, who was glaring alertly at the tall hill in front of us. "What time is it?" I asked him, still a little bit sleepy.

Alec checked his watch and replied harshly, "Almost four." I frowned, noticing the sharp edge in his voice.

"You should have woken me up half an hour ago," I told him softly, sitting up next to him and leaning against the rough tree trunk. "Why didn't you?"

Alec continued to stare at the empty hillside. "You needed to sleep," he replied simply.

"And so do you," I retorted, but Alec didn't move a muscle, so I sighed. "All right, what's the matter? You act crankier with every step closer to the camp."

Alec didn't answer right away; he just kept staring at the stupid hill instead. What was so interesting about it anyway? I was starting to get fed up with his strange actions, and so, with taut muscles, I just sat back, pausing to look up at the glittering stars in the clear night sky and subconsciously identifying familiar constellations.

Finally, he ran his fingers through his dark hair and spoke in a guilty whisper, "I should've told you this sooner."

"Should have told me what?" I looked over at Alec expectantly, waiting for an explanation.

"The Knowing didn't actually let me leave the camp to find you and the other gods. I sneaked out in the middle of the night," he confessed, wincing as if speaking the truth hurt him.

My jaw dropped in surprise and confusion. "What? Why?" I asked, getting slightly angry with him. The Knowing members probably thought he was dead! They wouldn't even be expecting us, which would make my job of convincing them to fight on our side a lot harder.

Alec frowned and rubbed his forehead, beginning again and assuring me, "Nearly everything I've told you has been the truth, except for that. I swear. It's just that when I told the leaders of the camp about my vision of the Oracle leading me to the Woods, they didn't believe me. So of course, they wouldn't train me to fight, especially since I wasn't sixteen and old enough to be trained in the first place. I tried to convince them otherwise, but they only forbade me to leave the camp and pushed back the real start of my training another few months as punishment."

"You've got to be kidding me," I groaned, and he shook his head solemnly. "Why wouldn't they believe you?" I asked, still slightly confused as to why the camp leaders would do such a thing. It sounded awfully ignorant to me. You would have thought that the Knowing would have wanted to find their beloved gods, but apparently not. Perhaps the Knowing was even more troubled than I had previously thought.

He sighed. "No one at the Knowing camp had gotten a vision like that in years . . . or maybe they had, and they just didn't want to admit it. To be honest, we hadn't gotten a sign from any god in about a century. Some people at the camp have even stopped praying as much as they used to and have started to believe that it's the *gods'* job to find *us*, but that made absolutely no sense to me.

If you had to teach yourselves everything, how could we expect you to find out about us?"

I nodded in understanding and admitted, "Yeah, we probably never would have found out about the Knowing if you and your father hadn't shown up."

Alec put his head in his hands, obviously distressed. "So that was about the time I started to train myself at night and prepare for the journey, even though my family was the laughingstock of the camp," he continued bitterly, hating to admit the weakness that was his family's identity in the Knowing. "Eventually, when I thought I was ready, I left. But my father wanted to come as well. He believed in me when no one else did, and now it's my fault he's dead," Alec finished, angry with himself. "And well, let's just say that the Knowing probably won't want to give me a homecoming celebration."

I sighed. "Hey, what's done is done, and at least you have most of the gods on your side," I comforted him, placing a hand on his arm, although I still wished he had told me all of this sooner. I hated not being prepared. It was downright dangerous.

"But it's not just about us and the rest of the gods saving the Woods anymore—it also has to be about fixing the Knowing. I don't want any other kids growing up like I did, victimized in such a corrupt society," Alec said wishfully, wiping his eyes. He paused and sighed. I watched as his brow started to furrow, but he stopped himself from frowning by giving me a pathetic half-smile.

Thinking about our destinies, like I always did at the back of my mind, I gulped and told him, "There will be plenty of time to fix the Knowing when this war is over, but right now, you should get some rest." But he shook his head stubbornly, even though he had dark circles under his eyes—obvious signs of fatigue. "Suit yourself," I added with a shrug and placed my head on Alec's shoulder, but he only sighed again and continued to glare at the hillside, too disturbed by the thought of the Knowing to even smile at my comforting gesture.

A few minutes later, we heard the sound of heavy footsteps in the grass making their way toward us, and my eyes flew open instantly. Instinctively, Alec and I both reached for the rocks in our pockets and simultaneously looked in the direction of the sound. My first thought was that the footsteps coming from behind us shook the earth a lot like Poseidon's, and I hoped they were Poseidon's, just so we wouldn't have to fight a monster there in the middle of the open field, where we had absolutely no territorial advantages.

But of course, Poseidon was at home in the Woods, and standing in front of us was a very chubby, fifteen-foot-tall monster of a man, who had one giant brown eye in the center of his forehead, and who was wearing nothing but an old brown loincloth. A Cyclops.

"You have got to be kidding me," I heard Alec mutter as we quickly stood up to face the gigantic man, now holding deadly swords instead of the dirty gray rocks.

The Cyclops stomped his large, bare foot in front of us, making the earth under our feet shake slightly and the flabby skin on his stomach roll. He pointed his sausage-like finger at Alec and me, and then his booming voice thundered in Greek, "Who do you think you are? You are in my territory!"

I gulped. Even though I knew revealing my identity probably wouldn't work, I figured it was worth a try and said in an equally powerful voice, "I am the goddess Athena, and I am the patron of this hero. I order you to leave us alone."

"Ha!" the Cyclops laughed heartily, studying us carefully. "You think I will let you go? I only obey Lord Poseidon, not silly little Athena."

I frowned and shouted back at him, "In your next life, I would recommend that you obey *all* of the gods. Now we will send you to Hades."

With that, the Cyclops made a fist with his hand, shook it in anger, then lunged at me, but Alec and I rolled out of the way in opposite directions. The Cyclops bellowed in rage while Alec and I continued to run circles around him, just wishing we had bows and arrows to kill the monstrous man quicker and easier. We made a few shallow cuts on his meaty legs and fat feet with our swords, but that really wasn't doing much to slow the Cyclops down. It only made the giant hop around on one foot like a madman, and we had to jump out of the way to avoid being stepped on.

"Arrgh!" the Cyclops yelled in frustration. "That's it!" Suddenly, the giant man picked his foot up and brought it down as hard as he could. The earth shook so much that Alec and I struggled to remain standing, although our focus changed when the Cyclops's hand reached down from the sky, aiming to grab me by the midsection. Alec ran toward me, but he was far away on the other side of the Cyclops and had no chance of making it in time to save me. Therefore, I could only brace myself as I felt the giant hand close around me and lift me high off the ground.

I gasped and let out a breath that I didn't realize I had been holding as my ascent reached a sudden stop. Admittedly, I hadn't seen what caused the stop, but I knew it had something to do with Alec. So I simply braced myself for impact with the ground—an impact I knew only a god would be able to survive without injury—as I felt myself slip between the Cyclops's fingers. A second later, I landed feet first in the grass before falling to my knees, rattled and off-balance. But I was safe.

That didn't seem to matter to Alec, however. Anyone could tell he was now downright furious as he pointed his shining sword accusingly at the Cyclops. "That's my patroness, you idiot!" he shouted menacingly in Greek, and I grinned proudly as my little hero chucked his sword as hard as he could, aiming straight for the Cyclops's huge eyeball. I decided to let Alec finish the fight on his own.

The Cyclops shrieked as the sword stuck in the brown iris of his eye, and he tried valiantly to pull it out, but his eye just started to bleed even more, turning the white part red and causing him to cry tears of blood. Taking advantage of the Cyclops's pain, which momentarily stopped the brute in his tracks, I tossed my own sword to Alec, and he ran rapidly around the Cyclops, making cuts and slashes wherever he could in the thick skin.

With a giant thud and a small shake of the earth, the Cyclops slowly fell to one knee, then onto his ugly face. Without wasting another second, Alec took a flying leap and repeatedly stabbed the Cyclops square in the back, pure hatred in his gleaming blue eyes and gold-green monster blood splattering all over his torso, until the Cyclops finally stopped moving. After a couple of seconds, the giant Cyclops crumbled to dust, and Alec dropped a few feet to the ground, landing on his feet.

Breathlessly, Alec staggered toward me with his arms outstretched, seemingly ready to give me a hug or something, but I only pulled away. "Look at you. You're covered in monster blood," I said to Alec, and for a second he appeared confused. I shook my head again, and Alec just frowned as he looked down at his jeans and shirt, which were formerly blue and red but were now almost entirely covered in the greenish-gold substance. Alec sighed, and then he too shook his head, a tiny hint of a smile playing across his lips.

"I wonder what the Knowing will think of us now," Alec stated grimly, gesturing to all the monster blood on his clothes as the swords he was holding abruptly changed back into rock form. He handed me my own rock, and I slipped it into my pocket.

"At least you'll be able to take a shower soon," I whispered to him brightly, and together we walked back over to our backpacks. We were both chuckling to ourselves and trying to catch our breaths, hoping we wouldn't be bothered by any more monsters. I doubted we would get much more sleep after that.

# Chapter 15:

# WELCOME HOME

Morning came quickly, with little sleep after Alec killed the Cyclops. Neither Alec nor I was very happy by the time the sun rose, until I pulled out some tiny boxes of cereal from my backpack that I had bought in the Kentucky airport.

Alec scarfed the entire box down in less than a minute, and although I took more time than him, we were still able to pack up the few things that we had and leave in less than ten minutes. We started walking north once again, on our way to the Knowing base camp. I would have called Zeus to give him an update and to find out about what was going on back in the Woods, but I hadn't even bothered to bring my cell phone, since I knew there probably wasn't going to be cell service where we were heading.

It was about eight o'clock in the morning when Alec and I hiked our way over the top of a large hill and stopped, looking down over a large dip in the rolling earth. Below us sat what I automatically assumed to be the camp, a collection of about thirty large, medieval-looking tents in deep purples, reds, and blues. In the center was a large, square wooden stage raised about three or four feet off the ground, and on the eastern edge of the Knowing establishment were a vegetable garden and two large corrals, each holding about fifteen to twenty well-fed horses. The hill behind it appeared to be dotted with at least fifty dark gray stones, which could only mark a cemetery.

On the opposite side of camp sat one of only two actual buildings there, and Alec told me that it held the showers and toilets and a small tattoo parlor, along with a working phone, which was strictly for emergencies. I immediately decided that calling Zeus would qualify as an emergency. After all, who knew what in the world Hades was doing right at that second?

Then, after staring at the view for a minute, Alec and I made our way down the hill. I noticed that a few large, muscular men who were wearing Grecian-style armor and who were situated at different points around the edge of the camp were looking up and pointing at us with what I hoped was enthusiasm. When I saw one of them quickly run into the largest tent in the camp, Alec explained, his voice unusually tight, "Those Warriors are just guarding the camp. Always on the lookout for monsters . . ."

As we got closer, however, I could clearly see the confusion and even anger written across the strong Warriors' faces. I frowned and muttered in confusion, "They sure don't look very happy to see us." And although I was certain that Alec knew why the Warriors appeared so angry, he didn't answer me, only keeping his gaze locked on the tents ahead of us. The air around us felt thick and tense (for more than one reason) as Alec and I passed over a dirt line drawn in the grass that circled the camp, and I looked down at it curiously. I had been inside the camp for mere milliseconds, yet I already felt enclosed and restricted.

"That's the boundary line for the camp, set up by the gods three or four generations ago. The Knowing base camp has been here ever since," Alec whispered to me from out of the corner of his mouth, answering the question he knew I had been silently pondering. "And un-Knowing humans, ones who don't have the Sight, can't see anything behind this line except grass, so they won't come near us. They have no reason to come over here."

More Warriors were appearing in front of us now. They ranged in size, but they were all men, none younger than eighteen or so, with bad sunburns and large, bulging muscles that had tiny veins popping out, possibly due to slight dehydration or a very recent workout. Furthermore, their muscles seemed almost artificial, or the kind that one tries too hard to attain—the kind that didn't come from real work, the kind that were slightly more gruesome than handsome, as opposed to the gods'. Even if the Warriors hadn't been wearing full-body armor and clutching the handles of their sheathed knives and swords, I wouldn't have trusted them.

"Whatever you do, don't panic. It will be over soon enough, once I straighten things out," Alec told me in a hushed voice. I would have reprimanded him for ordering me around, but the deadly serious expression on his face told me it was best to stay silent.

All of a sudden, one muscular man ran up to us and yanked Alec's arms, and then two other Warriors dragged Alec away from me. "No—" I tried to shout out, but I was cut off when another Warrior came up from behind me, stole my backpack, and blindfolded and gagged me. Meanwhile, a different one bound my hands behind my back, just like they were in handcuffs. With a cold shiver, I realized that they had me completely trapped for possibly the first time in my entire life, and I couldn't speak out because of the gag in my mouth. I struggled against their grip in vain as they dragged me into a tent and threw me down on a hard wooden chair, then took my blindfold off.

"Stay there," one of the large Warriors in rusted armor growled at me as he sat on a different chair, next to another Warrior blocking the tent door. I was really starting to dislike the Knowing, and I hardly knew anything about them.

I grew restless as I was forced to sit in the chair and wait. I supposed I could have been trying to escape, but part of me wanted to be obedient and was sure that the confusion would be sorted out quickly, as Alec had assured me. Curious, I tried to listen to what was going on outside, but I couldn't hear anything besides the cheers and shouts of the gathering crowd, which were getting louder and louder. Moreover, the two Warriors in the tent kept looking behind them, as if they too wanted to know what was happening. Whatever it was must have been good.

About another ten minutes had passed before the cheers abruptly faded away, and I guessed the crowd was trying to listen closely to hear something, so I strained my ears as well. As if on cue, a booming voice, which I assumed belonged to the Knowing leader, shouted from outside, "You flee the camp, you bring back an outsider, you get punished. Simple as that. Have you learned your lesson yet?"

The crowd was dead quiet now, but I still could not hear a reply from whomever the leader was talking to, probably Alec. "I think that's a no," the man's voice continued loudly, almost laughing.

And then I heard the crack of a whip.

I guessed the crowd had erupted in cheers again, but I did not hear them. Suddenly, I was angrier than I had ever been in my entire life. The blood pounded in my ears as it finally dawned on me: that sick, twisted Knowing leader was whipping—no, *torturing*—Alec for absolutely no justified reason at all. Punishing Alec, *my* hero, was a direct offense against me. And I had been trapped in the tiny tent with no idea whatsoever.

I leaped to my feet, muscles rippling as I tore through the thin, yellowing rope that had bound me to the chair, and I quickly untied the gag from my mouth. *Nothing* could stop me in that moment of rage. Glaring ahead, I pushed and clawed my way between the two dumbfounded Warriors and sprinted toward the noise, which seemed to be coming from the stage area.

Looking up, I saw a shirtless Alec, whose entire body, including his dark hair, was dripping with sweat, and his back was covered in what looked like pints of red blood. With a gag in his mouth, he was kneeling on the stage and slumped forward, being held up only by ropes binding each of his arms to separate wooden posts. The Knowing leader, a tall, muscular man with light brown hair that was slicked back with some sort of gel, stood above Alec, gripping a long leather whip in one hand, about to strike the little hero yet again.

Hyperventilating, I forced my way through the thick mass of Knowing members, who were too preoccupied with watching Alec to notice me. At one point, I passed a slightly plump woman with long dark hair and a similar facial structure to that of the boy on stage, and I knew she must have been Alec's mother. But she was ignoring her son's groans of pain, cheering along with the rest of the crowd and begging for Alec to be whipped again and again instead. The absolute worst part about the entire ordeal was that no one but me was even attempting to stop this injustice. In my entire life of fighting monsters, I had never seen anything so horrifying.

I shook my head in disbelief before I jumped onto the wooden stage and tackled the Knowing leader in one swift motion, pinning him down as I yanked the whip from his tight grasp. It took everything I had to restrain myself from killing the cruel man right then and there, for the overconfident way he carried himself implied that he had committed an unjustified crime of this caliber at least once before and, therefore, he deserved to die a slow, painful, dishonorable death at the hand of a god whom he clearly underestimated and did not respect. At that moment, I was not the least bit afraid to kill my first human; this one was just another monster that the world would have been better off without in the first place. However, there were around two hundred people—women and children included—watching my every move with a mixture of utter shock and maybe a little bit of fear. And to be honest, I didn't want to gain any loyal followers who would worship me only because they feared me.

Quickly, I stood up next to Alec, whose eyelids were fluttering as he struggled to remain conscious through the searing pain. Breathing hard, I wiped my sweaty brow and watched the Knowing leader with caution as he slowly got up off the stage in pure surprise. The crowd had also fallen silent once again, but this time it was because their oh-so-strong, unstoppable, beloved leader had just been brought down by a fifteen-year-old girl. I silently hoped to myself that the humiliation alone would be enough to humble him. Although killing or punishing him would have been fair and justified, it would have added yet another unnecessary spilling of blood to the heinous war that Hades was about to start.

But the Knowing leader simply sniffed and grunted as he wiped a drop of blood from his nose and glared at me with his evil-looking green eyes. I was not afraid. "Who do you think you are?" he yelled in English, right into my face. He was obviously not thrilled with my actions thus far.

Frowning, I wiped a few tiny drops of his disgusting spit from my face and replied loudly in Greek, so that the whole crowd could hear, "*I* am a goddess."

Gasps immediately echoed throughout the frantic audience, who appeared surprised that an outsider spoke Greek. A few men even laughed along with the Knowing leader, as if they thought I was a joke. Did I really look like I was joking?

"Prove it, *little girl*," the Knowing leader sneered at me, daring me to show him up once again. I only shrugged and pulled my black pocketknife out of my leather boot, where I had hidden it earlier in the morning. More gasps emanated from the crowd, and even the cruel Knowing leader raised his eyebrows.

"Yeah, you should probably search your prisoners a little better," I spat at him angrily.

The leader didn't reply, but just watched me carefully as I flicked open my pocketknife and stole a quick glance at Alec, who had his head bent over awkwardly and looked like he was unconscious. Knowing that I had to get him medical attention as soon as possible, I sighed to myself and took a deep breath. Then I made a cut about an inch long on the inside of my forearm, wincing only slightly as I dragged the tip of the sharp knife through my tan, glowing skin and watched the first drop of blood bubble to the surface.

Slowly, my shimmering golden blood dribbled down my arm, and the leader and the people in the front of the crowd who could see it yelped in unison, not quite believing their eyes. Without another word, I closed the pocketknife and shoved it back in my boot. Simultaneously, every single member of the audience knelt down on their knees, bowing to me out of respect. The Knowing leader knelt last, and he begged with a shaky voice, "I'm truly sorry for everything, my lady. Please, forgive me. Who are you?"

"Athena," I answered him bitterly, and a couple people in the crowd made strange noises of delight. I was one of their most loved gods, after all. But unfortunately for the Knowing, they were definitely not my favorite people.

"And apology not accepted. Besides, *Alec* is the one to whom you should really be apologizing," I continued, turning to face the rest of the Knowing and speaking to all of them in an angry snarl. "After all, it was *you* who refused to believe a loyal member of your clan! It was *you* who denied him his training and rights and forbade him to leave this wretched camp! And it was *you* who tortured him upon his return without letting him explain! Yet you still have the audacity to expect *me*, and *him*, to forgive you?! You must be out of your damn minds!"

Fuming, I turned on my heel and untied Alec's hands from the wooden posts. He collapsed onto my shoulder. I heaved him up as his blue eyes fluttered open once again, and I sighed in relief. Then I slowly helped Alec limp off the stage, taking the leather whip with me (I planned on destroying it later on) as the entire Knowing camp, in silence and in shame, watched us walk away.

"Get me a nurse," I ordered, my voice hoarse after yelling. On cue, a short woman in her forties wearing a simple blue dress with an apron was quickly shoved out from the middle of the crowd, and she nervously rushed over to help me with Alec.

She led me to the infirmary, a large purple tent that had a white flag with a red cross outside. Inside, there were five empty dark green cots and a large table with all of the medical supplies. The nurse and I placed Alec facedown on one of the cots to inspect his wounds more closely, but it was worse than either of us had thought. His entire back was covered with deep, crisscrossing gashes, and his blood and sweat were everywhere. The Knowing leader must have struck him at least thirty times.

I shook my head in disbelief and tried not to look too concerned as the nurse set to work cleaning the cuts. Alec yelled out in pain, and in a panic, he tried to push himself up off the cot, but he was too weak and collapsed back down in a heap, breathing extremely hard. Biting down on his lip so hard that it too started to bleed, Alec tried to get up for a second time and failed again, which sent him into another wave of panic, but I grabbed his hand firmly and knelt down next to him.

"Don't leave me," he whispered in Greek, tightening his white-knuckle grip with one hand on the cot's metal support bar and the other on my own hand.

"I wasn't planning on it," I told Alec truthfully, my voice almost catching in my throat. I frowned as he pressed his face into the fluffy white pillow on the cot and clutched my hand even tighter to distract himself from the pain. The nurse continued to clean his wounds in stiff silence.

Realizing I would probably be there a while, I sat down in front of the green cot, facing Alec and still keeping a firm hold of his one hand. Alec was gripping it so tightly that I was kind of surprised that the bones in my hand hadn't been crushed yet, but I didn't complain. Alec was enduring both physical and mental pain far greater than any of the gods had ever experienced thus far, and he deserved someone to be there with him.

I sighed when I took a closer look at poor Alec, who was now groaning in pain, for I noticed that his wrists were red and that the skin was peeling from rope burns. Frowning, I reached up with my free hand to push the dark, sweaty hair out of his eyes and touch his forehead, only slightly surprised to find that he was burning up. "He's running a fever," I told the nurse in a shaky, worried voice that was quite uncharacteristic of me, and she quickly handed me a cold wet blue rag, which I then gently placed on his forehead. Not trusting my voice any longer, I chose to stay silent after that.

A few minutes later, I had cleaned the raw skin on his wrists and was about to start bandaging them when Alec suddenly tensed up and cringed. I pulled the bandages away from his wrist instantly, thinking I had hurt him, but he only motioned for me to continue. "You probably think I'm weak after seeing me like . . . that," he mumbled glumly.

I just raised my eyebrows and told him seriously, "Someone who survives and stays conscious through more than thirty lashes is *not* weak. Plus, with your amount of training, I bet you could beat any Knowing Warrior in a fight."

Defeated and distressed, Alec only looked down and pressed his face back into the pillow, crushing my hand again as the nurse spread stinging antibiotic cream over the deep red gashes in his back. Just watching him, I had to bite down on my lower lip to stop it from quivering with guilt. I shouldn't have listened to him. I should have known he couldn't handle all of the Knowing on his own. Not yet anyway.

By then it was around noon, but I didn't leave to get lunch. I wasn't hungry, and I didn't really want to share a meal with the cruel Knowing people, who would have killed Alec if I hadn't intervened. So for hours on end, I sat in the medical tent gripping Alec's hand and solemnly watching him writhe in pain as the nurse treated his back. Even when the nurse was done, I stayed with the feverish Alec as he slept, knowing that he wouldn't trust anyone else there (and neither would I), although I too drifted in and out of sleep once or twice.

Outside, it was edging toward dusk, and eventually the nurse came over and tapped me on the shoulder. "Lady Athena," she said, bowing her head, "it is dinnertime now, if you want to eat."

I clutched my stomach, just then realizing how hungry I was, and nodded. Trying not to wake him, I carefully let go of Alec's hand and stood up to brush myself off. "What was your name again?" I asked the nurse. "I'm not sure you told me."

"Oh, I'm terribly sorry, my lady," the nurse quickly apologized. "I'm Jan."

I smiled and shook her frail hand. Becoming serious once again, I ordered dryly, "Stay with him and don't let anyone else in here. Please don't take it personally, but Alec does not really trust his people at the moment." She nodded in understanding, and then I walked out of the tent into the cool open air.

I followed the long line of people into the largest tent in the camp, a white, rectangular, circus-sized structure that I assumed to be the mess hall. When I finally reached the entrance, I walked inside to see that the entire mess hall was lit up by hundreds of small candles. Along the south side of the canopy was a long buffet table that held all the food. The rest of the tent was dotted with round tables that could each seat six people and were covered in simple white tablecloths.

At the far end of the tent, however, there was a lone rectangular table on a small, raised platform with five seats that were facing the rest of the people. Anyone could have guessed that this was where the leaders of the camp ate, and I couldn't help but notice that the seat in the middle of the table was still empty. The tall Knowing leader with light brown hair, who had been whipping Alec earlier in the day, saw me looking over and waved eagerly. I realized I would probably have to sit there whether I liked it or not.

Sighing to myself, I lazily dumped some chicken and pasta on my plate and made my way up to the leaders' table. The cruel Knowing leader from earlier quickly stood up and politely pulled out my seat for me, even though I didn't want him to. "It's good to see you, Lady Athena. We missed you at lunch," he said brightly, and I frowned. Did he really think I would just forget everything that happened that very morning? Frankly, I had thought he was smarter than that.

"I wanted to introduce you to my council," he continued. Pointing in turn to a short man dressed all in purple, a very hairy man in orange, and a blonde woman in white, he said in Greek, "That's Martin, Perseus, and Elizabeth. My name is Jason, by the way. I'm not sure we officially met earlier." I just nodded, not feeling the need or the desire to respond.

Suddenly, Jason stood up from his chair and cleared his throat before tapping his metal spoon against his wine glass to get the attention of his people. "Welcome, everyone, to our very special meal tonight. Before we eat, let us give thanks to our gods, and let us give applause for our guest, the wonderful and always wise Lady Athena." The crowds obediently erupted in applause and cheers but quieted down again when Jason continued, "Now, let us eat!" In a quick response, the members of the crowd gave a few whoops and then dug into their food.

Throughout the incredibly long meal, I couldn't help but notice that they all kept looking up at me, as if to see whether I liked the food or not. I found their stealthy glances kind of creepy, but even I had to admit that although the Knowing might have appeared cruel so far, they certainly made delicious food.

However, my whirling thoughts were interrupted by Jason when he asked, "So, my lady, how do you like our little camp?"

"It's very well organized," I said simply, not sure what else to say since I hated everything else about it at the moment. Jason only nodded eagerly, and then continued to eat his food and chat with his council. I tried to be polite and pay attention, but my mind was elsewhere. I found myself thinking of Alec, and my eyes kept drifting toward his mother, who was trying to eat, watch me, and talk to the other mothers with whom she was sitting, all at the same time.

Out of nowhere, a sharp pain stabbed my stomach, but this time it was out of guilt, not hunger. *Why am I here?* I thought. *I should be with Alec.* I gripped the table to stop my head from spinning, but then I silently cursed myself, because Alec really was fine on his own with Jan. I knew already that my heart was getting out of control, succeeding at overriding my brain with the emotions I tried so hard to ignore. *I don't love Alec, I don't like Alec, I don't trust Alec*, I tried telling myself, shaking my head back and forth, over and over again.

Eager to get out of the mess hall as quickly as possible, I finished my dinner before everyone else, not realizing I would be forced to politely wait in my seat until dinner was over. I tried to make my way back to the infirmary, but I was trapped in a sea of people, all begging for my attention. "How long are you staying? Why are you here? Can you bless my baby?" they exclaimed, and I frowned again; my head was starting to pound from all their shouting. Strangely enough, Alec's mother and Jason, who were smiling and talking in low voices just outside the mess hall, were the only people not joining in the excitement. They were far too involved with each other.

"Please, let me through. I will answer all of your questions tomorrow!" I yelled back at them.

Immediately they parted for me, not wanting to offend their beloved goddess in any way. I guessed they didn't want to risk losing an arm or something. I was beginning to realize that the Knowing were now on their best behavior because they knew how powerful I was, and although it was partly a good thing, it meant that I would probably not be able to see the full extent of the camp's corruption for myself. At least not during *this* visit.

Finally, I managed to make my way to the infirmary, where the distressed-looking nurse was standing over Alec, holding a bowl of tomato soup. I rubbed my forehead, trying to get rid of the headache, and breathed a sigh of relief when I heard the crowd outside slowly disperse. Jan just looked up at me, gratitude flooding her brown eyes, color returning to her pale face.

"He was freaking out when he woke, shouting crazy, crazy things. But now he won't eat anything, and he's still running a slight fever," she informed me hurriedly, and I reluctantly glanced over at Alec, who still had pain written across his handsome face. I couldn't help but notice that his dark jeans had fresh bloodstains on them.

I sighed as his sad blue eyes met my gray ones. "I'll handle him," I told Jan softly, taking the tomato soup from her hands and striding over to meet Alec. I carefully pulled my little hero off the cot and let him lean against me when he almost fell back down from the strain, and whispered to him, "Come on." Then I walked him outside to a spot in the grass with a clear view of the twinkling sky. I was especially careful not to touch his back because it was entirely covered with white bandages, some of which he had already bled through.

Even though we had only walked a couple of feet from the tent, Alec was tired and sweating by time we sat down. Clutching a stitch in his six-pack abs, he gasped shakily, "What made you think this was a good idea?"

I shrugged. "You needed some air." Then I glanced up at the sky, thinking of how we always sat on my roof at home after our late-night battle practices, and added, "And some stars."

When he didn't respond, I tried to feed him a spoonful of soup, but he immediately turned his head away. "Alec," I pleaded with him, "you need to eat." He looked me in the eye and frowned, but ultimately decided I was right and took the soup bowl from my hands. Or maybe he just wanted to make me feel better. It didn't really matter to me, just as long as he ate a little bit.

Very slowly, Alec worked his way through the tomato soup and stopped about halfway through, but I didn't press him to finish it. I was just glad he had eaten something to give him the energy needed to recover. Now, he just looked up at the stars and cleared his throat. "So," he started, his voice hoarse and falsely positive, "I'm sure you've already been asked this hundreds of times, but how do you like the camp?"

I sighed and thought for a moment, hugging my knees and glancing around at all the tents. "There aren't any roofs," I said bluntly, wishfully thinking of my own house, even though it was usually filled with angry shouts. It sounded like such a simple, spur-of-the-moment statement, but it meant so much more. Here at the Knowing base camp, the people thought they were so strong and safe, but really, they were just like the tents that they lived in—temporary and unstable. All of us were that way, actually, though some were obviously more stable than others. The Knowing had no idea yet that a huge war was brewing right outside their gates.

"Yeah," Alec whispered solemnly, hopefully getting what I was trying to say, "I never thought I would miss roofs so much." He ran his fingers through his hair in deep thought, and then we sat together in silence for a minute, staring at Artemis's beloved stars. Thinking of Artemis, I wondered if my good friend was preparing to hunt back at home. *Home.*

"You knew this would happen, didn't you? That you would be whipped," I accused Alec after coming to the realization quite suddenly, looking at him with sad eyes and wondering why he hadn't told me. Maybe I could have prevented it before anyone got hurt. He should have had faith in me.

Sighing, he nodded and admitted softly, "Yes, but I assumed they would give me a chance to explain first. That's what they used to do anyway . . . I guess things have changed since I left."

We returned to a state of silence, serene but sorrowful. I glanced around and realized that a couple of people kept peeking their heads out from behind tents to look at the two of us, but I tried not to let it bother me. Even though the Monster Watch had been mentioned in the newspaper several times when we were children and all of us gods were known for being exceptionally good-looking, I had never been treated like a true celebrity before, and I found it quite unnerving.

Alec was about to say something else, but I'll never know exactly what it was because just then, a little girl with a cute blonde ponytail who looked about five ran out from behind a nearby tent and jumped onto Alec's lap for a hug. I noticed Alec wince in pain as he just barely managed to give her a coherent greeting in between gasps. "Hi, Anna."

The little girl grinned and whined, "You didn't come see me earlier!"

"I was busy," Alec said with a grimace.

*Yeah, busy dying,* I thought to myself sadistically. Then an annoyed Alec looked to me to explain. "This is my little cousin." Unsure of what to say next, I simply raised my eyebrows and nodded, hoping the child would run away again.

Anna, who was still sitting on Alec's lap, squinted her big brown eyes and studied me cautiously. When she had had enough of silently scrutinizing me, she leaned over and tried to whisper in Alec's ear, but like almost all children, she actually spoke loud enough for me to hear her complete thought: "Your girlfriend is pretty." Slightly embarrassed, even though I had been complimented like this thousands of times before, I turned to hide my blush and pretend as if I hadn't heard her, but of course, Alec saw straight through my act.

"I know," Alec agreed with her, and I blushed again. "But she's not my girlfriend."

Confused, Alec's little cousin raised her eyebrows and asked him, "Well, do you want her to be your girlfriend?"

I had to put my head in my hands to try to stop myself from snorting in laughter, while Alec just blushed and looked shocked, like he didn't really know how to answer her. Anna was obviously too young to understand who I was. Alec probably didn't want to admit the truth, either.

But then I heard a gasp come from behind us, and Alec and I turned to look at what was going on. Alec's mother and another blonde woman had appeared in front of a nearby tent, and by the looks on their faces, they had obviously heard Anna ask the awkward question. The blonde woman rushed over and picked Anna up off of Alec as fast as she could. "I'm so sorry about that, Lady Athena," the woman apologized in Greek, bowing multiple times. "She's too young to understand what has happened today."

I nodded in understanding and replied with a wary smile, "I could tell; it's perfectly fine. Alec was just introducing me to Anna." Grunting, I pushed myself up off the grass and then helped Alec stand up slowly, keeping a watchful eye on his little cousin.

Anna's mother just frowned and reprimanded her child. "Don't bother Alec, honey. He's in a lot of pain. There are plenty of other people around who will play with you."

It became silent for a moment, and then meeting his gaze, Alec's mother gave a small cough to get his attention. "Oh, right," Alec said bitterly, suddenly becoming more serious. There was an edge to his voice that told me he knew exactly what his mother had been doing during his punishment.

"Lady Athena, this is my mother, Clara." Both Clara and I nodded and shook hands politely, although the image of her cheering for Alec to be whipped was still imprinted on my brain. I didn't think either Alec or I could ever forgive her for that, but of course, I didn't mention it.

"It's lovely to meet you, my lady. By the way, Jason wanted me to let you know that we have a small tent set up just for you," she said too positively for me to take her seriously. I only gave her a fake smile in return and nodded, and Clara turned back to face her son. "Are you sleeping in your usual tent?"

Alec frowned and shook his head, still leaning heavily on me for support. "I'm staying in the infirmary for a couple of days," he replied. Alec's mother just nodded solemnly, and then she patted his back softly, as if to comfort him somehow, though he still gasped in pain. My concerned eyes met his, but Alec only shook his head again, trying to tell me he was fine. Like I believed that.

Then Clara smoothed down her long dark hair and finished, "Well, good night, you two. Alec, it's good to have you back." I could feel the anger and disappointment simmering under her mask of happiness as she added pleasantly, "Oh, and welcome home."

She waved goodbye, taking Anna and Anna's mother along with her as she disappeared into the darkness, giggling something about visiting Jason again. It took me a moment to realize that Clara hadn't even asked Alec about what had happened to her husband, his father. This was the second sign of an affair I had seen, and still I said nothing to her or her son.

"This is not my home anymore" was all Alec had to say, under his breath and in response to his oblivious mother, to bring my attention back to him.

By the time I carefully laid him down on the cot, Alec was sweating like a pig again, so I grabbed the wet rag and silently brushed the hair out of his eyes before placing the rag on his forehead. "Sleep well," I told him. "Tomorrow, we tell them about the war."

"Athena, wait," he moaned softly, grabbing my hand before I could leave the tent. I couldn't help but tense up when my heartbeat started to race ahead of my brain, but it slowed down again to comprehend Alec's request. He continued, "If I make it out of this war alive, can I come with you back to the Woods? I can't stay in this hellhole any longer."

My heart broke, surprised that he even had to ask. After the whipping, I had automatically assumed that was what he wanted. "Of course," I said with a small smile. Then I gave his hand one last squeeze before I left for my own tent to get some rest. The next day was going to be a very long one.

# Chapter 16:

# A HERO AND A SPEECH

Running. I was running like a maniac through the woods. *My* woods. I would know those trees, those rocks, those leafy green ferns anywhere. But why? I did not know. I did not know, and it scared me. Because when you're the goddess of wisdom, you're supposed to know everything. Not knowing, to put it simply, was not good. Not knowing could be more dangerous than anything else in the entire world. Not knowing could get you killed. And I was not ready to be killed. I had lived through way too many monster attacks to die this early in life.

So I kept running. Running for my life—for anyone's life, really, because I had no idea what was going on. My feet had minds of their own as they raced through the forest that I knew so well, not slowing down even the tiniest bit for miles and miles.

And suddenly they stopped. My feet were now planted in the dirt, as if held to the ground by invisible superglue, and I couldn't move an inch. This was even worse than the running, but I forced myself not to panic. Instead, I took deep breaths, trying to calm down as I glanced around me.

But then my breath caught in my throat. I tried to scream out, but I could not make a sound. Because, lying at odd angles in the long grass was a girl, her wavy, shimmering, golden hair fallen around her perfect face, her expensive clothes covered in a fine layer of dust and dirt. This was the most beautiful girl in the world: Aphrodite. And she was dead.

I desperately tried to move my feet toward her, to somehow rescue the poor girl, but I could not move a single muscle. Suddenly, the world started to spin faster and faster, until all I saw and felt was blackness around me. However, the sullen, glassed-over but somehow still beautiful blue eyes of Aphrodite were still etched onto my brain, probably permanently. She did not deserve to die. I knew deep inside that I should have been in her place, for everything that I had done, for all the secrets that I had kept. Now more than ever, the part of my past no one else knew about, the arrow, was coming back to haunt me.

"*Help*," the seductive voice of Aphrodite called to me through the frigid darkness . . .

I bolted upright in a cold sweat as the blackness from my dream faded away, leaving only reality, though I still couldn't shake the vision of the dead Aphrodite from my mind. Breathing hard, I gripped the metal edges of my dark green cot, suddenly feeling homesick for more than one reason.

That couldn't have been just a dream, after all. No, it was too real. Every leaf, every rock had been right where it should have been in the forest. I knew the place like the back of my hand, every little nook and cranny. And I knew now that I had to get home. Here in the Knowing camp, I ironically had no way of knowing what was going on back in the Woods.

But, while rubbing my cold and clammy forehead, I remembered that Alec had mentioned a phone. Still, my breath came out shaky and untrustworthy as I put on some clothes and my leather boots to walk outside.

It was early in the morning, so only a few Warriors were awake. Like statues of old Greek heroes, five of them stood around the camp, fully clad in armor, staring blankly out at the air, which was thick with a sticky gray mist. It was gloomy rather than mysterious, and not silvery and beautiful like in the forest back home. Also, the tall, silent tents, completely closed, with no windows, seemed to loom above me like Hades's palace in the Underworld;

they were not friendly and welcoming like the houses and shops on Main Street.

Finding myself subconsciously comparing everything around me to the Woods, I frowned. Perhaps I was more homesick than I thought. Nevertheless, I made my way toward the main building that the Knowing camp had, which was supposed to house the phone.

This building was quiet and dark too, but the old wooden door was unlocked, and it creaked as I stepped over the threshold. On opposite sides of the common area, there were two hallways I remembered from earlier in the day—one on the right, labeled WOMEN, and one on the left, labeled MEN.

I searched down both hallways, then retraced my steps and searched the common area, which only had a black leather chair and a tangled mass of tattoo equipment in the corner. Frowning, I made my way back to the entrance to see if I had missed anything. I stood facing the quiet and sturdy door between the two hallways and was about to walk out into the cool morning air when I noticed something right by the side of the doorframe.

A few holes were left in the wall from screws that had been pulled out, and a faint brown line was stained on the wall, running in a large rectangle about the size of an old wall-mounted phone. A tiny hole revealed where the cord must have been attached. Chewing my lip, I reached out and traced the line with my finger, certain that this was where the phone had been. But why had the Knowing taken it down? From what I had seen the day before, I guessed that Jason had it removed because, as a connection to the outside world, it posed a threat to his power, which was based on the policy of isolation.

Suddenly the door creaked, and I instinctively grabbed the small knife from my pocket, narrowing my stormy eyes and shifting in place to strengthen my stance. I wasn't exactly sure who I expected to barge in, but I definitely wasn't expecting a fight, either. Just old habits, I guessed.

But then the pained face of none other than Alec stuck his head around, and his eyes brightened when they saw me. When they moved down, eyeing the open pocketknife in my hand, I quickly closed it and sheepishly looked back up at Alec. Instead, he only stared at the empty space on the white wall where the phone should have been. "It's gone," he whispered in Greek.

We must have stared together at the phone's old place for five whole minutes before I finally told him, "I have to go back."

Alec whipped his head around and narrowed his eyes. "Why?"

"Aphrodite. I think something's happened," I confessed with a sigh, and Alec shook his head, mumbling to himself as his face turned white with worry.

"I'm coming too," he proclaimed, determination burning in his deep blue eyes.

I frowned and crossed my arms. "No, I can handle this myself. I have a plan. You need to stay here and rally the troops and regain your strength."

Carefully, he placed his hands on my shoulders and looked me in the eye. "I *am* strong enough," he said, trying to convince me, but I noticed him wince just the slightest bit as he said this. After returning his hands to his sides, he continued, "And besides, these people will not listen to me."

"Yes, they will," I whispered, my gray eyes lighting up with an idea, and Alec just studied me curiously, wondering what ingenious plan I could possibly be thinking up now.

---

The entire Knowing camp was gathered at the square wooden stage, confusion in their eyes and in their voices as they gossiped among themselves, not exactly sure what was going on. Some were still yawning, trying to wake themselves up, while I stood on the stage facing them, dressed in a blue-and-white traditional Greek tunic that someone had laid out for me in my tent. After they all finally quieted down, I yelled out, "I call upon Alec of the Knowing. Come up to the stage."

There was movement in the crowd, and then Alec, looking slightly bewildered (I hadn't told him the plan), was pushed toward the stage. His shirt must have been irritating the deep wounds on his back because he was no longer wearing one, and so all of the girls were staring at his abs. Most of the men, however, stared only at the white bandages which covered his entire back and had bright red blood seeping through. Breathing hard and obviously in extreme pain, Alec still managed to climb up to the stage relatively easily. He stood up to face me in silence, his blue eyes full of questions.

"Kneel," I told him, and he obeyed, bowing his head. While he might have demanded an explanation of what was going on if we were back in the Woods, where he was also my friend, here he did not because he probably would have been punished even more for questioning a god. Alec was strong, but I was not sure that even he could withstand two whippings in two days.

I continued, "I require your sword."

Alec frowned, no longer trying to figure out what I was planning, and reluctantly pulled the small gray rock from his pocket. When he squeezed it and the long, shining blade popped out, the crowd gasped in shock. They had never seen anything like it, but then again, they hadn't met the handy Hephaestus of this generation.

Alec handed the sword to me carefully, and I gripped it with two hands, holding it so that the tip was pointing toward the ground. He was still frowning, and the dark look in his eyes told me that he thought I was making a mistake. But there was no mistake. I was always right, after all. I always had a plan.

"You don't have to do this," Alec murmured through clenched teeth, so no one else would hear.

"Yes, Alec, I do. You've earned the title of hero, and the Knowing will just have to deal with it."

But Alec continued to argue under his breath. "Athena, you can't force me to help them learn how to fight properly. They don't deserve my help. Trust me when I tell you they are not the good guys."

"Maybe not," I agreed quietly, looking him in the eye. "You can just think of it as keeping your friends close, but your enemies closer. You *are* the one who said the Knowing needed to be fixed in the first place."

At this, Alec finally nodded in agreement and lowered his head once more so the ceremony could begin. Smirking, I took a deep breath and began in a raised voice, "Do you, Alec, swear to do no harm to the innocent, and to punish the guilty only in a fair manner?"

"I do," he said firmly, trying to keep his voice from shaking.

"Do you, Alec, swear to uphold the honor code of a Geek hero and to never turn a blind eye on someone in need unless otherwise justified?"

"I do."

"Do you, Alec, swear to educate and train your people in the ways of the Greeks, but protect the secret of the myths against outsiders?"

"I do."

And finally the last question, but perhaps the most difficult to answer: "And do you, Alec, swear to obey and protect your Greek gods in every way possible, even if the sacrifice is the life of a loved one or your own?"

"I do," he growled fiercely and without the slightest hesitation, like the Nemean lion, his blue eyes gleaming. I knew my little hero was not afraid of anything in that moment.

I smiled proudly to myself, flipping the sword around in my hands casually, as if it were only a pencil, and the crowd watched me in stunned silence. I think they were shocked I was naming Alec a hero, but then again, they didn't even know half of the things he had done. So I flipped the sword around one last time and swiftly brought it down in a stabbing motion as the Knowing crowd gasped, sure I was about to accidentally kill Alec. You would have thought they had a little more faith in their own goddess of wisdom and war.

Finally the sword slammed into the stage, and the tip stuck right in the thin line where two wood panels met, just over an inch in front of Alec but exactly where I had been aiming. And my little hero didn't even flinch. I supposed you could say he passed the final test.

As the crowd let out a collective sigh of relief, I grinned again, and Alec looked up to meet my gaze. I yanked the blade back out of the stage and carefully placed the flat edge of the shining sword on Alec's left shoulder for a second, then moved it to the right as I finished the ceremony.

"Then I, Athena, your patron goddess of wisdom, war, and skill, name you, Alec, the first official hero of Mount Olympus of the twenty-first century," I finished with a triumphant shout, and the crowd erupted in a tremendous cheer. I smiled, even though I knew most of them were probably cheering for me more than Alec, as he was still a traitor in some of their cold eyes.

I handed the sword back to Alec, and he let out a deep breath, turning to give the crowd a short nod of gratitude. The two of us stood up there for a couple of minutes, anxiously waiting for the rest of the Knowing to stop clapping so we could move on with our day. However, I couldn't help but notice that a group of tough-looking teenage boys at the back of the crowd was glaring at Alec, not even bothering to applaud with the rest of the crowd. I would have to mention it to Alec later to see what that was all about.

---

It was finally time for breakfast, so the entire camp headed into the mess hall, where we received our food. I would have sat down with Alec, but I thought it was still best to eat at the table with the rest of the Knowing camp leaders, so I had to watch wistfully as Alec sat down by himself at an empty white table. You might have thought that he would be super popular now that he was an official hero, but all of the teens kept shooting him dirty looks full of jealousy, and, as usual, the adults and small children stuck to each other like glue.

Alec had just started to dig into his scrambled eggs after the Knowing had said a prayer to the gods when the same group of guys who had been glaring at Alec during his hero ceremony came up behind him. They were laughing, but the grins on their tanned, oily faces were not friendly. Their eyes were filled with a cloud of anger, and their movements were cold and calculated—the look that Ares always wore when he was hungry for blood and revenge.

I frowned and gulped nervously as the four of them slapped Alec on the back in what might appear to be congratulations. Alec clenched the silver fork he was holding with a white-knuckle grip as he tried to hide the pain when the first boy's hand collided with his ripped skin. Three more boys followed the first, each slapping Alec on the back right where his wounds were, and I could see the anger flaring up in Alec's blue eyes as he struggled to control himself. I sighed in relief only when the boys sat down at another table, laughing up a storm and finally leaving Alec alone.

But it wasn't over yet.

Another group of younger boys saw what the first group had done, and they too stood up and started making their way toward Alec. I knew that this would be Alec's breaking point, but I still held my breath, hoping he wouldn't do anything to wreck his new image. At the same time, I wasn't planning on intervening; I knew this was his fight.

Before the other boys could reach him, however, Alec saw them and stood up, looking them right in the eye and daring them to make another move. All eyes in the mess hall swiveled toward him. The boys immediately halted, and Alec said something else to them, but he was all the way on the other side of the mess hall, so I couldn't hear what was said. Then he turned and met my gaze, and I nodded to him, giving him permission to leave before anyone else could bother him. He bowed one last time and left the mess hall in a rush.

Of course, I had to be sociable, so I reluctantly stayed and finished my breakfast along with everyone else. I was about to leave and go find Alec when Jason pulled me aside. "My lady," he began with a slight bow, "not that I don't respect your judgment, but why did you make Alec a hero? He's just so . . . young. And you of all people would know that most of the other famous heroes were more than ten years older than he is now."

"You will understand my choice soon enough. But what *I* want to know is why your only emergency phone was taken down," I replied with a frown, annoyed that he questioned my authority. After all, I knew Jason's real problem with Alec was *not* the hero's abnormally young age, though his ceremony was indeed a step in the right direction toward terminating the policy of having to be sixteen to start battle training, the policy that had left Alec completely defenseless on the eve of his quest to find the gods.

Jason gulped guiltily, and his brown eyes looked to the floor. This was obviously something he didn't want to talk about. "It was being . . . misused," he lied. I was starting to get a feel for how corrupt this base camp really was. It seemed to me that the leaders—Jason in particular—destroyed or punished anything or anyone who might be a threat to their power.

"If you're smart, you won't lie to me again," I hissed. "Now, I am planning to leave here tonight, but first, I must make an announcement. And I would reinstall that phone if I were you. It will probably save some lives," I told him mysteriously, leaving half of the story out. He looked at me quizzically, but I only turned around and left the mess hall, annoyed.

I sighed as I stepped out from the mess hall and into the bright sunlight, but my thoughts of corruption were interrupted by loud cheers coming from behind a large blue tent. Naturally, I went to investigate.

When I arrived on the scene, a large circle of people were standing and cheering, blocking my view of whatever was happening in the center, with evil grins on their faces. I quickly pushed my way through to the front and found Alec, dressed in full, poorly fitting armor, holding his sword, ready to attack. The boy he faced was the same age, the blond who had been the first to slap him on the back in the mess hall during breakfast.

"What's going on here?" I asked an average-looking boy with brown hair standing nearby, and even more people started to gather around the fight. It appeared as if the whole camp wanted to watch.

"Brady challenged Alec to a fight," he said, pointing to the blond boy, "and Alec accepted."

I frowned in thought, deciding not to intervene, even though I knew it was a bad idea for Alec to be fighting with the unhealed wounds on his back. Although I generally believed that people should battle only if absolutely necessary, this was an exception. All around the camp, I could tell that people did not think Alec was worthy of being a hero, so this was Alec's chance to assert himself as the alpha male and to prove them wrong.

The crowd gasped as Brady lunged at Alec, but Alec easily blocked his sword and swung back. They went back and forth, back and forth, blocking each other's swings, each one failing to get a clean hit on the other. Most of the crowd was enthusiastically chanting "Brady! Brady!" over the sound of clanging metal, and I shook my head, disgusted. I knew Alec was hurt, but I also knew he could fight way better than that. He was a hero, for crying out loud, and Brady was leaving big, gaping holes in his defense. Hence, I guessed that Brady had just started his battle training.

"Alec," I said, getting the hero's attention for a second. He paused and glanced over at me, beads of sweat just starting to slide down his brow. "What the hell are you doing?" I asked him with a small frown. He raised his eyebrows in a rare moment of confusion, and I snapped my fingers at him. "Hello? Fight, you idiot."

He grinned at me, then lunged like a lion at Brady with renewed strength, catching him off guard. Swing after swing hit Brady directly in the side, on a thick part of the armor, since Alec didn't really want to hurt Brady too badly.

Alec swung again and stabbed Brady square in the breastplate, and this time Brady fell back into the grass with a thump. For a second no one moved as Alec triumphantly held his sword at Brady's neck, a small smirk on the hero's handsome face. The entire crowd, except for me, wore expressions of shock during the moment of silence.

But then, enraged battle cries sounded throughout the mass of people as all three of Brady's friends jumped into the crowded circle, swords at the ready. Alec's jaw dropped in wonderment along with the rest of the crowd's, and he glanced back at me again for permission to take them out. I just nodded at him impatiently; I knew he could take all three of them down in a matter of minutes. And besides, I could tell from looking at the others' weak stances that they, like Brady, hadn't had too much training.

Alec waited for the first boy, a chubby one, to lunge and he easily blocked the swing of his sword, then whirled around to parry the stab of a tall skinny boy. Breathing hard, Brady got up and stood next to Chubby, the two of them waiting for their turn to strike again. But Brady's third friend, a scrawny little fellow, ran at Alec like a bull. For this, Alec didn't even bother to swing his sword; instead, he just used his foot to kick Scrawny to the ground. After all, the very best warriors can use their own strengths and surroundings as weapons.

I snorted at the poor brown-haired boy as he fell, but then looked up to see Jason, who was standing just inches behind Clara, so close that his breath must have been blowing through her hair and rolling down her neck. If she even noticed, Clara didn't seem to mind at all. Watching Alec with a sudden great interest, he scratched the tiny brown goatee on his chin in thought as Alec continued to fight, and I smiled to myself; Jason was finally paying attention to someone besides himself and the rest of his council.

Alec blocked and lunged at both Brady and Chubby as the two attacked at the same time, and was knocked off balance. This only seemed to anger Alec, and he got up, seeming to forget his pains and attacking with even more rage but also with strategy. Again and again, the four boys attacked Alec and failed to make a mark. Alec knocked Scrawny to the ground yet again, but this time much harder than before, and Scrawny looked around in a daze, as if he had a mild concussion.

One by one, the other boys fell—Chubby, then Tall Skinny, and finally Brady again. The four boys sat on the lush green grass, panting as they stared up at Alec in surprise and pain. Alec just straightened up and twirled his sword around in one hand like it was almost weightless, and then he challenged, "Does anyone else want to fight me?" The crowd said nothing, their eyes wide in shock, including those of Jason. Satisfied, Alec squeezed the hilt of the sword and it retracted, forming itself into the small gray rock once again.

I stepped up beside Alec, checking my watch. "Four minutes and twenty-nine seconds," I told him, frowning in mock disapproval. "I could have done it in less than two. Needs work."

Alec rolled his eyes, but then he bowed because he had to, here in front of his elders. "With all due respect, Lady Athena," he began in an equally mocking tone, pausing while he tore off his borrowed armor, followed by his shirt. The girls in the crowd behind him giggled, and the boys just snorted. "This needs work too," he finished, motioning to the bloody bandages on his back. I just grinned playfully and pushed him along toward the purple infirmary tent.

The rest of the crowd watched with great interest as I turned back to acknowledge them. "If any more of you have problems with my hero, you will take it up with me from now on. As you can see, Alec is quite capable of beating all of you," I announced, raising my voice, and they all nodded quickly and dispersed. Even Jason shot me a small look of approval as he ran he fingers through his light brown hair, and so I took a deep breath of relief; they finally understood and respected my choice, at least somewhat.

---

The crowd whispered in confusion. I guessed making two important announcements in one day was unusual, but hey, so was I. I paced the wooden stage, waiting for the Knowing to quiet down so I could speak to them, and glanced at Alec, who was standing on the stage next to me and actually wearing a shirt again.

When the crowd quieted, Alec nodded, showing me that he was ready to start, and I took a deep breath before announcing, "I know you all have been wondering why Alec and I are here." Grumbles of agreement passed through the crowd, and I continued over them, "Well, I'm sorry to say that it's not a happy visit. I apologize for calling upon you so suddenly, but there is a war about to start, and, unfortunately, the Olympian Council cannot fight Hades and all of the monsters in the world alone."

Horrified gasps sounded from all around me, which was not unexpected. Some people even started to whimper and cry, but I could not stop now. These people had to be warned, even if I didn't like them very much.

"Yes, that's right, we need reinforcements. So we need you. All of you, whether you are defending the base camp or my own home, the Woods." I paused, letting this information sink in a little more. "Alec and I will give you more details later on, but I also need to tell you that I am leaving tonight," I stated, and even more people started to cry. Alec and I only exchanged shocked expressions, wondering what was wrong with them. Crying wasn't going to help anything. It never did.

Someone lost in the crowd called out to me, asking why I had to leave the camp defenseless. I sighed, but eventually admitted, "I had a vision, and all I'm going to say on the matter is that the rest of the gods are in great danger. You'll just have to trust me. In the meantime, I am leaving Alec here to train and organize the troops. I can personally assure you and I think that by now you too have all seen that Alec is quite capable of doing this. I hope that he and the troops will meet the Olympian Council at the camp by Pan's hideout within two weeks. Don't worry; Alec will lead you there safely."

After I motioned to Alec, he cleared his throat and began, "I know many of you still distrust me because I left, but you have to understand that I did it for the gods, and that I really did have a vision." Alec paused, and I heard a few exasperated groans from the crowd. He looked back at me, so I gave him an encouraging nod. "I don't care whether or not you believe me, but you all must get past our differences so we can fight together to save the world! I don't know about you, but I do *not* want to die." At this, the crowd cheered like crazy, and I smiled with Alec, giving a sigh of relief that he was finally gaining the respect he deserved.

When the Knowing quieted down a little, Alec finished, "We must get to work right away. Lady Athena and I will inspect and critique your form before she has to leave."

When he took a deep breath and stepped back, the crowd started to talk again and disperse, but I quickly stopped them with the raw power of my voice. These people would do anything for me, and yet they did not even know me. I would never fully understand that.

Then again, I had also seen what they were like before they knew I was a goddess. So maybe their dedication too was just an act.

"One last thing," I told them. "I'm not going to lie; this will not be easy. Many of you will die, but I can assure you that it will be for the greatest cause you could ever fight: to protect the world. I know your numbers are not many, so I am begging all boys and men over the age of twelve to train for battle. As of this moment, the age restriction on battle training has been abolished."

I paused to let the whoops of excitement from the teens die down before adding, "I know this goes against the ancient Greek custom, but I am also inviting women to fight—only if you really want to, of course. Remember that we also need nurses and medics. And thank you. That will be all," I said, sighing as I turned away from the petrified Knowing faces.

"Well, you just blew my speech off the map," Alec sputtered, wiping the sweat off his brow.

I just smiled, giving him a sympathetic pat on the shoulder, and together we walked toward the battle-training center. We had a whole lot of work to do.

## Chapter 17:

# A GOODBYE PARTY?

I walked with Alec, following the Knowing leader, Jason, toward the training area at the other end of the large encampment. I paused, tightened my side ponytail, and cast Alec a curious glance. "So who were those guys who attacked you earlier?" I asked him, wanting to find out more about the crazy people with whom he used to live.

Alec sighed, staring at the long green grass under his shoes as we walked slowly along. "Enemies," he answered vaguely, chewing his lip and avoiding my gaze. "I seem to have made a lot of those." He sighed again and kicked a tiny rock, sending it flying forward.

I snapped my fingers in front of his face to get him to look at me with his deep blue eyes. "Winston Churchill once said that having enemies is good. It means you've stood up for something, sometime in your life." Alec looked up at me with a new respect, wonderment in his eyes. I just shrugged. "It's one of my favorite quotes."

"It's the best I've heard. Although I don't have any other friends who are insufferable know-it-alls with smart quotes for every occasion," Alec said with a smirk, turning to look out at the hazy horizon, but his attention returned when we reached the training area.

"Hey! If I'm so insufferable, why do you hang out with me?" I stuck my tongue out at him. "And you don't even have any other friends besides the gods!"

"Ouch. That hurt," Alec said, though he brightened up and added with a wink, "but it's so true."

I just looked forward at the training area. In front of us was a large sword-fighting arena with marble and stone stands built into the hillside, like the ancient Greek theaters. On one side of the arena was an archery range, and on the other was a large barnlike shed, which I assumed was the armory, but I didn't get the chance to ask because Jason clapped loudly and began to shout to his people.

"All right, everybody put on your armor and grab your weapons. Then we'll have all the sword fighters split into groups. Archers, just go to the archery range and start shooting," he ordered in his most commanding voice, which was really just a whimper when compared to Zeus's, and his people immediately responded.

In a huge wave, they surged toward the brown shed, confirming my suspicion that it was indeed the armory. When most of the people had pushed their way back out, they began to split into groups. To give the sword fighters a chance to regroup, Alec and I made our way over to the archers, who were already in a line, shooting at colorful targets set up about seventy feet away.

There were only about ten archers, though, many fewer than I would have liked. But I didn't complain. Instead, I sat on a wooden bench facing the archery range as the archers—eight grown men, one younger boy, and a girl—picked up arrows one by one and sent them flying through the air toward the circular targets.

Nervously, every single one of them would turn around after they shot, as if looking for a sign of my approval. I could tell that my presence distracted them, because almost every one of them actually hit the target only one out of five times. I sighed, and Alec dropped his shoulders in defeat, obviously noticing the same thing I had, and assured me they didn't usually shoot so badly. I knew if they kept shooting that badly, however, our side of the war would be in serious trouble.

I grunted and got up off the bench, thinking that these people needed a serious pep talk, so I clapped my hands together to get their attention. "Okay," I said with a long sigh, a little louder and more intimidating than I meant to be, and they dropped their weapons in frustration. "I can tell you are nervous with me here, but I also know you can shoot a lot straighter than you are shooting right now. And I'm sorry to say that this isn't going to cut it." I paused and watched the archers as they shifted and squirmed under my powerful gaze. "So either pull yourselves together or die. Your choice."

The ten archers muttered among themselves and reluctantly returned to their stances, aiming their arrows at the targets once again. I motioned for Alec to follow me, and together we stopped by each archer in turn, trying to give them pointers. I'll admit that I wasn't nearly as good as Artemis or Apollo, who managed to hit the bull's-eye almost every single time, but they had given both Alec and me a couple of lessons before we had left the Woods in case we came across a situation like this. I caught Alec's eye once again, and we couldn't help but smile in remembrance of our battle with the Stymphalian birds.

First, we started with the older men, who seemed to have things under control after I gave them the motivational talk. Each one of them had hit the bull's-eye at least three times when I had finished, and I quickly picked out the best archer of the group, a blond man who looked to be around age thirty. Next, I moved on to work with my two younger students. They stopped shooting and lowered their weapons when Alec and I walked over and turned to study their targets, and I smiled, raising my eyebrows at their results.

The boy with dark hair and brown eyes, who looked about twelve, had eight arrows stuck in the bull's-eye ring on the target—just as many as any of the older men had. The freckled girl, who looked about fourteen, only about a year younger than Alec and I, and who had her sleek black hair tied up in a ponytail, had also done much better than I expected. Her target had a respectable five arrows in the red bull's-eye, and I nodded to the two of them, showing that I was impressed.

The girl and the boy, who I thought looked similar enough to be siblings, exchanged relieved glances once they saw my amused expression, then they looked back up to me. "How long have you two been shooting?" I asked them.

"About two years," the boy with dark hair answered. "But we had to train in secret, especially since we aren't even of training age. Our dad got us started early. He's over there at the end of the line."

"Actually, all of the archers had to train in secret at one point or another," the girl added.

I nodded, and Alec muttered bluntly, "Sounds familiar." I sighed, rubbing my forehead, still not understanding why the Knowing would forbid archery training, let alone why they would place an age limit on battle training, so I asked the two about it. Surprisingly, they weren't sure, but Alec was ready with the answer. "The Knowing chooses to believe Ares," he said with obvious disgust. "That all archers are cowards because they don't do hand-to-hand combat."

"Then the Knowing obviously needs to update their views on such matters," I said, remembering how Ares would always tease Artemis and Apollo about that, until one day in the forest Artemis had knocked Ares out cold by hitting him square on the back of his thick head with her bow. It had served him right, in my opinion.

I smirked at the memory, and Alec only whispered to me harshly, "No, the Knowing need to update their views on *a lot* of matters."

Ignoring him for the moment, I turned back to the boy and girl. "What are your names?" I asked them politely, eager to get to know more of the Knowing people, specifically the younger ones with the brightest futures.

"I'm Hannah, and this is Ben," the girl answered with alacrity, gesturing to the boy next to her. "It's an honor to meet you, Lady Athena."

I nodded and told them seriously, "Well, thank you for volunteering to fight. I think that is very brave of you, no matter what anyone else says."

Hannah and Ben blushed sweetly, and I found it hard to believe that Alec and I were just a little older than the two of them. They seemed so much younger and more innocent than we were, although I supposed they hadn't seen nearly as much death and destruction as we had, or faced as many of their fears. Based on what Alec had told me about the Knowing's murky past, I doubted these two had ever even been outside of the base camp before.

Frowning, I tried to rack my brain to remember the fears I had, but strangely enough, I couldn't think of any. Did my human part, Ashley, have any fears? I wasn't even sure anymore. I supposed my biggest fear would have been the death of my friends, the gods, but I wasn't worried about it; I knew they could handle themselves better than anyone else in the world. After facing so many horrific monsters, I guessed the rest of the gods and I had become sort of immune to fear and its side effects. Maybe that was why we felt and acted so much older. After all, wisdom does not just come with age, but also with the things you have seen.

Then again, maybe that was just part of being a god.

I shook my head to clear my thoughts, but Jason's booming voice cut through the air. "Hurry up! Let's get to work, sword fighters!" he yelled from behind Alec and me, somewhere near the arena. I took this as a sign that it was time for Alec and me to leave the archers to practice on their own for a while and give the sword fighters some tips. I looked over to Alec questioningly and he nodded in agreement, starting to lead me toward the arena. I smiled; somehow we always knew what each other was thinking.

The sword fighters in the arena stood in two groups, which I hoped were based on skill level because there were so many different-sized men clad in Grecian armor, holding shiny swords and spears of various lengths and weights. The bigger, well-muscled ones had tattoos of monsters crawling or slithering like snakes up their tanned arms and torsos, and I tried to hide my frown; I'll admit that I thought having one or two tattoos was cool, but having too many was just gross.

Tightening my ponytail before getting to work, I suggested to Alec, "You take one group, and I'll take the other." He nodded and peeled off, heading toward the smaller group on the left.

Sighing, I strode slowly toward the larger group. I assumed it was the group of more experienced members because the men were slightly older and more buff. They all turned to face me immediately, their gleaming eyes studying me carefully—maybe a little too carefully. Smiling self-consciously, I told them, "Okay, I'm assuming you all know how to fight pretty well, so I'm going to pair everyone up, and you can all practice sparring." They nodded stiffly, and I walked around the group slowly, pairing people up no matter their size. The most able hero could win any fight.

"Remember not to actually hurt your partner," I said clearly, and a few reluctant grumbles passed through the group but quickly died out. The feistiest of the men lunged at their sparring partners before I could even finish my instructions, and soon the sound of clanging metal drowned out the sound of my powerful voice. I made my way to each pair of fighters, yelling tips at them over the background noise. They all obeyed my commands beautifully, and by the end of the fights, they looked almost half as good as Alec.

Thinking of Alec, I paused as the Warriors regrouped with new partners and glanced over toward the other group of younger Warriors. They too were paired up, but they were just practicing the most basic stabs and parries, as most of these Knowing members had not had any training because they were still too young, according to their society's outdated standards. Meanwhile, Alec wandered about between the smaller men and teens, trying to avoid being hit by the occasional swing-and-miss at the same time as shouting orders. Surprisingly, I even saw Brady and his crew, the ones who had fought Alec earlier, obeying the hero with a newfound respect.

Nodding in approval at no one in particular, I returned to inspect the fighting of my own group of Warriors. I continued to give them pointers throughout the sweltering afternoon, and slowly the men improved. Every once in a while, I would take a look back toward the archery range, where it appeared as if they had also listened very well to my advice, since each target was empty of arrows except for large clusters in the red bull's-eyes. Smiling out of pride, I sat down to watch the Warriors as they finally finished their training for the day with basic group formations. When I decided they looked good enough, I let them leave to shower before dinner.

Then I looked for Alec, who was nowhere to be seen, although I knew that his group's practice had ended a bit earlier. Sighing, I made my way back over to the tents to clean myself up, but a huge monster of a man—literally, he was one of those guys with tattoos of monsters covering his entire torso—stopped in front of me.

I craned my neck upward to look him in the eye instead of straight at the giant purple and green Hydra on his bare chest. I couldn't help but notice that the way the man's chest moved with every breath made it look as if the Hydra were real, and brought back fond memories of the Monster Watch's early days roaming about the forest.

"Yes?" I asked him politely. "Can I help you with something?"

He cleared his throat and, in perhaps the deepest voice I had ever heard besides that of an angry god, said, "I am Nicholas." He stopped abruptly, as if waiting for me to say something even though I had absolutely no idea why he was there in front of me. I simply raised my eyebrows, peeling my eyes away from the Hydra again, and he continued, "Jason wanted me to tell you that he is preparing a goodbye party for you."

"A party?" I clarified, thinking how stupid and irrelevant a party would be at a time of war like this. But then again, maybe it was a good distraction, a good excuse to lighten the mood of the worried Knowing people. It's a well-known fact that the ancient Greeks loved to party.

"What kind of party?" I mused, narrowing my eyes at him.

The brutish man named Nicholas scratched his head stiffly. "A regular party? You know, with dancing and music and food. You know?" he said awkwardly, not sure how to explain any further. "It's going to be after dinner, just outside the mess hall, by the stage," he finished quickly and gave me a bow, then headed off toward the mess hall tent. I followed him with an exasperated sigh.

---

Dinner passed slowly. As usual, I sat at the front table with Jason and his council members, and Alec sat alone at a small, round table below. I tried to make eye contact because we hadn't even really seen each other or been able to talk in private since before lunch, but he was too involved in scarfing down every last bit of chili that was in his bowl. Slightly annoyed, I turned back to the conversation I was having with Jason, but it was nowhere near as interesting as my usual conversations with the Monster Watch and the rest of the gods.

One by one, people left the mess hall to gather at the party outside the canopy. The sound system screeched as someone tried to adjust the volume and start playing some music. Jason, who was sitting next to me, turned and whispered in my ear, "The nurse, Jan, has prepared a dress for you. It is in your tent. The tunic you wore earlier has also been cleaned." He gave me a short nod before heading outside with his council members, leaving me alone in the mess hall with my thoughts.

*A dress? Seriously? Nicholas hadn't told me it was a* formal *party!* I thought in disgust, pushing myself up out of the chair and whining to myself.

After all, the only reason people dressed up was to show up everyone else and to look as important as possible, when, in reality, the people who actually *were* important would dress pretty much the same whether it was a formal party or not, because they had to look good to earn the respect of everybody else anyway. Take the president and first lady, for example, or even some of the gods, specifically Aphrodite. But really, the gods didn't need to dress up to convey their power; their stances and attitudes were more than enough.

*Screw it,* I thought silently to myself, deciding that I was not going to go to the party in a dress. I was feeling too lazy to change, and the Knowing couldn't exactly punish me if I didn't obey their stupid, outdated, unjustified rules.

I walked outside into the warm, cloudless night lit up by the bright moon and stars to find a mass of people both young and old crowded around the small wooden stage, and music blaring from the black speakers set up there. A long snack table was set up along one of the sides of the mess hall, where some adolescents were clustered in tiny groups, appearing too nervous to ask each other for a dance. The youngest children were playing a game of some sort while running in circles, and the older teens were in their usual groups, dancing the night away and singing along to the song quite obnoxiously. Adults were either dancing slowly in pairs or sitting in folding chairs on the sidelines, supervising their children. I was the only female in the vicinity not wearing a dress, and all the males were just wearing jeans and nice collared shirts.

Sighing, I decided that the safest option for avoiding having to dance with someone was to head for the snack table (after all, that is the whole point of having snack tables at parties), even though I had just finished dinner. Jan, who was watching over the snacks, was about to hand me a glass of alarmingly bright red punch when another hand slapped mine away from the cup. I didn't have to turn around to know it was Alec; he was the only Sighted person I knew who was daring enough to do something of that nature to a god or goddess.

"Dude, just let me have some punch," I told him, shaking my head.

He grinned at me, his eyes shining with mischief. "I figured you would ignore the dress code," Alec said while inspecting my skinny jeans, cropped white tank top and black leather combat boots. To be honest, I probably looked more like a cute biker chick ready to hit the road than a party girl ready to dance. But then again, I noticed that Alec's old blue T-shirt had a few noticeable bloodstains, so he was in the same boat as me. We made quite the pair.

I shrugged, since he wasn't wearing a collared shirt like the rest of the boys, and answered, "I'm allergic to dresses." Alec only snorted, looking unsurprised. "So how was your set of Warriors?" I asked him.

He returned my shrug. "Fine. Some are pretty scared, of course. Mostly the younger ones."

I nodded, because that was to be expected. "And yours?" Alec asked in turn.

"Fine," I agreed, glancing to my left, where Nicholas stood talking with a few women, his muscles ready to rip open his tight red polo shirt. "Some of those guys are huge."

Alec grinned knowingly, but then his expression became slightly more serious. "Speaking of Warriors, I was thinking we should take the archer Hannah with us in the first group going back to the Woods. Artemis probably would like her," he suggested.

"Are you kidding me? Hannah's female and an archer. Artemis would *definitely* like her," I responded with a grin, leaning on the snack table. "Smart plan."

Alec shrugged nonchalantly but agreed with a wink, "I learned from the best. Plus, everyone knows Artemis hates guys."

"Well, she tolerates you," I pointed out as I watched him down a cup full of punch in only one gulp. "I think she was actually warming up to the idea of the A Team."

"Only because you accepted me as a friend first," he argued playfully.

"I accepted you as a friend *reluctantly*," I reminded him, crossing my arms. "Remember? I still think you're dangerous. Even more dangerous than before, actually."

"Athena, you have no one but yourself to blame for that." He laughed heartily and ate a couple potato chips before brushing off his hands. Knowing that what he said was absolutely true, I sighed forlornly as I reached for a glass of fruit punch again. But again, I was denied.

Alec caught my hand in mid-reach and smirked. "Come on, let's dance. This is my favorite song." And when Jan shot Alec a stern glance from behind the table, he quickly added, "My lady."

My eyes widened in shock as he started pulling me toward the crowded dance area on the grass. "I don't know how to dance!" I protested, trying weakly to pull away.

Dancing was one of those things that made me feel awkward no matter what. Maybe it was just the compromising positions. I would have rather fought a monster, no offense to Alec. Not even Zeus could get me to dance with him at our eighth-grade graduation dance.

Alec's handsome smile just grew bigger. "Liar," he accused me, shouting over the blaring music. "You know everything!"

My face was probably tomato red from blushing as Alec pulled me in closer, placing his hands softly on my hips. I reluctantly laced my hands around his warm neck, and he blushed as well. We slowly swayed to the music, although I wasn't really paying attention to the song, and I wouldn't really call it "dancing" because we only took a couple of lazy, half-hearted steps throughout the whole thing. Honestly, we probably looked like idiots just swaying there in the middle of a huge mass of people, but even as a few of them shot us dirty looks, I couldn't say that I really cared what they thought about us at that moment.

I tried to focus on something other than his hands on my hips to keep myself from completely losing my mind, but I only felt my heartbeat flutter more as we continued to talk. I knew I wasn't supposed to be doing this with him, feeling this way about him (I wasn't even sure what that "way" was yet), though there was really nothing I could do. And I absolutely hated not being able to do something about it, hated it more than anything else in the world. I just had to prevent it from happening as much as I could, although slow dancing with Alec was not a good start . . .

Then again, when did dancing—well, swaying in place—ever hurt anyone? For that one night, I didn't want to believe in the rules of being a goddess. For that one night, I wanted to feel young and dumb and thus rebel against the order I had followed for so long. But only for that night.

He gave me a small smile as we continued to turn in place, even though some fast-paced song was playing over the speakers now. "Why are you doing this?" I whispered to him, though I wasn't completely sure I wanted to know the answer.

"Because . . ." Alec's voice trailed off as his gaze dropped to the long grass. I looked at him expectantly, and he finally admitted with a confused and exasperated sigh, "Because I—I think I love you."

If hearts could shatter to pieces but continue beating, that's what mine did. I closed my eyes and let out a shaky breath, because this was exactly what I had been afraid of. Hearing the words come out of his mouth now only made them seem more powerful, and I didn't understand why he acted upon those feelings—rarely, yes—but he shouldn't have been acting upon them at all, and he *knew* that. Alec fell in love with me even though he knew better than anyone that he couldn't have me, a virgin goddess.

*But why?* I thought to myself. *Maybe it wasn't really him. Maybe it was a trick. It had to be a trick, right?* There was an explanation for everything, and I was determined to find out what it was.

"No, you can't . . . me? No. Wait, did Aphrodite put you up to this?" I muttered angrily. "Because I will *kill* her."

Alec interrupted me, shaking his head and running his fingers through his dark hair. "It wasn't Aphrodite. I swear. I don't know why this happened. It just did, okay?"

Dubiously, I looked into his deep eyes, but I could tell he was telling the truth. We were confused, hurt, and angry—with each other as well as our individual selves—but unfortunately for both of us, there was nothing we could do about it. "Let's just forget about it. Who cares, anyway?" he said with a surprisingly positive smile. Slightly confused, I plastered a grin on my face and rolled my eyes as he spun me around, keeping time with the thunderous music. Alec's ability to leave all of his feelings behind in the blink of an eye amazed me; he was better at it than some of the gods—much better than the jealous Hera, anyway.

---

My mind wandered for the rest of the evening, distracted by the lingering thought that I should have left the camp already, that I could leave Alec behind to let us dwell on his confession separately and alone. I had no idea what was going on back in the Woods, but after my dream of the dead Aphrodite, I knew that it could not be very good at all. I also couldn't help but wonder if there was a specific reason why Aphrodite was the target, and not some other god.

Trying (and failing) to forget our worries, Alec and I were laughing at a dumb joke when I heard a small cough coming from somewhere behind me. It was Jason, trying to get my attention. I felt Alec protectively tighten his grip on me, but Jason did not seem to notice, as his green eyes bore solely into my stormy gray ones. "Excuse me, my lady," he began, bowing his head and studying me suspiciously. Maybe I looked like I was having *too* much of a good time with Alec. Oh well. "Can I talk to you in private for a moment?" he asked, though I could tell this was more of an order than a request. I nodded with a sigh as Alec reluctantly let go of me, and the warmth of his arms around mine suddenly vanished.

Remembering that he was supposed to be polite and submissive around me, Alec quickly said, "Thank you for accepting my request for a dance, Lady Athena. It was an honor."

Playing along, I returned Alec's wary smile, and he bowed to me while simultaneously keeping one watchful eye on Jason. Once Alec had returned to the snack table, out of earshot, Jason swiveled his head to face me. "How do you like your party?" he asked me politely over the loud music, though I was pretty sure he knew I hadn't talked to anyone else there besides Alec.

"This is great," I lied, when in truth, it totally sucked. I didn't even know these strange Knowing people, and they definitely didn't know me as well as they thought they did.

"But something tells me there's another reason you came over to talk to me."

"I just wanted to say that I now fully understand your decision to make Alec a hero," Jason started, and I had to stop myself from rolling my eyes at him. All he knew was that Alec could fight; he wasn't there when Alec walked straight to Hades with his head held high or trained for hours on end in the middle of the night, and he definitely wasn't there when Alec went on his journey all the way to Washington to find the gods.

"But unfortunately, some others here are concerned, so I came over to inform you that Alec . . . well, he was always extremely smart, but before he left to find you, he became very rebellious. Ignoring the rules and fighting with other boys, like Brady, for example." Jason paused and studied me for a moment. "Are you all right? You look troubled."

*Yeah, troubled by you,* I thought, but of course, that would have been a very rude thing to say to him out loud. Frowning while thinking about the way the other boys had bullied Alec after his hero ceremony that morning, I demanded, "Did anyone here ever stop to think that maybe Alec *wasn't* the instigator of those fights? Because it seems to me that everyone here is determined to tarnish his record." I paused, and Jason just gulped nervously, knowing he had angered me. "Unlike you people, I don't care about his bad reputation—only what he does to fix it. And in my book, becoming a hero at such a young age pretty much fixes it."

Jason bowed his head under my steely glare and apologized. "I am truly sorry."

"Do I look like I care?" I snarled, but I was suddenly interrupted when my head started spinning out of control. Even though I had been standing firmly in place, I stumbled and tried to regain my balance in vain. My vision blurred while the piercing screams of dozens of people echoed through my brain, but somehow I knew that the mysterious phenomenon was occurring only to me. I winced and rubbed my forehead, trying to get rid of the terrible screams, though I was unsuccessful and fell to my knees hyperventilating. Determined to hold onto reality, I clenched my fists and held on to a few blades of the long grass with a white-knuckled grip.

From somewhere behind me, I heard Alec's worried voice yell, "Athena!" And I was certain he was racing over to my aid, but a sudden chill overcame me, and I started to shake uncontrollably, like a leaf. Then everything went black as I collapsed on the soft grass, and I could hear and see no more of the colorful world.

"*Help me,*" the flowing voice of the beautiful Aphrodite made its way to me once again through the lonely darkness, like it had in my dream, as another warning of things to come—that is, if something bad hadn't happened already.

All I could think was that I knew I should've left that damn camp sooner.

# Chapter 18:

# COUNTDOWN

It was still dark in my head, but I slowly started to regain feeling in my limbs, and the first things I felt were my arms tingling from the warm touch I knew immediately was Alec's. My heart started to race as I concentrated, trying desperately to hear and see the world again.

"What did you do to her?" I heard Alec hiss angrily, probably directing the accusation at the untrustworthy Jason. As my eyes struggled to flutter open and color returned in place of the blackness, I just barely managed to channel enough energy to squeeze Alec's hand to let him know I was fine, and he instantly returned his focus to me.

His blue eyes lit up as they met mine, but his eyebrows were still knit together with worry as he carefully helped me sit up on the grass, keeping his arms around mine for protection. I stiffened, knowing that letting him get that close to me was a bad idea in the long run. At least leaving the camp would allow me to put some distance between us, and hopefully some of our problems.

Finally, Jason seemed to wake up from his bewildered trance, and he ordered to no one in particular, "Get her a drink." Then he asked, "Are you okay, my lady? What happened?"

Alec shot him an annoyed glance and looked back to me before I answered quietly, "I have to go now. Honestly, I should have left sooner."

Jason raised his eyebrows in surprise and smoothed down his light brown hair, which he had been pulling at in anguish, before protesting, "But you just passed out! Surely you need to rest?"

Alec glared coldly at Jason and said curtly, "If she says she has to go now, then she goes now." Unlike Jason, Alec knew better than to argue with me at a time like this . . . well, at any time, actually.

Brushing a few pieces of grass off my white tank top, Alec leaned down toward me and asked again, "What *really* happened?"

I sighed and whispered into his ear so no one else could overhear; I didn't want to worry the Knowing people any more than I already had. "Aphrodite" was my one-word explanation, but Alec nodded in understanding because I had told him about my dream early that morning.

Jason gave the two of us a confused look, as if he wanted to know what was going on as well, but he didn't get the chance to press it because Jan returned, holding a glass of lemonade with ice. She carefully pushed Clara, who had been clinging fearfully onto Jason's arm, out of the way and handed the glass to Jason, who then gave it to me. Slowly, I took a sip, but started coughing in shock over the taste. The surprised Alec quickly sat me up straighter and started to rub my back, trying to end my little coughing fit. He glanced at me with a questioning look, but instead of a spoken answer, I handed him the lemonade. Alec raised one eyebrow at me, and I just nodded.

The people who were crowded around us only gasped in shock as Alec shrugged and took a huge sip of lemonade from the tall glass. I knew what they were thinking. *What just happened? Did Alec really just drink from the same cup as a goddess? Is that even allowed?*

But really, it didn't matter what they thought.

After swallowing the light yellow lemonade, Alec made a very unpleasant face. Looking terrified, Jason sputtered worriedly, "Is something wrong with the lemonade?"

"It tastes terrible," Alec said, shoving the glass back into Jason's hands.

Jason's face turned as white as a sheet of paper in horror and embarrassment. "But," he started, "it just came from the regular batch of lemonade. What could be wrong with it?"

Alec and I glanced at each other sheepishly. Because truthfully, there was nothing really wrong with it; both of us knew that. But when you're used to enjoying the very best lemonade in the world, lemonade-flavored powder mixed with water just can't compare, and it comes as quite a shock when you're not expecting it.

"Uh, never mind," Alec responded quickly, realizing that right then was not a good time to be picky. "Just get some horses ready. I will be escorting Lady Athena to the bus stop."

Jason nodded obediently, though he still looked quite confused about the glass of lemonade in his hand. Meanwhile, Alec helped me up and walked with me to the little tent where I had stayed the night. I quickly collected in my backpack all of my belongings, which wasn't much—only my clothes and money. I made sure that I had the rock-sword in my pocket and that my pocketknife was still safely hidden in my leather boot. Finally, I slung the black backpack over one shoulder and nodded to Alec, who then turned around and walked out toward the large horse corral, where almost everyone in the Knowing camp was gathered, eager to say goodbye to their lovely goddess.

Jason emerged from the crowd leading two medium-sized horses toward us, one black and one a silvery gray. "Here you go, my lady," Jason said as he handed me the reins of the gray horse and gave the black horse to Alec.

I gave Jason a quick thank-you and carefully mounted my horse as I prayed in a quiet mutter, "Poseidon, please make these horses behave." Beside me, Alec did the same. I did know how to ride adequately (every once in a while Zeus took me with him to fly through the puffy clouds with Pegasus), but horses just weren't my favorite creatures. After all, they were Poseidon's sacred animals, not mine.

"I am also sending Nicholas along with you, for extra protection," Jason added, and I nodded because it really was a good idea, although Alec didn't look very happy about it. Shrugging, I turned around to see Nicholas sitting atop a huge flame-colored stallion.

Suddenly, I heard a loud wail from the mass of people, and Alec's little cousin, Anna, burst out of the crowd and started tugging at Alec's leg from down on the ground. Alec blushed, obviously embarrassed, and whispered to her ungratefully, "I'm coming back, you know." Anna just looked up at him with her big brown eyes and then glared at me like this whole thing was my fault, which I guess it was, in a way. Anna was about to say something, but Clara pulled her away and returned to Jason's side, as usual. Yes, I thought, the two were definitely more than friends or clan-mates.

Smiling weakly, I cleared my throat and faced the Knowing people one last time. "Thank you for having me. It is unfortunate that I was only able to stay for two days, but duty calls." I paused to take in the solemn looks on all their faces one last time, and then said, "Good luck, and do everyone a favor by staying alive."

Sighing, I gave my horse a kick, and then Alec, Nicholas, and I took off into the night, desperately hoping we wouldn't run into any monsters on our way to the bus stop where Alec and I had first arrived in a taxi.

---

The wind blew my long hair wildly around my face even though it was tied back in its usual ponytail. Together, we galloped as fast as our horses could run through the quiet night, the bright stars lighting the way for us across the seemingly endless rolling hills. I supposed if I were particularly bored, I could have used the time and the horses' approximate speed to calculate how many miles we were from the camp, but my mind was elsewhere. Horrible scenes of a dead, broken Aphrodite covered in dirt and leaves, lying in our forest, haunted me as Alec, Nicholas, and I rode on. I kept shaking my head as if it did some good, and I tried in vain to refocus my attention on just making it all the way to the bus stop quickly and safely.

But of course, even that was too much to ask for.

As the three of us came over a hill, I frowned at the dark, looming figure below us. It was indeed a huge monster, although it did not appear violent and bloodthirsty from afar. It was crouched patiently, like a cat, almost as if it were waiting for us specifically. The strange creature had yet to move a single muscle except for the slight twitch of her lion tail every couple of seconds, though I was certain she had seen us because her bright yellow eyes were locked on us.

Yes, this was, in fact, the infamous Sphinx: a lion with the face of a woman, a scaled chest like a snake, and the huge wings of a bird. I exchanged worried glances with Alec as we slowly rode up to meet her, and the Sphinx stood up to her full fifteen-foot height, glaring down at us with merciless eyes, her golden coat shining in the moonlight. Nicholas, Alec, and I quickly stopped the horses, but they began stomping their hooves nervously.

"Hello and welcome. I am the Sphinx, as you probably know. You three look mildly intelligent, so maybe you will be able to answer my riddle," she began in a low growl, and I rolled my eyes. She had no idea just how intelligent I was. But then her gaze shifted to the brutish-looking Nicholas, and she frowned. "Then again, maybe not."

Now it was my turn to frown; she had no right to judge him like that. "Excuse me—" I started, but I was interrupted.

"Oh, be quiet, Lady Athena," the Sphinx said, and I raised my eyebrows, waiting for an explanation about how she knew who I was. Noticing my bemused expression, she explained, "I would know your annoying, radiating aura of wisdom anywhere, in anybody. But unfortunately for you, even gods cannot pass by me without solving the riddle." I raised my eyebrows again in surprise. I had a radiating aura of wisdom? Cool.

Suddenly Nicholas chuckled, and Alec and I winced, knowing that was a bad idea. "Sorry to upset you, but we could always just walk around you. You're really not that great of a border patrol."

*Nice job, Nicholas. Way to offend a hungry monster,* I thought sarcastically.

"I think I'll be having a good meal tonight," the Sphinx hissed angrily through her sharp, clenched teeth, shooting Nicholas a stone-cold glare. If the stare of a Sphinx could kill, poor Nicholas would have died right there on his horse.

I explained quickly, "Please, don't kill him. He doesn't know what he's saying. I bet he's never even been outside of the Knowing camp before. And besides, I'm the only one who will be passing." At this, the Sphinx slowly turned her huge head to face me, with her bushy light brown eyebrows raised and her hair falling elegantly over her broad shoulders.

"All right, then. But do not be fooled, stupid man," she said slowly, looking right back at Nicholas, "because an invisible border lies behind me, and you will not be able to cross it unless you solve my riddle."

Nicholas gulped nervously, and everything was quiet for a moment as the Sphinx thought of the perfect riddle, one she hoped would stump the goddess of wisdom. I took a deep breath, trying to concentrate. I couldn't take anything for granted; if I didn't guess the riddle correctly, she would most likely eat me alive, and probably Alec and Nicholas too, if they couldn't escape in time. Talk about pressure.

Minutes seemed like hours as the Sphinx continued to think, wasting my precious time. I was about to ask her to hurry up, but then her pupils dilated slightly, and she finally began, "Ah, this one I think is quite appropriate for you. Ready? You only have one guess." I nodded, eager to get the whole thing over with.

"A dog runs into the woods. How far does it go?" she asked, and I raised my eyebrows; I had no idea how she knew about the woods, but I didn't let that distract me.

Breathing calmly, I pictured the woods in my brain. I was running through the tall trees and leafy ferns uncontrollably, and suddenly I realized that this was the same winding path that had led me to the dead Aphrodite in my dream. Gasping in shock, I opened my eyes again before my dream self could reach the poor girl. It was a sight I didn't want to see any more of than I absolutely had to. So I gulped and closed my eyes to picture the woods again, but this time safely from above.

"Halfway," I said aloud, barely even hesitating, and I opened my eyes to see the Sphinx tense up, confirming my suspicions. "The dog can only run halfway into the woods before it is heading out of the woods, a phenomenon I've experienced on a daily basis for years."

"Perhaps that riddle was too simple," the Sphinx mused, though she didn't seem very upset that I outsmarted her so quickly and easily. "But I will keep my word, Lady Athena." She gave me a curt nod, lifted one wing, and said, "Until next time." I sighed in relief and dismounted my gray horse, glad to hear that the Sphinx was on my side, for whatever reason.

Then I turned to Alec, handing him the reins of my mare, and he took them silently. "I want you two to run away right now. I don't trust this Sphinx," I whispered to him, and he nodded in agreement. "Just . . . don't die."

Alec nodded again, his blue eyes full of the pain that came from knowing he was being left alone again. "Jason is reinstalling the phone at the camp. I'll call you every day with an update," he promised with a tight voice, and I knew an update was just going to be an excuse to be able to talk to me.

I smiled because I suddenly realized that I didn't even care all that much about an update, just as long as everyone I truly cared about was safe. But I couldn't let *him* know that.

"Hurry up before I change my mind," the Sphinx hissed, and her giant yellow eyes flashed at me. Was that anger or something else in her eyes?

*Note to self: Certain monsters can be very impatient, even with gods.*

I turned back to face the two guys on their horses. "See you in two weeks," I said to Alec and Nicholas brightly, as if everything was going to be perfectly fine. Which it definitely wasn't.

Nicholas just nodded in agreement, but Alec added eagerly, "Hopefully less."

With that, the two of them started galloping in the other direction, toward the base camp, before I could say anything more. I watched them disappear safely over the hill and into the black night before turning around, hoping that I had helped to change the Knowing's old-fashioned ways at least a little bit, even though I had only been there for two days. Perhaps all the Knowing really needed was proof or confirmation of their neglected beliefs.

Without wasting any more time, I ran under the Sphinx's raised golden wing, through the invisible gateway, and sprinted toward the bus stop without a second thought. According to Alec, I wouldn't have to wait too long to catch a ride to the airport; time was my only enemy for the moment.

---

I finally reached the bus stop about half an hour later, sweating only slightly after running so hard for so long. I checked my watch as I sat down on the hard, black metal bench. Five minutes to wait. With a little luck, I would be home in the Woods around lunchtime the next day, maybe a little earlier.

*But don't get your hopes up,* I told myself bitterly. Because, in general, we gods were anything but lucky.

A few minutes later, the bus rolled up, and I quickly jumped on, handing the driver the fare on my way to sit at the back of the empty bus. I didn't really expect anyone else to be on a bus out there in the middle of nowhere at eleven-thirty at night anyway. Sighing, I leaned back in my seat and closed my eyes, ready for some rest before I had to wake again.

However, sleep did not come to me that night. Every tiny rock the bus drove over jolted me wide awake, but that didn't even matter. Each time I thought I was finally drifting off to comforting black nothingness, I found myself running along that same dreaded path in my beloved forest toward Aphrodite, hoping that somehow the dream would end differently for once, but of course it didn't. I ended up gasping for air each time I awoke, so I wouldn't have been surprised if the driver thought I was having asthma attacks or something. Honestly, I was surprised she didn't ask if I needed medical attention.

Eventually, I gave up on sleep and resorted to staring out the bus window into the starry night, wondering if Alec was asleep yet. But knowing him, Alec probably wouldn't get a wink of sleep either, until he knew I was safe, relatively speaking. He really needed to stop worrying about me and focus on keeping himself alive instead, especially since his falling in love with me was definitely *not* part of my master plan.

About two hours passed before the bus finally arrived at the airport, and I hopped off eagerly, almost running into multiple people as I rushed through the sliding doors and headed for the ticket line. When I finally made it through security without even needing to say a word, I walked toward the gate, checking behind me every couple of seconds for monsters. Even when I sat down in one of the cheap leather seats in the waiting area, my heart continued to race, and I knew it would not stop until I was home with the gods, the only people I really trusted besides Alec.

My flight was finally called a few hours later, and I boarded the plane at almost six in the morning, hurriedly snagging the window seat in my row.

The plane was almost empty, which was good. If a monster had somehow sneaked on board, I would have needed as much room as possible to fight. Taking deep breaths, I reached into the pocket of my jeans, gripping the cool, gray rock for comfort, and then I leaned back in my seat as the plane engines roared to life.

---

The flight had been going quite peacefully, with no interruptions by monsters trying to kill me or annoying people trying to talk to me, but, as some say, all good things must come to an end. The plane was less than half an hour from landing when it suddenly shook as if I were on the ground in one of Poseidon's earthquakes. I gripped the armrests tightly and gritted my teeth, ready for the pilot to tell me to prepare for a crash landing, but luckily, that didn't happen.

"I'm sorry to inform you all that our arrival time has been delayed due to major turbulence caused by thunderstorms in the area," the monotone voice of a flight attendant suddenly cut through the silent plane. Many of the passengers who were awake exchanged annoyed glances and checked their watches impatiently, but I knew better than to feel unconcerned or merely bothered. After all, this thunderstorm was not some random weather event brought on by an area of low or high pressure that could be predicted by any capable weatherman; this was the result of an epic war of the gods, something only my father, Zeus, could conjure up at a moment's notice.

I just gulped and shut my eyes, praying for the storm to pass quickly as a sign that everything was okay.

The plane seemed to take ages to land, but the rain had eventually slowed to a drizzle and then stopped, and it was clear enough for me to actually see out of the little window next to me. When the plane finally stopped at the gate, I raced off the plane with my backpack slung over one shoulder, heading for the nearest exit as quickly as possible so I could hopefully flag down a taxi before a monster had the chance to get me.

By then, it was nearly ten in the morning, and I was rushing along through the nearly empty airport, minding my own business and about to take a deep breath in relief because no monsters had popped out from behind a column yet, when the unthinkable happened. "Ashley? Is that you?" a gruff voice called out in the hallway.

At first, I kept walking as if I were in a daze; I did not recognize my human name or the gravelly voice until a few seconds later. I supposed I hadn't been Ashley in so long that I had forgotten what the name sounded like, how Ashley herself was supposed to act. But really, it had only been three days since I had acted as Ashley back in the Woods, which also meant that the rest of the gods and I had only about three weeks left to stop Hades and his monster army. Time really does fly when you're trying to save the world before summer is over.

"Ashley!" the man yelled at me again. I stopped for a second to think but did not dare to turn around as the thick fog in my head finally cleared, and I suddenly came to my senses, remembering everything at once. "Ash—"

*No, not* him, *it can't be*, I thought. I took off in a sprint straight toward the exit before he could even finish saying my human name. However, the man kept yelling my name, and I knew that he was running after me, but there was no way I was going back to him, not this time.

Following the lighted exit signs, I pushed past everyone who was in my way without apologizing, but there was no time for that anyway. My only goal at the moment was to get away from that unforgivable man and into a taxi as fast as possible. Glaring ahead at everyone around me returning my dirty looks, I raced like a cheetah toward those wonderful sliding doors to freedom, though I knew I had probably lost him already. Let's face it; he was an out-of-shape, middle-aged man and I was a fit goddess, so there was really no comparison.

Still, I did not stop to check and see if he was following me as I burst out into the cool morning air and screamed, "Taxi!" I looked around wildly, then ran to the nearest little green taxi and jumped in, buckling right up. "Go!" I yelled loudly to the driver, desperately hoping I hadn't accidentally said it in Greek, because I was pretty sure I hadn't spoken more than a few words in English in at least two days.

But thankfully the driver understood me, and the tone of my voice must have spooked him because he stepped on the gas pedal right away, and I was thrown back into my seat as the taxi screamed around the tight corners of the small airport parking lot. Hyperventilating, I gripped the seat cushion in front of me for dear life.

"Where to?" the driver asked, his voice shaking slightly as he seemed to calm down a little and started to fully analyze the crazy situation. But then his dark eyes brightened as he turned around in his seat, studying my face, and exclaimed, "Hey! I know you!"

My eyebrows rose in the surprise of seeing the lively, dark-skinned face of Larry, who had driven Alec and me to the airport only three days before, though right then I didn't have time for proper greetings.

"The Woods," I answered him grimly in English. "Get me there as fast as you can." Then Larry gave a short nod and turned left out of the parking lot, heading swiftly down the highway without asking any more questions.

Sighing in relief, I glanced back at the front of the steely airport just in time to see none other than my damned human father scratching his head in confusion and anger, as usual, obviously wondering where the hell I had gone. I guessed he had finally decided to return to my mom and me from Paris—for now, that is. He had already had his turn to leave my mother and me in the dust multiple times before, and now I was able to give him a piece of his own medicine. I really was not in the mood to make up more lies about my trip to Kentucky and why Martha was no longer with me. So I just smiled to myself in satisfaction, sinking down in my seat and resting my head in my hands.

Approximately a hundred miles until we reached the Woods, until I reached home.

---

Time could not pass quickly enough. I tried in vain to force time to move quicker by both tapping my fingers on the seat and humming the song that Alec and I had danced to the night before, much to Larry's annoyance. When he gave me the evil eye for probably the third time, I gulped and sheepishly stopped tapping my fingers, turning to face the dirty window instead. Sighing, I watched as we blew by the evergreen trees lined up like soldiers on the side of the highway, and I looked up at the sky every once in a while to check for even the slightest change.

Now, the sun was hiding nervously behind large silver clouds, but it definitely wasn't raining, which was a good sign. In other words, Zeus wasn't too angry at the moment.

Eventually giving up on being patient, I leaned my head back on the seat and shut my eyes, hoping for a small nap. But as you probably guessed, that's not what happened. Almost right as I closed my eyes, bloodcurdling screams echoed through my brain, and I didn't even bother asking Larry if he had heard something weird. The burden was mine alone, there in the tiny taxi without the other gods.

My eyes flew open again as I shuddered, getting a bad feeling that the visions would not subside until I made sure Aphrodite was okay, assuming she was still alive by the time I got home, of course. Frowning in thought, I turned to look out the window again, but my vision suddenly blurred, and images of random rocks and trees from inside the forest flashed through my mind. Again, I took slow, deep breaths and gripped the seat in front of me for support. Gritting my teeth, I forced my pained eyes to obey me and take a look at my small watch.

Thirty minutes until home, until war. My life was like a constant countdown, always ticking on toward unthinkable tragedy.

As you can imagine, the rest of the ride slowly became worse and worse, and soon I was not even able to block out the horrible images of the dead Aphrodite. All I heard was the sound of screams pounding in my ears, with only the occasional touch of reality. Larry's voice called out to me through the chaos to ask if I was okay, but he seemed so far away.

Unable to string together a complete thought, let alone words, I simply nodded and turned my head to where I knew the taxi window was, though all I could see was the thick forest surrounding me. Because I couldn't let Larry think anything was wrong, I silently forced myself to keep calm, taking deep breaths as the little taxi slowed down. I couldn't tell if we had arrived at Main Street, or if we had been stopped in the middle of the road by some horrifying monster.

"We're here, miss," Larry's friendly voice informed me, and I smiled in relief. Countdown over—for now.

I reached into my backpack and pulled out a wad of crumpled cash, handing the entire thing to Larry, even though it was way more than the actual fare. "Keep the change," I told him with a quick smile, my blurry vision finally starting to clear. Then I leaped out of the taxi without another word, rubbing my eyes and leaving Larry sitting in his cab in utter shock.

I blinked away the last few blurs, and they slowly disappeared from my sight, leaving only beautiful reality. I breathed in the familiar smell of the evergreens as a cool breeze tousled my long hair. Smiling, I walked on the wet pavement past the old brick gas station and the cozy-looking shops along the empty Main Street, thinking about how relieved I was to finally see those old yet strong buildings instead of dark, collapsible tents. Although its appearance was rugged and a little rough around the edges, the tiny town was still comfortingly cute and welcoming. Home sweet home.

"Ath—Ashley!" the loud voice of Zeus called out from behind me. I wasn't even looking at them yet, but I could feel the air—suddenly lighter and stickier than before, almost making my mind buzz uncontrollably—radiating with three distinct kinds of power from three different gods. This was an effect of the gods' power that I had never really noticed before. I guessed I was only aware of it now because I had spent so much time away from them and my home.

Grinning, I whirled around to face the Monster Watch before running straight into Zeus's arms for a warm hug. He only breathed a sigh of relief and hugged me tighter, and for a second, the sun actually peeked out from behind a cloud. The huge smiles on all three of their faces told me that if Aphrodite was dead, they didn't know about it. The fact that none of the other gods had received the vision of the dead goddess meant her fate was somehow connected to Alec's recent confession and to the part of the prophecy I should have told everyone about sooner, the part that resulted in me escaping that godforsaken arrow . . . but I digress.

"It's good to have you back," Apollo said in English with a handsome smile, tussling my hair in a brotherly fashion and making me forget my worries temporarily. I smiled back and punched him in the arm playfully.

"You know you're home, like, way early, right? Like, almost two weeks early," Poseidon commented, his blue eyes gleaming as he ran his fingers through his black hair.

With that, I suddenly remembered my real reason for racing back to the Woods. "Where's Aphrodite?" I asked in a hushed voice in Greek, finally pushing Zeus and Apollo away from me.

Poseidon grinned, obviously not noticing the gravity of my tone, and responded in English again, "Whoa, slow down for a minute. You just got here!"

I grabbed the collar of Poseidon's old blue T-shirt, jerking him in closer so that his face was mere inches from mine. "Where. Is. Aphrodite?" I growled at him in Greek, the tone of my voice dead serious. This was a matter of life or death for a fellow god, not fun and games anymore. The fate of Aphrodite awaited us deep inside the woods like a ticking time bomb waiting to blow.

A new countdown had just begun.

Printed in the USA
CPSIA information can be obtained
at www.ICGtesting.com
JSHW022330140824
68134JS00019B/1397

9 781630 474461